SHIVAREE

TO FELIX

ALSO BY J.D. HORN

WITCHING SAVANNAH
The Line
The Source
The Void
Jilo (a Witching Savannah prequel, coming in 2016)

SHIVAREE

A NOVEL

J. D. HORN

47N★RTH

Published by 47North, Seattle

www.apub.com

Amazon, the Amazon logo, and 47North are trademarks of Amazon.com, Inc., or its affiliates.

ISBN-13: 9781503949485
ISBN-10: 1503949486

Cover design by Shasti O'Leary-Soudant/SOS CREATIVE LLC

Printed in the United States of America

This is all Flannery O'Connor's fault.

AUTHOR'S NOTE

This is a work of Southern Gothic fiction. Please be advised that this story contains elements of emotional, physical, and sexual violence that some readers may find disturbing.

PROLOGUE

Conroy, Mississippi—July 8, 1953

Ruby awoke with no illusion that she was unchanged.

There was music. She recognized the tune. "Glow Worm." A man hummed along to the melody.

She was lying flat on her back on a cold, hard surface. The feel of it, running the length of her body, told her she was naked, but the thought of being uncovered didn't bother her. She'd long since given up on modesty—or had it abandoned her? Either way, it didn't matter.

The world around her held no shape or form. There was nothing but a salmon-pink glow, like she had closed her eyes to savor the sun on her face. That was it, she realized—her eyes were closed, and the light she faced was bright, but cool. She tried to open them, but they wouldn't respond.

"Let's get you ready for your big date, my pretty one," Ruby heard a man say. She tried to place the voice—it was somewhat familiar—but she couldn't. She tried to open her mouth and speak. To ask him where she was, but she couldn't. "Your father believes it will be a small event, but I think you should expect a crowd," the man continued. "A lot of folk around here gonna be glad to see the last of you." She felt a hand brush her face, a thumb and a forefinger force open her right eye. As the hand pulled away, she saw a smile, framed by a full beard. "Most folk hoped when you two moved away that'd be the last you'd be seen around these parts." The beard was dark, but streaks of gray had begun to form in it.

"Yes, young lady, a lot of people gonna be glad you're gone for good," the man said, "but I'm not one of them. I've missed how you two kept everybody jumping around these parts. Been downright dull without you." Again the hand touched her face, its fingers opening her left eye. "There you are," the bearded man said. She tried to focus, but the lamp above his head formed a halo over him, the bright light obscuring his features. "Besides, your friend Dylan was always good to wet a man's wick during a dry spell."

A syringe appeared before her. "Just a little disinfectant," he said, and flooded her eye with a liquid that smelled of rubbing alcohol. It burned like liquid fire. She tried to fling her arm before her face, but it wouldn't move. "And again," he said. The syringe hovered over her left eye. She tried to call out. To tell him to stop, but she saw a slight bend in his hand, and the liquid filled her other eye. Her vision was blurred in both eyes, but she could see his movement, the burst of light as he turned away. Her vision cleared in time to see him turn back again. The syringe was still in his right hand. His left reached toward her, and turned her head to the side. His touch was gentle.

With her right cheek turned to the surface, she could see that she lay in a shallow ceramic tub, the glare of the overhead light reflecting on its glossy surface. His hand, now gloved, touched her lips; his thumb and two fingers opened her mouth. He put the syringe between her lips and sprayed the foul liquid into her mouth. As the solution entered her, something awoke within her, excited, then repulsed at the mixture it was tasting.

Something else had invaded her, had taken up residence in her. During the weeks of fever dreams, she had sensed it, lurking on the periphery of her awareness, but now she felt its presence as surely as if it had always been a part of her. Somehow she knew, she would never be alone, with her own thoughts, in her own body, again. Another flood of the spray angered her guest, but the man turned her face back up to the light, and used a dry cloth to wipe off the liquid that had spilled from her mouth onto her cheek.

"There, not so bad, was it?" he said.

She heard a door creak open. "I got 'er clothes from the Judge's maid," another voice, one Ruby had no trouble identifying, called. A wave of conflicting emotions hit her. The mention of her father, whom everyone knew as "the Judge," and their maid Lucille, combined with the sound of Charlie Aarons's voice, made for an odd cocktail. A father she detested, and the woman who'd been the closest thing she'd ever known to a mother, being talked about by the most disgusting excuse for a man Ruby had ever known—and she'd spent time in Hollywood. It sickened her to think Charlie had touched her belongings.

The man near her raised his head. "Charlie," he said, "my good and faithful part-time servant. It's good to know I can always count on you to show up to work early . . . when it's a young one." The man hovered, still holding the cloth to Ruby's face. "Well, come in, come in, and have a good look," he said. "We both know it's moments like these upon which you build your dreams, and I'm sure you want to see before we get to the cutting."

Ruby fixed on to his last two words, and tried to cry out, to tell him that they'd made a mistake, that she was still alive, but the only sound was the shuffling of Charlie's shoes.

His wrinkled face and bushy grizzled beard appeared over her, his milky cataract eye joining its partner in running the length of her. "Did you do that?" Charlie asked, pointing at her chest, the spot where there had been carved an intricate, yet ugly, triple star joined together by curved lines and small circles.

"No, of course not," the man with the dark beard said, shaking his head. "She came in with that. God only knows what kind of trouble she got up to in California."

"Why she blue?" The old man's head tilted as he inspected her.

"Well, Doc McAvoy thinks it's something to do with the drugs she did out in Hollywood. Says they affected her ability to absorb oxygen . . ."

"To do what?"

"To breathe, Charlie," the man sighed. "To breathe. I don't know if that's the case, but if the good doctor says it is, and if the Judge doesn't disagree, then I'm not going to either. Gonna be a closed-casket service because of it."

"Then why'd you make me go fetch her dress?"

"Because we couldn't just bury her like this, now could we? Wouldn't be Christian." Ruby watched as he balled up the cloth he'd been holding. The hand lifted and tossed it to the side. "You still doing work on the side for the Dunne family?" the man asked.

"Yeah, what about it?" Charlie's tone was defensive.

"Nothing. I don't care what you get up to when you aren't working for me. I was just wondering how young Elijah's taking all this. I suspect that other than her father, he might be the only man on earth who'll mourn this child. And just between you, me, and the little miss here, I'm not so sure about her father."

His words struck home. If she were dead, truly dead, Ruby knew the only thing the Judge would feel was relief. Relief that she could no longer act in ways that made him appear the fool. But Elijah. Elijah would care. He'd forgiven her.

Her interest in Elijah had started out as a cruel joke, but she'd come to love him. He'd been the only one ever to see through her wickedness and discover a spark of the girl she might have been, if only things had been different. If left alone, Elijah might have found a way to save her soul.

But they hadn't been left alone. She'd been forced to let Elijah believe she was a whore, and she saw no little irony that after losing him, a whore she had become. If she had to do it over again, she would kill the men who'd driven her and Elijah apart. The men who'd forced her to let him believe a lie, so she could protect him from the one truth about herself she suspected Elijah could never accept.

If she could have another chance, if she could wake from this nightmare, she'd kill them. And she'd send the rest of Conroy to hell with them.

"I don't know." Charlie's voice sounded distracted, irritated. "I get what they tell me to do done, and I go home. The rest of it is none of my business."

"Really, now, Charlie," the man said, "it wouldn't hurt you to show a little interest in your fellow man."

"I don't care . . ."

"All right," he said, "all right." The hand that had held the cloth lifted as he signaled Charlie he'd heard enough. "Get out of here and let me work. I'll call you when I'm ready to move the body."

Charlie hesitated, allowing himself one last long gander, before turning and shuffling back to the door. He pushed through it with more force than when he'd entered. Ruby heard the door flap back and forth a few times before settling closed.

She tried again to signal the bearded man, to move a finger, to bat an eye, but she remained frozen.

"That is one filthy old son of a bitch," the man said, "but he works cheap." The man walked a few steps away. When he returned, he fed a long needle with black thread. "But you probably don't need me telling you that. Seems like you knew just about every sordid detail there is to know in Conroy." His left hand opened her mouth, the right slid the needle inside, and he pressed the tip of it through the center of her tongue. "Come to think of it, I should've held an auction for the right

5

to sew that pretty mouth of yours shut. Bet a lot of people would have bid for the right." He chuckled to himself, but the laughter died away.

"I do apologize," he said. "That was uncalled for, even if that tongue of yours ruined lives." He pulled the needle through and pushed it back up into her mouth, just a bit behind the jaw. "I did always wonder if old Tom Wallace's suicide had something to do with your shenanigans. But I guess you're taking that secret with you now, aren't you?" He pointed the needle back up through her jaw and then paused. "My, my, young lady, but you did have some sharp ivories." The needle poked up right in front of her bottom teeth. "Would've taken a brave sinner to march past those pearly gates."

He began sawing with both ends of the thread, and she felt searing pain as it cut through the soft tissue. He stopped and then worked the needle through her gum behind her upper lip and through her left nostril, looping it back around and through the right. The sharp point pierced her septum; then he brought the needle back out through the left nostril of her nose. He placed a hand under her chin.

"There, that looks real nice," he said. "Course no one's going to see it, but you were such a pretty girl. I want to do a good job for you." He released her, and she divined by the movement of his hand that he was tying off the thread. A moment later, a flash of a scalpel severed the needle he'd been using from the thread. He turned, Ruby reckoned to return the needle to where it was kept, and his mind seemed to make a connection between his actions and the record player that had now gone silent.

Ruby heard a faint scratching sound as he started the music over, dropping the player's needle onto the disk. "Shine, little glow worm, glimmer, glimmer . . ."

"Well, my dear," he said, leaning back over her, "it would seem a shame to gum up those eyes, especially since we're closing the lid on your casket. I'll make a deal with you." He placed his palm on her forehead, and slid it down to close both eyes at once. "You keep these closed, and I won't glue them shut, all right?" The world returned to a salmon-colored glow. "No peeking now."

Somewhere nearby a machine hummed to life. "I'm afraid we're done with the pleasantries," he said. "Time to get down to the real business." In the next moment, Ruby felt the blade of the scalpel press into her neck.

She felt the blade begin to cut into her. *At least it will be over soon,* she thought. *It'll be over. I'll really be dead.*

But then Ruby felt her heart begin to beat—unaware till this moment that it had been still—as something inside her sprang to life and began racing through her veins. She felt it slither through her, forming an endless loop, like a snake swallowing its own tail. Pa-dum. Pa-dum. Pa-dum. The sound of her heart throbbing roared in her ears.

She had sensed a presence, during the fevered, dreaming days that had preceded, lurking silently on the edge of her awareness, drawing closer with each approaching dusk. But now it was there, with her, inside her. Stretching itself, taking stock of its new surroundings.

A command that did not come from her echoed within her mind, and the hand holding the blade froze. The scalpel dropped, clanging as it fell to the porcelain. She heard soft footsteps as the man moved away, then the machine's humming stopped with a click. Ruby knew it had been switched off.

Somehow this thing that shared her body had taken control, forcing the man to leave her, to leave them, alone.

Across the room, the music stopped playing, and a hissing scratch began as the player's needle slid to the end of the groove. Her ability to hear grew magnified, and the sound felt as if it could rip off the top of her head. All of her being became focused on it, wishing it would stop, willing it to stop. And then it did.

A cool peace fell on her as the needle was lifted from the record and its arm dropped back to the holder. Another click, and the player was stopped. She felt the thing within her probe her mind, and the noise around her lessened as it adjusted itself to its new home, tempering its natural senses to a level her body could tolerate.

It hadn't happened to her as she lay dying—a fact that she must now accept—but her life did begin to pass before her, one flash following the other so that years passed in a blink. As the thing within her took her inventory, odd and distant memories jumped to mind, images nearly forgotten springing up as fresh as the day they were formed and playing out before her mind's eye as if she were sitting in a darkened theater. Short but telling scenes: a lit match, an animal trapped, a child losing an eye. The images sped up so that her conscious mind could no longer track what it was seeing, but Ruby knew the thing inside her was pleased with what it had found there.

She felt it relax. It had weighed her in the balance, and determined that it had found a partner capable of the violence it craved. It tried to move her, to help her rise. She felt a pulsing tremor start in her hand, but then it stopped, and the force within fell back, seemingly exhausted. The markings carved in her flesh burned as sharp as when they were first cut, and with a single rush, her heart stopped beating.

But still Ruby remained awake and aware. A hunger began to fill her, but it was more than physical. An obsession closer to a craving for opiates descended on her; the depths of it told her that it was not hers alone, but shared with the other within. Again, her hearing sharpened, and she remembered the bearded man who remained there with them, the sound of his pulse as clear to her naked ear as if she were wearing a stethoscope.

Ruby joined her will to that of the creature within her, and she heard the creak of the man's leather-soled shoes as he crossed the room, drawing near her, near them. Again, the man opened her eyelids. The light overhead still shone too bright, but now he leaned over her in a way that shaded her eyes, so that she could make out his features. She would have expected his face to show fear, but instead, he looked down on her, beaming, an insipid schoolboy smile on his lips, his eyes warm and tender. He gazed on her as if he were in love.

She felt the thing within guiding his movements. His right hand reached out and brushed her temple, but her temple hadn't been his intended target. He found the scalpel where it had fallen, and she heard two snips in quick succession as he undid the ends of the thread he'd used to secure her mouth, slipping his fingers inside and unraveling his careful handiwork.

He raised his hands, now both within her field of vision. He lingered, staring into her eyes as if asking permission, the sharp of the scalpel pressed against his left wrist.

Yes. Yes, she thought, even though she wasn't consciously sure what the thing within her desired. The man sucked in a breath as he traced the blade along the wrist, then turned it so the first few drops of blood fell onto her lips.

Ruby's mind protested, saying that she should be disgusted by the taste of blood on her tongue, but that voice quickly faded. Joined with the entity, she found herself caught up in the rapture of feeling another's life force feeding into her, warming her, renewing her strength. But in those first moments the entity had not yet been strong enough. The ecstasy she had been experiencing came crashing down around her, ripped away as their control over the source of the feast broke.

The man roused himself and cursed, seeming to believe he'd cut himself by accident, or at least trying to convince himself that was the case. He called out for Charlie and then turned his attention to wrapping his wrist.

"Clean her up," he commanded as the door creaked open. "Clean her up and get her dressed. I need to get her boxed and out of here."

ONE

September 6, 1953

The smell of smoke and creosote seeped through the broken window-pane. Glass lay strewn everywhere. A burning cross cast a glow over the yard and illuminated the men—four, no, five of them—with pointed white hoods pulled over their faces.

"Mama?" Joy's small voice called out.

"You get on back to your bed," Lucille whispered fiercely to her daughter. "No, stay back," she ordered as the girl tried to come closer. "You will cut your feet. Now you do as I tell you."

Coarse laughter, followed by a rock crashing through another of the window's panes. "You go on, now, Lucille," one of the men in white shouted. "You send that boy of yours out here to talk to us."

She crept up to the side of the window, taking quick peeks through the broken glass, while making sure to keep out of range of any further projectiles. "What you want Willy for?" she called out. She heard a noise behind her and turned to see her twelve-year-old son standing wide-eyed and frightened in the doorway. "What you done, boy?" she asked in a hushed voice.

"I ain't done nothin', Mama," Willy responded.

"You just send him out here, Lucille," another of the men called. He sounded tired, like he had other places he'd rather be. Terrorizing her children was an inconvenience for him.

"Not till you tell me what you want with him." Lucille tried to keep her voice level, but inside she was quaking. Her husband, Jesse, would have known how to handle these men. He would have gone out there and offered them a comical act like Stepin Fetchit. He would have disarmed them with his smile. Convinced them they'd be better off at home in their own beds, with their own wives. But the government had shipped Jesse home from Korea in a box and now everything—raising the children, feeding them, protecting them from the monsters in white who came after dark and desecrated the Lord's own holy cross—had fallen on her.

"Lucille." The first man's voice pulled her back. "You send the boy out here. If he will stand and take his punishment like a man, we'll go and leave you alone." Lucille peered out the window again so she could take another glance at the men. One of them carried a bullwhip, she noticed. She *knew* these men. She recognized Bob McKee and Sam Jessel by their voices. Dowd Johnson, the one with the whip, she knew by his bulk. These three always traveled in a pack, so that meant the others were probably the Sleiger siblings, Walter and Wayne. One of their regular gang was missing. Probably guarding the back door. All the same, she'd pretend never to have laid eyes on any of them, as dispelling the myth of their anonymity would inevitably mean death for her and her children.

"But I ain't done nothing, Mama," Willy pleaded.

Lucille waved her hand at him in a downward motion. "Shhh!"

"But I ain't," the boy whispered.

"Lucille, don't make us come in there to get him. If we gotta come drag him out, we won't just whip him, we'll string him up and burn that house of yours down around you. Now what's it gonna be?"

A thousand thoughts rushed through her mind at once. There was a chance the back of the house had been left unguarded—it was their only chance. "You take Joy, and you see if they anybody in back. If they ain't, you take her and you run. Don't you stop till you get to Pastor Williams's house, you hear me?"

"But what about you, Mama?" Willy's eyes had flooded with tears.

"Do as I say," she hissed at her son, knowing full well that these would most likely be the last words she ever said to him if he managed to escape with his sister. She had to keep the men engaged, give her children a chance to slip out unnoticed. She turned back to the window. "What you say my boy done?"

"He done took something what didn't belong to him, that's what he done."

"That can't be. My Willy, he ain't a thief. I raised him better than that."

"You calling us liars, Lucille?"

"Why, no, sir, I ain't saying that at all. I'm just saying they's been some kind of mistake."

"No mistake. They was a witness."

Lucille swallowed hard and stepped in front of the window. "I'm sure you are all good Christian men. You tell me what the boy took, and I'll make right for it. I'm his mama. You let the blame of what he done fall on me."

"You gonna do that, boy?" Dowd raised his head and yelled into the darkness. He flicked the whip out to its full length and lashed at the ground. "Are you gonna show that you a man? Or do you plan on shamin' your daddy's memory by letting your mama take your punishment for your sins?"

"No, sir," Willy's voice called out from the tree line. Lucille's heart sunk at the sound of his voice. He'd managed to sneak past the men unnoticed, but he must have been too worried about her to flee.

"You run, Willy," Lucille screamed and raced to the door, barely noticing the pain as a shard of the broken glass punctured her foot. She threw the front door open and ran out, but by then it was too late. All she could do was watch helplessly by the light of the burning cross as Willy walked toward the men, his whole body trembling as he stepped into the unholy glow. Lucille scanned the surroundings for Joy, relieved at least to see she'd had the sense to stay hidden.

"I ain't taken nothing, Mister," Willy said to the closest man. "Honest, I ain't."

"You bring that lying little sack of shit over here," Dowd said to the Sleiger brothers, cracking his whip. "He'll own up to it soon enough." They advanced on the boy's slight figure and dragged him over to Dowd. "Turn him around." Dowd came closer and thrust his hand through the collar of Willy's nightshirt, ripping it open down the back.

"No," Lucille pleaded, falling to her hands and knees. "Please don't hurt my boy. I'll do anything. Use that thing on me, if you need to use it, but don't hurt my boy, Mr. Johnson." She'd no sooner said the name than she realized her error. Dowd turned to look at her and reached up to pull off his mask. He handed it to one of the Sleiger boys. "I will deal with you later," he said, pointing at Lucille. "Hold him," Dowd commanded, and Sam stepped up to assist the other Sleiger.

"Mama," Willy yelped as his arms were pulled tight to each side, exposing the whole of his back. Dowd took a few steps rearward and brought the whip up, the leather whistling through the night air as he brought it down for the first lash. Lucille closed her eyes and sank to the ground. She could not bear to watch.

But there was nothing—no sound of the lash breaking open Willy's skin, no cry of pain. Lucille opened her eyes to see that Dowd, and his whip, had inexplicably vanished.

A cry of terror came from just beyond the point where the light from the burning cross gave way to darkness. Dowd screamed again— for the screams were his, that was unmistakable—then there was silence.

"What the hell?" Sam shouted, loosening his grip on the boy enough for Willy to break free of him, though the other Sleiger still held him tight. The sound of footsteps beyond the circle of light was almost deafening in the astonished silence. Someone—*something*—was circling them.

She followed the sound with her eyes. A blur crossed her field of vision, followed by a shriek. This time she sprang up from the ground, taking advantage of the men's surprise to pry Willy from Wayne Sleiger's hands. He was too startled by what was happening to put up a fight. She pulled her son close. "Where's your sister?" she whispered.

Willy nodded toward the well, where a shadowy movement betrayed the girl's presence. "You get her to Pastor's. You do as I say this time, or Joy's blood is gonna be on your hands. You hear?" Willy nodded, and Lucille watched as he pulled off his ruined nightshirt and took off barefoot, dressed in nothing but his underpants. Soon, his shadow joined that of his sister. The two clasped hands and headed for the trees, in the direction of their pastor's house.

Lucille wanted to chase after them; the pull of her heart should have been enough to cause her feet to move. But some force held her here. Something stronger than her own will, stronger than her own fear, demanded that she remain.

She watched till the last glimpse of Joy's white gown disappeared into the growth, then Lucille turned back to the scene unfolding behind her. By the light of the burning cross, she now only counted three men. They had clustered together in a tight group. Walter, the taller of the Sleiger boys, the one who had been holding Dowd's hood, had now disappeared. The remaining men unmasked themselves, trying to get a better view of the unseen predator circling them.

"What the hell is that thing?" McKee asked the others, his voice shaking.

"I couldn't see nothing. I just felt it move past me," Sam said in a hushed and cautious voice, circling the area, the cross at his back. "I think it done killed Dowd."

Lucille had heard the sounds of a man dying in agony before. There was no question in her mind that Dowd was dead, maybe Walter too.

Wayne Sleiger looked panicked and was calling out his brother's name in all directions. The other men stood perfectly still as they listened. No response came. A gust of wind rushed around the men, causing the flames on the cross to dance and sputter. As the remaining men tried to get their bearings, Lucille moved back toward her house, testing the invisible bounds she felt holding her, seeing how much play they would allow. "I say we get out of here," she heard McKee say, his voice unsteady. "I refuse to stand here and let that thing, whatever it is, pick us off one by one."

A woman's deep, sultry laugh rang through the night.

"Miss Ruby?" Lucille whispered under her breath. The adrenaline that had failed her all along suddenly rushed up in her. Her heart beat in loud and painful thuds as she continued to edge back.

"What was that?" McKee asked, then he took note of Lucille's movement. "Where the hell you think you goin'?"

Lucille froze, but before she could answer, there was another rush of wind, followed by a blur of movement and a loud snap. Then Bob McKee's body lay on the ground before them, his head wrenched clean off his neck. In spite of the horror she'd already felt, there was something so unnatural about seeing McKee's head roll over his once white but now bloodstained hood. Lucille wondered if it was all a dream. The moment stretched on for longer than it should have, as though time had slowed to molasses. She watched on, removed and dispassionate, as the remaining men succumbed to panic. Sam Jessel jumped away from the bouncing head only to bump up against the cross and set fire to his robes. He flailed around screaming, calling for help, but there was no help to come. Lucille turned away from the sight.

Lucille deafened her ears to the sound of Jessel's cries. She felt the power that had held her here begin to loosen its grip. She started walking toward her house, for the first time favoring her wounded foot.

She ignored the sound of Wayne Sleiger as he screamed the Lord's Prayer. His words were cut off after "thy will," anyway. If Wayne called out for mercy before his death, Lucille didn't hear it.

She went inside her house and pulled out the cardboard suitcase she'd used for her honeymoon. She didn't have a car, and the station-master knew better than to sell her a ticket. A powerful man, a man who believed he owned her, Ruby's own father had forbidden her to leave town. But while Lucille knew she'd never make it out of Conroy, Mississippi, she'd be damned if her babies lived and died here.

TWO

Willy shifted his weight, trying to find a place on Mrs. Jones's lap where her bony knees wouldn't poke him.

"Stop squirming," the beanpole of a woman complained.

Willy's mama looked back over her shoulder at him. "You sit still," she said, her voice quiet and tired, but still firm enough to make him settle.

Pastor Williams's Nash Suburban was built to provide a comfortable ride for five, maybe six if those passengers didn't like pie.

Most mornings, other than Sunday, the car was already filled to its limits, its wood sides straining to contain the pastor's wife, Willy's mama, and four other ladies, three of them widows like his mama, one of whom liked to say she was a good as widowed, what with a bone-idle husband like the good Lord had given her. These women, like his mama, lived outside Conroy, but worked as maids in town. There was no bus that ran out that far, so Pastor Williams took it upon himself to make sure they would have transportation from their homes, some as far as five miles from Conroy, into town where they earned their living. Mrs. Williams, the pastor's pleasant but ample wife, always rode along for propriety's sake, sitting between the preacher and whichever of the women he picked up last that day.

"It's too hot for my jacket," Willy grumbled. His mama had dressed him and Joy in their best, Willy in a suit and tie, Joy in a frilly white dress with a blue cardigan. They'd worn the same outfits to Sunday school just yesterday. At church, he'd been roughhousing with Joe Turner till Mrs. Wiley, their Sunday school teacher, threatened to make them go out and cut a switch. They settled down right fast then.

Yesterday, he never imagined that today he'd be leaving home.

"You keep that jacket on," his mama said. "Don't you take that thing off till you up with your auntie, you hear me?"

"Yes'm," he said. Last night, after she joined them at the pastor's house, he'd watched as she undid the lining and slid an envelope inside before repairing the jacket. She'd told him the envelope held a letter for his auntie, and what money she had to help take care of them till she could send more. His mama said they'd only be away a couple of weeks, but he knew full well she'd put everything she'd set aside in that envelope.

Most mornings this time of year—at least since his daddy had been gone—Willy and Joy said good-bye to their mama, and waited for the pastor and his wife to come back and carry Willy to school, and then bring Joy back home with them. Willy wouldn't be going to school today. He wouldn't be going to school for a little while, his mama said, at least round here.

A bump in the road caused him to bounce on Mrs. Jones's knee and hit his head on the roof. "Ow," he said, rubbing the side of his head, though the blow hadn't really hurt, and it had been the top of his head rather than the side. Mrs. Jones shifted her legs. "Why don't you stop squirming," he muttered.

A sharp "Willy" from his mother's lips caused his mouth to clamp shut, but only for a moment. "Those men were lying. I didn't do anything wrong. I don't see why we gotta go."

"I know, baby," his mama said. "I know they were, but you can't talk about those men no more. You never saw them, and you don't know what happened to them."

But Willy had seen the men, and it puzzled him that the pastor didn't get on his mama for telling him to lie. He waited until he figured Pastor Williams had time to say something, but the man kept quiet.

"Last night you said Miss Ruby killed them. I heard you say it, Mama."

"Your mama was mistaken," Pastor Williams's voice boomed in answer. Then it softened. "Ruby Lowell is dead, and Ecclesiastes tells us that the dead sleep and know nothing, 'neither have they any more a portion forever in anything that is done under the sun.' That means Miss Lowell couldn't have been there." He paused. "No, your mama was just upset. Scared for you and your sister. She doesn't really know what happened to those men, and neither do you, so you keep still about it like your mama told you."

Willy felt like he'd been chastened, and for no good reason. He sulked for a few moments, then decided to ask what he really wanted to know. "How long we gotta be up north anyway?" He hadn't wanted to, he didn't want to act like a baby, but as he posed the question his voice caught in his throat and he started crying, setting Joy off wailing again.

Worse, his mama started crying, too. She tightened her grip on Joy, and patted his sister's head. "Shhhhh, baby."

"You gonna have a good time up visiting your auntie Hettie," Mrs. Green said, patting his knee. "Ain't that right, Lucille?"

"That's right," his mama said, her voice full of cheer. She pasted a big smile on her face, and used the back of her hand to wipe the tears from her cheeks. "I done told you, Auntie Hettie's gonna love having you two for a visit. You are gonna like it up there, Mama promises. Auntie Hettie and Uncle Ernie live in an apartment in a real nice town."

"What's an apartment?" Joy's question came out muffled, her head buried in their mama's shoulder.

"Well, it's like a house, but it's like a whole bunch of houses put together." His mama shifted Joy so that she could see her face. "You are gonna have a whole bunch of kids your age to play with. A whole bunch of new friends."

From what Willy could see of his sister, she seemed unconvinced, her eyes wide, but her mouth pinched in tight. "Why can't you go with us?" Joy asked again. Even Willy had lost count of how many times, but he kept quiet. He, like his sister, hoped his mama would have a change of heart.

"I done told you, baby. The Judge, he can't get along without your mama. But it ain't gonna be for long. You two will be home before you know it, and complaining that you got to stay here with your tired old mama, rather than visit your fancy new friends up north."

Joy stretched up, looking over their mama's shoulder directly into his eyes. He knew his mama was fibbing, so he turned his head to watch out the window.

"What's the town called again?" Mrs. Green asked, sounding like she'd be excited to be going in Willy's place.

"Highwood," his mama said, "and Hettie works for a real nice family real close to there in a place called Lake Forest. Don't that sound nice?" his mama asked, but didn't wait for a reply. "Auntie Hettie said they's a lake there bigger than you've ever seen, right behind the house where she works."

"Why, that sounds real nice," Mrs. Green said. She patted his knee again, causing him to look at her. "Real nice."

"I've been up to that area," the pastor called back to Willy. "You like snow, don't you? I remember your mama telling us how excited you were the first time you saw it." He paused. "Up there, you're gonna see snow piled up almost as high as you," he said and laughed.

"What are they gonna do for coats?" his mama asked, sitting up straighter, and clasping Joy even tighter. It worried him that he could hear the worry in her voice. "It's gonna get real cold up there soon, and Willy done outgrew the coat he wore last winter. I didn't even think . . ."

"The good Lord is gonna provide," Pastor Williams interrupted her. "You just have faith. We'll pass the plate this Sunday, see to it your sister can buy good, sturdy ones for them." The pastor's promise seemed to make Willy's mama relax. She slid back down, and commenced to rocking his sister like she was a real baby, not the six-year-old she was. She might not be a baby, but she was still too little to realize they were gonna be gone a lot longer than their mama was letting on. Willy wished he couldn't tell his mama was lying to them either.

As they drove past, Willy's eyes were drawn to a couple of people walking along the side of the road. He turned to look at them, as they in turn followed the passing car with their gaze. A skinny white boy in a plaid shirt and blue jeans, followed a few feet behind by an old woman, limp gray hair hanging pretty much down to her waist.

"She the one sending those letters?" Mrs. Williams asked, and Willy turned back to see the preacher's wife staring over her shoulder at the two they'd just passed.

The pastor nodded without ever taking his eyes off the road. "That's what we reckon. The scripture quoted was spelled correctly. Everything else was spelled phonetically, like the words were being guessed at."

"What letters are these?" Mrs. Marshall asked, piping up for the first time.

"Nothing at all, sister," Pastor Williams said. "Just the ramblings of an uneducated zealot more interested in watching the end of the world than making it a place Jesus would be proud of. Every church within twenty miles of Conroy, white and black, got one. Some written by hand, some carbon copies. But they're just a bunch of nonsense, really."

"What did these letters say?" Mrs. Marshall pressed the reverend.

Mrs. Williams looked back and shook her head. "Our Lucille doesn't want to hear any of this now. And it isn't really appropriate for the children to hear."

"I want to know," Willy said, curious only because the details had been labeled unsuitable for him to receive.

"Mrs. Williams said no," his mama said, this time turning back so she could trace a finger along his cheek. Something about that gesture frightened Willy. It didn't feel like a "watch your mouth," it felt like a good-bye.

"Suffice it to say," the pastor said, "she spoke of end times and quoted Exodus 12:22. You can look that up for yourself, sister, when you get home tonight."

"I can look it up right now," Mrs. Marshall said, tugging a well-worn black leather-bound Bible from her large purse. Willy watched as she flipped open to the passage, and read silently to herself. "Hmmm . . ." she said, closing the book and returning it to the bag.

As they drew nearer to town, a wall of fog enveloped them, making it impossible for Willy to pick out most of the familiar landmarks. They rode on, no one speaking, till the car passed a nearly concealed sign that Willy knew to read "Welcome to Conroy," even though he couldn't make out the letters today.

It was his mother who broke the silence that had fallen over them. "You'd better let us out a good distance from the station, Pastor."

"Don't be ridiculous, Lucille," he said, "I'm taking you and the children to the station. Gonna make sure they get off all right."

Willy could see Mrs. Williams's shoulders tense.

"I can't let you do that, Pastor. If the Judge finds out you knew about my kids leaving . . ." She stopped short, and her face turned ashen. "We should've gone to the station in Tupelo, or maybe Muscle Shoals. What if the man at the station recognizes the children? What if he won't sell us tickets?" she said, her voice coming out in a higher pitch, her words coming more quickly.

"Pull over here," Mrs. Green commanded with an authority Willy had never heard before in her voice. From his perch on Mrs. Jones's lap, Willy could see Mrs. Williams reach over and gently place a hand on her husband's forearm. He turned his head, giving her a quick glance, and eased the car to the side of the road. He shifted the gear to park and killed the engine.

The pastor climbed out, then circled around the back of the car, opening the front door—Willy's mama's door—first, and then Willy's. Willy slid off Mrs. Jones's lap, and stood watching as his mama tried to pass Joy to the pastor so that she could more easily get out of the car. Joy refused to be handed over, tightening her arms around their mama's neck.

The pastor stepped back, out of the way, and Willy's mama shifted her feet to the ground. "It's okay, baby," she said to Joy. "Mama's got you." She placed her hand on top of the girl's head to keep it from getting bumped as they exited the car, and stood, turning and facing Willy with a smile. She shifted Joy into one arm, and motioned Willy forward with the other. He took a couple of uncertain steps toward her, knowing that if he didn't slow all this down, soon he'd be missing her. When he reached her side, she wrapped her free arm around his shoulders and pulled him into her. "You getting so big," she said as if she'd hadn't noticed his growth before. "You gonna be taller than me when . . ." She fell silent.

"Help me out, Mary," he heard Mrs. Green say, and craned his neck to see Mrs. Jones offering a hand to the older lady. Mrs. Green slid out of the car, and ambled toward them, moving slowly. "My hip is acting up again," she said rubbing her side. When she got to them, she grasped Willy by the shoulders and pulled him back from his mama. "You all go on now, Pastor," she called out to their companions. "I'm gonna take care of this. Make sure these children get to go on this special trip." Willy turned to see her beaming down on him.

Mrs. Jones slid back into the car without another word, closing the door behind her, but Pastor Williams hesitated. "Are you sure about this, sister?"

"Course I'm sure," she said, releasing Willy and waving her hands to shoo the pastor away. "That white man who sells the tickets, he knows you, 'cause folk around here are worried about what you up to in 'that church.' He knows Lucille 'cause the Judge told him he'd better recognize her. But an old woman like me and a couple of Negro children? Even if he bothers to take a look at us, he's ain't gonna look at us twice."

Pastor Williams nodded, then went and opened the trunk, pulling out the case their mama had packed for them and a tin he'd seen Mrs. Williams fill with cold chicken and biscuits drizzled with molasses. He handed Willy the tin, and set the case by their mama's feet. He squatted down so he looked Willy straight in the eye. "You need to be a man for your mama, and keep an eye on that little sister of yours. Don't you let her out of your sight, not for one second. You see to it you two get up to your auntie's place safe. You hear me?"

"Yes, sir," Willy said, feeling a weight fall on his shoulders.

The pastor rose and then leaned in to place a kiss on Joy's cheek. "You do what your brother tells you."

"No," Joy said, and buried her face back in their mama's shoulder.

The pastor placed a hand on Joy's back. "You do what your brother tells you," he repeated, though this time it was clear that his words were a command, not a request. He cast Willy one last look, then went back to the car, firing it up and pulling away. Within moments, its taillights faded into the fog.

"Now, children," Mrs. Green said, "I need you two to take a moment and give your mama all the loving you can." Her words caused Willy to feel nervous butterflies in his stomach. "You two gotta say your good-byes here before we get to the station, 'cause we're gonna play pretend once we get there."

"Play pretend what?" Joy pulled her face back from their mama's bosom, and faced Mrs. Green with an upturned chin and wary eyes.

"Well," Mrs. Green said, her voice taking on a musical quality. "We are gonna play pretend that your mama, she ain't your mama, and that you two are my grandbabies, been down here visiting for a spell, but now heading home. Your mama, she ain't gonna come all the way in with us. She gonna wait across the street and watch us play."

"I don't want to play that," Joy said.

"Ah, sure you do," Mrs. Green said, "it'll be fun." Mrs. Green nodded at their mama, signaling with a small gesture of her hand that Joy needed to be put down.

Willy could see his mama was fighting back tears as she lowered Joy to her feet. "You a big girl now," she said. "Too big for your mama to carry." Still, Joy resisted the separation, wrapping her arms tight around their mama's skirt.

"Go on," Mrs. Green said, nodding toward his mama. "You go give her a hug, too."

Willy didn't have to be told twice. It suddenly dawned on him that this was happening no matter how much he or Joy protested. Their mama pried Joy loose, then knelt down so that she could hold them both at once.

Too soon, Mrs. Green came and took Joy by the hand. Joy tried to tug herself away, but Mrs. Green held firm, and soon Joy surrendered. Mrs. Green held out her free hand to Willy. "Hand me that tin. I'll carry it, and you and your mama take turns with the case."

THREE

The world outside the window disappeared in a blink as the train drew near Conroy. One moment it was there, the next, Corinne saw nothing but a swathe of dirty white. Fog, denser than any she had ever witnessed, had descended on the train, swallowing it whole. Unlike the cascading mists that crept over San Francisco's Twin Peaks, this fog seemed like a rigid and unyielding curtain.

"It's the paper mill that causes it," said an elderly man across the aisle. Corinne spotted a leather satchel on the seat next to him. His case was distinctive, and it marked him as either a doctor or a veterinarian. There was something prim about the gentleman—the crispness of his collar, the careful way his manicured hands held his hat on his lap, the precision of his tie's four-in-hand knot. No, this man did not spend his days plodding around pastures. Then again, maybe Corinne had just grown accustomed to a rougher crowd, people for whom fineries were unaffordable luxuries.

"I'm sorry?"

"The fog. It's steam from the paper mill." He nodded toward the window. "Please allow me to introduce myself. My name is McAvoy, Wilson McAvoy."

"I am pleased to meet you, Dr. McAvoy."

He narrowed his eyes in puzzlement, but then he caught sight of his own case, and a smile tilted his lips up. "Ah, you are a very observant young lady . . ." His pause implied a question.

"Corinne. Corinne Ford."

"Well, Miss Ford, be glad the train won't stop in Conroy long, because the smell the plant gives off is rather pungent. I, on the other hand, do not share your luck. I run the infirmary at the mill and do most of the doctoring around the county."

"I'm a nurse myself," she volunteered.

"Is that so?" he asked, and turned a little so that he could see her better. "If I may ask, what is your destination?"

"I'm actually getting off in Conroy also," Corinne said. In Korea, it had seemed the most natural thing in the world to accept Private First Class Elijah Dunne's proposal of marriage and agree to follow him wherever he called home. War gave every situation a heightened sense of urgency. While in a war zone, there was not an abundance of time to consider options; one simply looked for the most expedient solution to the problem at hand. The promise of a new beginning with the handsome, if somewhat callow, soldier she had nursed back to health in Korea had been Corinne's solution. With it would come a new name and a new home, thousands of miles from San Francisco, a place to which she could never return.

Corinne's nursing skills, combined with an urgent need to flee, had led her into the Army Nursing Corps. And the Nursing Corps had led her to Incheon, on the west coast of Korea, not much below the now all-important 38th parallel.

For a moment, Corinne was not on this train to Conroy, Mississippi. Instead, she was walking through a boxcar in a refugee train, dousing the displaced with DDT to control the pests they carried on them. On the first of those trains, when she still believed the conflict would be short and the riders soon returned to their homes, she tried to offer comfort, to hearten her charges, though few of her words were understood. On the last train, just a month before she herself left Korea, she avoided the eyes of those she sprayed and bandaged. And she no longer flinched as she covered the corpses that would be removed from the train, freeing up a bit more space for those who might still live.

If she wanted to sleep at night, Corinne needed to believe in the righteousness of her experiences overseas. If the American troops had been more successful over there, the sound of the brass bands would have drowned out any questions of whether the military involvement had been right or wrong. Only in defeat did the country fall quiet enough for the small questioning voices to be heard. But what was done was done, and what had been lost was lost. She squelched the plaintive voice inside herself, pushing it into a little box and locking it up tight.

"I've faced worse," Corinne said, more as an encouragement to herself than as a response to her fellow traveler. Two years of the smells of blood and feces in tent hospitals and trains. "Much worse," she said and offered him a grin.

"You from up north?" her companion asked, causing Corinne to wonder why he'd made that assumption. "Your accent," McAvoy explained.

"Oh, no. Out west. California," Corinne said, suddenly tiring of the old doctor's attention. Intentional or not, he was forcing her to relive too many memories. The scents and sounds of war gave way to the feeling of a gun recoiling in her hand. Her mother's screams and the sight of her stepfather clasping his hand over a wound and tumbling forward. If only she'd had the nerve to kill him outright, she might have been able to go home after a while.

"The fog burns off around noon," the old man offered by way of apology. "At least it usually does. And you'll get used to the smell quickly. I barely notice it any longer, except after I've been away awhile. Pardon me if I am being intrusive, but I feel compelled to ask: What could possibly bring a young lady such as yourself to Conroy?"

The trained slowed and blew its whistle to announce its impending arrival. "A proposal of marriage," Corinne responded.

"Then I suppose congratulations are in order," he said, his words partially muffled by the sound of the train's brakes.

"Thank you." Corinne acknowledged the expression of good will with a smile and a slight nod. A nagging voice told her that she should be glowing, a blushing bride-to-be, but this was as close to effusive as she was likely to get at the moment.

"May I inquire as to the name of the lucky young man?" McAvoy said and stood. "Conroy is a small town; if he's from around here, chances are good I know him." He chuckled. "Truth is, chances are good that I *delivered* him." The doctor offered Corinne his arm to help her rise. She took it, allowing him a sense of gallantry, even though she trusted her own strength to stand.

"Elijah Dunne," Corinne said, leading the doctor to the exit. His silence caused her to look back at him. McAvoy's complexion had gone gray.

"Mr. Dunne," he said, with a smile that looked about as genuine as the one Corinne had pasted on her own face. "Didn't have the pleasure of bringing him into the world, but I did nurse him through a bout of measles. He's a fine young man. A hero. A credit to his country." The doctor rattled off these rapid-fire platitudes as he hastened Corinne off the train.

He stopped in his tracks once he'd guided her onto the platform and, after a little more consideration, added, "He'll always have that limp, but they did a fine job of saving his leg." Corinne had played no small part in that concerted effort. "I hope his buddies keep his injury in mind on your wedding night." He smiled at Corinne's perplexed expression. "We got us a little tradition in these parts called shivaree. Folk gather outside the new couple's house and make all kinds of racket. Try to force their way in. If they manage to get to the groom, they'll spirit him away before . . . well, before he gets the chance to enjoy his newfound conjugal rights."

Corinne shook her head in disbelief.

"No, I'm not kidding," the doctor continued. "The poor fellow gets dumped miles from home, and sometimes spends his whole wedding night just trying to get back to his bride. It's gone by the wayside for the most part, but the rowdier boys 'round here still keep it alive, and your Elijah's friends have oft been counted amongst the unrulier."

Corinne wondered if the old doctor was just having her on. "I'm sure that may have been true when he was younger . . ."

"I must be off now," McAvoy interrupted her, seeming not to have noticed she was speaking, "but I wish you two young people the best. If I can be of any service, you know where to find me." He nodded in the direction of the pulp plant. "Just follow your nose."

The steam from the train, as it fired up and chugged away, spilled into the thick haze like milk pouring into cream. The porter, a black man in a black hat with gold trim, emerged from the fog, his body not appearing to possess three dimensions until he drew near enough to pierce the mists. "Passengers' waiting room straight ahead, Miss," he said. "I'll bring your bags around for you momentarily."

"Thank you," Corinne said, "but I was told that there would be a car waiting for me?"

"No, ma'am. No cars waiting, but I am sure your escort will arrive shortly. You just go on in and make yourself comfortable. I'll make sure you are informed as soon as they arrive."

Corinne thanked the porter and approached the building. Perhaps it was the fog that had delayed Elijah's arrival? But no, if the fog's appearance and disappearance could be timed, as the doctor had implied, then Elijah would have factored in its presence. Her hand connected with the door as another thought occurred to her, sending a shock through her system. Perhaps Elijah had changed his mind? He had been sent home with a Purple Heart six months before Corinne could arrange to be decommissioned. His letters had come regularly for three months straight, but then a month, perhaps six weeks, had passed without her receiving a word from him. He began corresponding again without providing any explanation for the break. Corinne had assumed his intervening letters had simply been lost. She shook off her worry. Coming here, marrying him. Those were the right choices. This was her new life, and she might as well embrace it.

She pressed the latch and pushed the heavy door open. Dark faces turned up to look at her, a mixture of apprehension and curiosity playing on them. A woman, not much older than Corinne herself, stopped in the process of gathering her belongings to look at her through tear-reddened eyes. Corinne could tell without asking that the other woman had just said good-bye to someone she held dear. Her sense of loss was so acute that it reached out through her eyes and needled at Corinne's heart. "Oh, no, Miss." The porter hurried up behind her. "This here is the colored waiting room. I'm sure you'll be much more comfortable in the big waiting room. Here, let me show you."

"Sorry," Corinne said and let the door close. It banged shut with a much louder *clack* than she would have wished. Once it was closed, she noticed the sign reading "Colored" for the first time. She had nursed white soldiers, black soldiers, Oriental soldiers, and civilians. All of them with the same red blood.

"Nothing to be sorry for, Miss. You just follow me, and we'll get you settled."

Corinne had just turned to accept his invitation when she heard an unfamiliar voice calling her name. "Miss Ford? Miss Corinne Ford?"

She couldn't make out anyone's features in the fog, so after a moment she stopped trying to pin down the source of the voice. "Yes. I'm Corinne."

A man with a long, steel-gray beard waded to her through the thick air. "I'm Charlie Aarons. I work for the Dunnes. I've been sent to fetch you."

"Oh?" Corinne asked. "Is everything all right? Elijah had written that he'd be here himself to meet me."

"Don't you worry none. Everything's fine. Elijah just has his hands busy with a difficult foaling. Thing's coming out wrong way first." He clasped his dirty hand over her shoulder and guided her in a bum's rush away from the platform.

Corinne knew she was marrying into a farming family, and difficulties with horses and other livestock would inevitably arise from time to time. Rather than allowing herself to dwell on the fact that Elijah hadn't arrived as promised, she decided to dive head-on into the role of farmer's wife. "Take me to him. Perhaps I can help."

The old man fixed her with his gaze and smiled. One of his eyes was covered in a cataract; it was unlikely that he could perceive more than shadows through it. His other eye remained a sharp, burning blue. "Good Lord, no," he said. "That ain't no kind of thing for a lady to get herself into."

"But I'm a trained nurse," Corinne protested.

"I ain't questioning that, but Elijah's mother told me to bring you straight to her, and she's the one who pays my wages, so to Mrs. Dunne we go. Boy," he said, addressing the porter.

"Yes, sir?"

"Put the young lady's bag in the back of my truck, and there'll be a shiny new dime in it for you."

"Thank you, sir," the porter said and, shifting the bags under his arms in order to get a better grip, crossed over to the decades-old red Ford truck that had emerged from the fog. As he neared the bed of the truck, Corinne jumped at the sudden sound of snarling and barking. Three enormous brindle canine heads with cropped ears reared up over the side of the truck, saliva flicking as they growled and showed their fangs.

The porter reacted by jumping back, but he kept a tight grip on the bags he carried. "I'm sorry, sir, but I don't think your dogs are gonna let me get any closer."

Charlie doubled over with laughter. "You right about that one, boy."

"It's all right," Corinne said. "Leave the bags there, I can manage."

"Sorry, Miss," the porter said.

"You have nothing to be sorry for." The porter tipped his hat and headed back toward the station.

"Wait a moment," Corinne called to him. "Aren't you forgetting something?" she asked, turning to Charlie.

The man stroked his grizzled beard. "No, don't think so."

"You promised this gentleman a dime."

Charlie narrowed his eyes and leaned in toward her. "I promised this *boy* a dime if he put your cases in the back of the truck. They ain't in the back of the truck, are they?"

Corinne shook her head, sickened by Charlie's behavior, but not secure enough in her new surroundings to call him out. She dug into her coin purse and found two quarters. She approached the porter and held them out to him. "Thank you."

The porter looked past her without meeting her eyes. "Oh, no, Miss. I can't take your money off you. The gentleman is right. I didn't earn it." The look on his face caused Corinne to glance back at Charlie. The old man's glower served as a warning sign to the porter, and she knew she'd be doing him no good if she insisted. She returned the coins to her purse.

"You have a good day, Miss," the man said and hurried back to the station.

Corinne wondered how a man such as Charlie would have found himself in the Dunnes' employ. Elijah had seemed to be great friends with Washington and Jones, two of the black soldiers in their unit, playing cards and drinking with them. Corinne didn't believe he harbored racial hatred, or would condone this uncouth man's treatment of the porter. She decided she would have some words with Elijah about his employee's behavior, but for now she would say nothing.

Corinne picked up her bags. They were heavy, but she was used to moving dead weight. Charlie made a motion to help. "I can manage," she cut him off.

"Have it your way," Charlie said, shrugging as he walked around the truck to the driver's side.

Corinne approached the bed of the truck and hefted the heavier of the two bags. The dogs snarled at her in unison. Corinne stopped and fixed her eyes on theirs, one after the other. "I am not afraid of you." One of them lunged toward her, and in spite of her determination not to show fear, she pulled back. She looked up to see Charlie staring at her, the corners of his mouth turned up.

"Down," he commanded, and all three dogs collapsed. "Go on," he said to Corinne. "They ain't gonna bother you now. You just got to show them who's in charge. It's the natural order."

Corinne didn't respond. She tipped the first bag over the side of the truck and into the bed. One of the dogs shifted, but they all stayed in prone positions.

She picked up the smaller case. "I'll keep this one on my lap."

"Fine by me," Charlie said, "but we need to get a move on. The farm's a good twenty miles from here, and if we miss the next ferry 'cross the river, we won't get across till past lunchtime."

FOUR

Wilson McAvoy took advantage of the empty infirmary at the mill to get out and check on his godson, whose Christian name was Ovid, but who was known around these parts simply as "the Judge." Locals joked that a man brought before the Judge was just as likely to face the noose for jaywalking as for murder, and McAvoy had to acknowledge there might be a tinge of legitimacy to the jest. Truth was, the man for whose moral upbringing he shared responsibility had grown into a cold-hearted bastard with a twisted sense of justice that had little to do with the law he'd vowed to uphold. The only reason McAvoy felt compelled to look after him was his fond memory of the man's father.

McAvoy hesitated before knocking on the Judge's door. He'd stopped by several times in the two months since the death of Ovid's daughter, but nearly every time the maid Lucille had turned him away, saying the Judge didn't feel up to receiving visitors. Wilson couldn't just walk away, though. A brief feeling of regret caused his shoulders to slump. Hell, Ovid might be "the Judge" now, but Wilson had helped bring him into this world almost half a century ago. He had slapped his ass and then heard his first cry. That he should feel such ambivalence toward the grown man hinted at his own failure to honor his duties as godfather.

He only wished he'd been around to help with Ruby's birth, for then he might have saved Ovid's wife. Perhaps Ovid's soul wouldn't have atrophied if his bride had survived. But there was no use playing the *what if?* game. Ovid's wife was dead, and now his daughter was gone too. And while McAvoy's regret over Ruby's mother's death was real, the guilt he felt over Ruby's demise knocked the wind out of him. He'd done all he could for her, but it would've been better for everyone if she'd never come back to Conroy. Half the town had shown up for her funeral, not because they mourned her passing, but because they wanted to make sure she was good and gone. She'd been her father's daughter all right—the worm-ridden apple hadn't fallen far at all from the tree. If he had stepped up earlier, when she was still just a girl, maybe he could have set her on a different path. But he hadn't, and he'd go to his grave regretting that he'd let Ovid mold her into his own image. *What if, what if.* There they were again, those words. Perhaps those two tiny words were bound to be the heavy burden of any man who'd lived long enough.

Wilson considered heading back to the mill, but he stopped to ring the doorbell. He waited, taking in the late afternoon sun that had finally managed to pierce the pulp plant's haze. There was no answer. Now, *that* was unusual. Lucille was ordinarily here at this time of day. He rang again, then circled around the porch to try and peek through a window. The curtains were pulled tight. He returned to the door and placed his hand on the handle, easing it open. "Lucille? You here?" he called, even though he knew she would have heard the bell and opened the door if she were. "Ovid? It's Wilson."

He stepped over the threshold and closed the door behind him. Instantly swallowed by the gloom, he banged into the hall table with his ever-ready medical bag. He waited until his eyes could adjust before carrying on down the hall. "Anyone home?" To the right was the sitting room. Even though the heavy red velvet curtains had been pulled shut, there was more light here than in the hall. The air was still and hot in the house, nearly as warm as it was outside even though all the light had been blocked from the house. The curtained crimson rectangles that glowed on the western wall of the room provided the only illumination. Wilson made his way toward the rightmost one, reaching out to pull open the drape.

"Don't." Ovid's voice came from the room's darkest corner. Wilson looked over to see his godson slumped over in the wingback chair that sat there. Even in the somber light, he could tell Ovid was in bad shape. "The light bothers me. I've had such terrible headaches lately."

"Why didn't you tell me?" Wilson said, taking note of the man's labored breathing. "Lucille should have had the sense to call."

"I forbade her."

"Well, that woman has more sense than to listen to you when you are in this state. Where is she, anyway?"

"I don't know."

"It isn't like her to be late."

"Not once in ten years," Ovid said, seemingly exhausted from their short conversation. Wilson reached over to the table beside Ovid's chair and turned on the lamp. His hand brushed a silver-framed photo of Ovid's daughter, taken when she was as tiny as a porcelain doll. It teetered, but McAvoy managed to right it before it toppled. Then his eyes fell on Ovid. The sight of his godson nearly made him gasp. He wasn't yet fifty, but he'd aged a decade since Wilson had last laid eyes on him some weeks ago. Ovid's jet-black hair had turned a steely gray, and his skin showed an odd bluish cast and looked bruised and purple beneath the eyes. Despite the heat, he was dressed in a heavy overcoat with a thick knitted scarf around his neck. Wilson tried not to show his shock. Without waiting for an invitation—or permission—he sat his bag down on the table and went to Ovid's side. Taking the man's hand, he worked his fingers down to his wrist. The pulse was weak, thready. The skin cold.

"Lucille been feeding you right?" he asked.

"I don't really have much of an appetite anymore."

"And how are you sleeping?" Wilson let go of the wrist and fetched his stethoscope from his bag.

"Nightmares," Ovid said as if that were a complete answer. Wilson put the stethoscope into his ears and opened his friend's coat to place the diaphragm against his chest. The man's heartbeat wasn't racing, but it was still too rapid for a resting state. He undid the scarf.

"I'm so cold," Ovid protested, but Wilson paid no heed. He ran his hands over the lymph nodes. They were slightly swollen, and a little bruising was evident on the right side of the neck.

Wilson ran his hand down Ovid's stomach. "Tell me if this hurts," he said, pressing in. A flinch was the only answer. "Well," Wilson said returning his stethoscope to his bag, "I don't know what's causing it, but you, my friend, are showing clear signs of anemia."

Ovid said nothing. He didn't seem interested one way or another. He reached up and wrapped the scarf back around his neck.

"We should get you to the hospital in Tupelo, have them run a few . . ."

"No. No Tupelo. No hospital. I can't be seen like this. You know that."

"But Ovid, you can't just hole up in here and expect people not to talk. When did you last preside over court anyway?" The Judge waved his hand in the air like he was trying to shoo away a lazy fly. From the gesture, McAvoy surmised that Ovid's official duties were the least of his worries. McAvoy always made an effort to overlook the less savory aspects of Ovid's *dealings*, but the Judge's extracurricular business activities were obviously what was weighing on his mind.

McAvoy had fulfilled his duty to the Judge, and Ovid had rejected his opinions and advice. He had loved Ovid's dad, yes, but the son had not inherited the characteristics that had endeared the father to him. He allowed himself to wonder if the world would be a better place without the Judge in it. Perhaps the best course was to do what little Ovid would allow him to do, then let God do the deciding. "Well, don't you worry. We'll get you fixed up right quick. I'll get Lucille to start you on a diet with plenty of iron. And I'll drop by later with a couple of seco-barbitals to help you sleep."

"I don't want pills."

Wilson cursed himself for his own stupidity. Ruby had developed a taste for barbiturates, even before she'd taken off. They'd been trying to wean her off of them, when she up and disappeared. "I'll drop a couple off anyway. Take 'em, don't take them, but you need to rest."

"I should have never let him take her," Ovid said. McAvoy knew whom he was talking about, of course—the man he blamed for Ruby's drug use, the one who'd later stolen her away from Conroy. "I should have known the son of a bitch was trouble and turned him over to Frank and Bayard." It was a well-known secret that Bayard Bloom and Frank Mason acted as the Judge's enforcers and, McAvoy reflected, executioners. This was no world of innocents, though, so he'd waste no tears for the missing. It had been this pair of ruffians the Judge had tasked with going to California to retrieve Ruby. McAvoy cursed their success in the job.

"I should have killed him myself," Ovid said. "If I'd known she'd run off with him like she did . . ." He struggled to catch his breath. "I mean, damn it, Wilson. All his talk of movie stars and his pretty ways. I thought the boy was one of those *introverts*. It never occurred to me that she wouldn't be safe with him. I'd've had his balls for cufflinks if I'd known the truth. How did they get their hands on drugs anyway? Must've been through the coloreds."

McAvoy understood why the Judge was mystified. After all, the Judge controlled all trafficking in the three surrounding counties, outside of a few daring fools who had begun to make inroads in the area with goods obtained from sources in Memphis. He didn't like the direction in which Ovid's thoughts seemed to be headed. It'd be just like the Judge to order a few disciplinary strikes against the entire community, just to send a message to the few who'd misbehaved, so he presented his godson a different and more distant scapegoat. "I understand the boy frequented jazz clubs in Biloxi. Those musicians are walking apothecaries." He patted the Judge's arm. "But you need to calm yourself. It won't do you any good to think about it now."

"He's the one who put that motion picture nonsense in her head, you know . . . That they could go out to Hollywood and become movie stars, the both of them."

A remarkable face surfaced in Wilson's memory, a young man with golden curls, nearly indigo eyes, hollow cheeks, and Roman nose. Any number of people might have made fools of themselves over that face. Really, it came as no surprise that a beautiful, bored girl like Ruby had fallen under his sway and attached herself to his dreams.

"I've asked myself a thousand times," Ovid continued, "where I went wrong with her. I thought I'd raised her better than that. But when it came down to it, she ran off like a blue-tick bitch in heat."

McAvoy decided to let Ovid pretend he'd been a good father. Ruby was gone and buried. No good would come from criticizing the man now, and maybe a little pious fiction would help Ovid pull himself back together. And who was he to cast stones? McAvoy had his regrets, just like Ovid did. "Well, what's done is done. Now we need to work on getting you well again."

"I just can't figure out how they got their hands on the money to leave town. That boy never earned an honest dollar in his life."

"Well, Ovid, there are many ways to turn a dishonest dollar," Wilson said, instantly regretting the irony of his words, but Ovid seemed to take no heed. "We need to get you up to your room. You think you can make it if I help you?"

The Judge stayed deep in thought, and it wasn't clear whether he was considering the weighty issue of his daughter's fate or the question of his own remaining strength.

The doctor turned at the sound of approaching footsteps. Whoever had entered the house must have come in through the kitchen. "Lucille?" he called out.

"Yes, sir," Lucille responded. "Oh, Doctor McAvoy, it's you," she said as she moved into the room, a mixture of pity and fear crossing her face as she took in the sight of her employer. "It's good you came."

"You should have called me, Lucille," Wilson said, taking care to sound duly stern.

"I know, sir. I wanted to, but . . ."

"No buts, Lucille." The severity of his tone caused her to wince. "No excuses. Now I need you to help me get the Judge up to his room."

"Yes, sir," she said and rushed forward to assist him.

"How long has he been like this?"

"Well, sir, he ain't really been himself since . . ." she started, then stopped herself. Wilson understood the rest. Just after Ruby's passing. "But he didn`t start feeling poorly till last week. He's much worse than when I seen him last, at Saturday lunch, that is. He just said he was a little tired when I was leaving, but . . ."

Wilson calculated the amount of time the Judge had been on his own. Just shy of forty-eight hours. "Okay, Ovid, on three," he said, although he wasn't sure the Judge had even heard him. He positioned himself on the Judge's right side and signaled with a nod that Lucille should support him on the left. "One, two, three." Wilson nearly toppled over when the weight he'd been expecting didn't manifest itself. He was amazed by how light the man had become. The Judge was wasting away. "Lucille, you run up and make sure his bed is ready. I think we can manage on our own."

Lucille acknowledged the command with a curt nod and headed

immediately toward the stairs. "I don't want to sleep," the Judge murmured into Wilson's ear.

"You need your rest. We're putting you to bed so that you can get it."

"But the nightmares. I can't stand them."

"They're only dreams. They'll pass."

The Judge grasped his upper arm, much more tightly than Wilson would have suspected his remaining strength could manage. "She comes to me, Wilson. Ruby comes to me, and her eyes are on fire. Blue like the center of a flame."

"That's enough, Ovid. It's only your illness working on your grief. Speak no more of it . . . to anyone." Wilson assisted the much younger, but strangely aged man to the foot of the stairs, then helped him begin the arduous climb. Lucille met them at the head and, slinging the Judge's arm over her shoulder, helped him the rest of the way to the foot of the bed.

Once the Judge was sitting steadily enough, Wilson pulled Lucille aside. "The Judge seems to be suffering from anemia and exhaustion," he said under his breath. He reached into his own wallet to pull out a five-dollar bill. "You get on down to the butcher and pick up some liver—chicken, beef, I don't care what kind. Fry it up light so it's still good and pink and get it up here as quick as you can."

She nodded and lowered her hand so that he could place the bill in it. "And Lucille," he said as she was about to leave the room, "tell no one about the Judge's condition. You hear me?"

"Yes, sir." She turned and hurried down the stairs. He heard the door close softly behind her.

"Let's get you undressed," Wilson said, turning again toward his patient, who didn't seem to have processed what was happening. He pulled off Ovid's scarf and removed the man's coat, revealing the dirty white shirt and gray pants he had on underneath it. "These things, too." After helping Ovid out of the shirt, he shifted him so that he was lying flat on the bed, his head cradled in a pillow. That done, Wilson tugged off the patient's pants, leaving him in nothing but an undershirt and briefs. Ovid's right thigh was marked with a streak of dried blood, which he tried to hide with one hand.

"Let me see it," the doctor commanded, pushing his hand aside. The flesh on the thigh had been severely bruised. Wilson leaned in closer to investigate the wound. "Son," he said with a whistle, "any idea how you got this?"

Ovid closed his eyes tight and shook his head.

FIVE

Death, everyone knew, was meant to be the end, but it wasn't, at least not for Ruby. She was awake and aware. She felt both pleasure and pain. Only those things she'd previously counted as essential, breath and a steadily beating heart, had deserted her. Still all the old angers and attachments clung to her. She nursed the same wrongs. Ached over the same missed opportunities, felt shame over the same missteps, mistakes that now surely should no longer matter. No, the grave had brought her neither eternal rest nor release.

At first, Ruby would have rather died out in California, her cold body incinerated—just as those who had infected her with the parasite had planned to do—to keep her from coming back. But she hadn't died there. She'd been brought back to Mississippi, back to the Judge's house, even though she'd sworn to herself she'd never spend another night under his roof.

If her father had let her go, the nightmare would have ended, but he had seen her as his personal property, and there was no way he would have simply allowed her her freedom. So he had her transported home, where those ignorant of her condition had allowed her body to transition from the life into which she'd been born to this new tomb-born existence.

It had almost felt like flying as the pallbearers lifted her casket up, and like being rocked in a bassinet as their uneven steps caused her body to sway inside the metal box. Even though she was swaddled by padding and secured by steel, even after she'd felt them rest the coffin on the waiting bier, her hearing remained clear so that each voice reached her. Each tiny laugh. Each whispered expression of joy that she was now gone for good. Only Lucille's voice, raised in song, carried tones of loss, of regret.

Hardest of all had been Elijah's absence. She'd let her mind pick its way through the insincere platitudes, and all-too-sincere expressions of joy, trying to uncover a single utterance that might have belonged to Elijah. She imagined that he'd been too devastated to come, or perhaps that he'd taken his own life so that he could join her in whatever world awaited. She'd since learned that both suppositions had been laughably wrong. The thought of her naïveté led her to reach out and claw plaster from the wall beside her. The thing within her listened on, communicating through images the pleasure it took in her plans of vengeance.

It had seemed like an eternity before she felt the first tremor of movement play out along her fingers. She came to learn that it had actually only taken around three days from awaking in the funeral parlor to regaining full mobility. In between, she lay motionless in the dark, with nothing to comfort her other than the entity's presence. Quickly she grew used to sharing her mind and body with it, coming to think of it less and less as a parasite, and more like a twin soul, a part of herself that had been missing, a partner in the devastation she was about to let loose on the place of her birth.

She had come to rely on its instincts, on its magic—for that was the only word she could think of to describe its abilities—that it seemed to delight in sharing with her. It freed her from the casket, and unlocked the gate of the mausoleum with only a touch. It showed her how to hide from the daylight, and how to feed off the blood of dumb and lumbering animals until together, they were strong enough and quick enough to take down a running man. When it led her to come to this house, she didn't question it. She followed its tug without a single qualm.

This place seemed to have been created for her. While the houses of the living rejected her—a force she didn't yet understand held her just beyond the threshold—the old Cooper home had wanted her, welcomed her. It called to her almost as if it were a radio station broadcasting on the same frequency into which she was tuned. The thing within her had heard the house's call, and caused her to bound along, her feet rarely touching the earth as she tore through the wooded ravine that separated the cemetery from the edge of the farm, the fields long since fallow, where the house sat.

Nearby, the train tracks took a sharp turn to avoid the bend of the river. Trains had to slow at this point, so it had become a customary place for the dirty vagabonds who traveled in boxcars to jump on and off. This area proved prime hunting territory, as the hobos often traveled alone, and were sure never to be missed. No one would come looking for them, so there was no chance of discovery.

Kudzu vine, rapacious and never sleeping, had nearly swallowed the old Cooper house whole. The slanting wood structure would've long since disappeared from sight were it not for the teenagers of Conroy, who came, year after year, wave after wave, drawn at first by the thrill of visiting a place where multiple murders had taken place, then by the convenience of a spot where most adults who'd known the Coopers couldn't bear to visit. For years, the teenagers had kept the front porch and entrance clear of the vine, but they'd stopped visiting the house since Ruby had claimed it, even if they themselves couldn't quite say why.

Darkness calls to darkness, horror to horror. Ruby once thought of houses as lifeless structures, nothing more than a joining of wood and stone and plaster. Void of personality and incapable of feeling or memory. She knew better now. She'd been drawn to this suffocated and decaying house, left so long without regular inhabitants, and stained, physically and psychically, by bloodshed. The Cooper family murders had taken place in a time before Ruby could remember, twenty or more years before, but the stains left by the slaughter, both mundane and mystical, were still there for anyone who cared to look. Before, Ruby had never cared to, but the thing within her seemed to relish the crimes it could still taste, nearly as fresh as the day they'd been committed. And the house tried again and again to speak to her, eager to replay its trauma.

Pay it the slightest attention and shadow would thicken, edges sharpen, and the image of Mr. Cooper would appear, limping and bleeding from where his wife had managed to stab him in the thigh before he ended her with his axe. The visions that arose didn't match the timing of the sound that accompanied them; Ruby had many times watched Cooper's lips moving, calling sweetly out to his children, long after she'd heard their terrified cries.

A few precious yards of the house's entrance remained bare of the creeper vine, but growth over the rest of the place had been left unchecked. Ruby had ordered the boy Merle to see to it that the front window was boarded over, making it safe for her to visit the front of the house during the day. She could move freely through the rest of the place without further precaution. What little sunlight pierced the house's other windows was dyed a dim bottle-green by the leaves of the knotted kudzu that had covered them over.

Ruby examined the blue pallor of her skin given an even more otherworldly sheen by the filtered viridescent sunshine. She could bear this sunlight; it didn't scald her and send her fleeing for the closest source of cool and comforting shade. Ruby didn't know why this light should be different from sunlight filtered by shades or curtain. That light still caused her skin to redden painfully within moments of exposure.

Perhaps the plant fed on and absorbed the wholesome part of the light that was noxious to the thing inside her.

The thing to which she'd been joined relished the procession of images, turning its focus to the bloodshed again and again, like a child demanding to be told the same bedtime story night after night. Ruby, fascinated at first, now found the house's reminiscences tiresome. She coaxed the thing within her to look away, knowing that the seemingly solid man, once ignored, would dissolve back into shadow. Besides, Cooper's bloodshed only amounted to two tears in a bucket compared to the fate she'd planned for Conroy.

SIX

A horn sounded outside, and Ava Dunne removed her soiled apron, folding it to hide the blood from the chicken she'd just cut up, and laying it on the counter. She swatted away a fly that circled the dismembered bird. The horn sounded again. "All right, all right, I'm coming." She smoothed her dress and headed toward the sound, the heels of her black flats clacking out a staccato beat on the newly laid linoleum. She pushed through the swinging kitchen door and headed down the Oriental runner that led to the front door.

She looked through the door's window to see Charlie standing next to his red truck, one hand snaked in through the open window, preparing to honk the horn again. She opened the door wide, and reached up her right hand to touch her throat. "Charles Aarons, if I have told you once, I have told you a thousand times. This is a civilized household. I will not have you announcing your arrival as if you were Gabriel himself." This was not the first impression she had hoped to make on her soon-to-be daughter-in-law. She turned her head slightly in the hope of seeing past the glare on Charlie's windshield. After catching a glimpse of his passenger, she forced a smile to hide her disappointment. "A drab girl," she thought. "A practical girl," she rephrased it to sound better to her own mind. The young woman opened her own door and climbed out of the truck. This Corinne had a sturdy frame, she immediately noticed. "She's no Ruby," she thought, and then she breathed a quiet sigh of relief. "She's no Ruby."

"Welcome," she said, opening her arms and stepping down the stairs off the porch. "Welcome." Corinne placed the bag she'd been holding on the ground and after a few moments' hesitation circled around and reached into the truck bed, tugging on the handle of a larger case. "Good heavens, Charles. You help her with those bags, and don't make me tell you twice." Charlie ran his hand down his beard, mumbling something under his breath as he did so. "Don't you back-talk me." She stepped off the final stair and crossed over to Corinne. "Welcome," she said for the third time, realizing that she was at a loss for anything else to say.

Corinne matched Ava's frozen smile with her own awkward grin. "Thank you."

"I am so sorry that Elijah wasn't able to meet you as he'd planned."

"I understand," Corinne said, showing no sign of hurt feelings or resentment. "A breech birth is difficult."

"Well, yes, and he and Clay, my husband, Elijah's father, have been with the poor mare since dawn." The two women regarded each other nervously. "Come in," Ava said remembering herself. "You must be exhausted after your trip. Perhaps you'd like something cool to drink, or maybe just a short lie down?"

"Oh, no, I'm fine. The sleeper car on the train was quite comfortable. Especially after two years of sleeping on an army cot."

Ava was surprised at how easily Corinne spoke of two years spent living in a war zone. Elijah still had nightmares. He tried to deny it, but Ava could hear his cries in the night. She always wanted to go to him when he was suffering, but Clay would never let her. Clay wanted their son to be tough, to deal with his problems like a man; funny since

Clay himself tended to look for his courage in the bottom of a bottle. But Ava knew her place. She held her tongue, and did as her husband commanded.

"Leave it," he'd say. "Elijah didn't have to go." That much she knew was true. He was the only son of a farm family. Going to war had been his choice.

"If anything, I'd really like to go assist with the foaling," Corinne said, pulling Ava back to the present moment.

"Oh, dear, no," Ava said, amazed by the very thought of it. "Animal husbandry is man's work. You just come in and freshen up before the men return from the barn. Charlie," she addressed the old man, "you put Miss Ford's bags out on the back sleeping porch." She turned to Corinne. "You will be much more comfortable there. It has been positively stifling around here over the last few days."

Charlie made a struggle of lifting Corinne's larger bag. "What'd you pack in here, bricks?" He staggered over to her and held out a hand for her second bag.

"No, I'll take this one." Corinne clutched the smaller bag tightly.

"That's where she keeps the hooch," Charlie said to Ava and laughed.

Ava shook her head, but her lips tipped up in a small smile. "I must apologize for Charlie. He is a good man. Deep down, at least." Then her attention was captured by the unexpected sight of Conroy's new police car—a Hudson Hornet, Clay had told her—pulling down the gravel drive.

"Is everything all right?" Corinne asked, turning to watch as the black-and-white came to a stop.

"Of course, dear." She tried to smile reassuringly, but the police had never come to her door before. Sheriff Bell, a lean man in his fifties with a drooping gray mustache, exited the passenger's side. His deputy, Rigby, had grown up with Elijah. Younger but thicker than his superior, Rigby climbed out and followed the sheriff a few respectful paces behind. "Good afternoon, ladies," the sheriff said, tipping, but not removing, his hat.

"Sheriff," Ava responded, the word teetering between an acknowledgment of his presence and a question as to why he had come.

"Your Elijah wouldn't be around today, would he?"

"Why, yes, he's in the barn with his father. This young lady here is his fiancée," she added, not sure herself why she felt the need to explain Corinne's presence.

"Congratulations, Miss," the sheriff said, tipping his hat again in Corinne's direction.

"What seems to be the trouble, Sheriff?" Corinne asked. Ava blanched. This girl was a bit too direct for her taste. She'd have to learn her place.

"Oh, no trouble at all. Nothing for you to worry about." The right edge of the sheriff's mustache raised up. Ava took it to be his version of a smile.

"Well, like I said," Ava dove in before Corinne could overstep again, "my son is with his father in the barn. One of our mares is having a difficult foaling. They've been out attending her for quite some time. Poor thing must have finished delivering by now. I'm sure they'll be back soon. You are more than welcome to wait inside, if you'd like, or . . ."

"Why do you want to see him?" Corinne interrupted.

Ava's hand went up to her throat as she looked at the woman who was soon to be her daughter. "I am sure that if the sheriff wanted to share that with us, he would have done so without any prompting." How had this girl been raised?

The sheriff chuckled and stroked his mustache. "Don't worry, Miss. We were just wondering if he'd seen either of the Sleiger boys last night. They never came home, and their mama is worried about them. We wouldn't make much of that," he said, nodding toward his deputy, "other than the fact that they didn't show up for work at the mill this morning either."

"These are friends of Elijah?" Corinne asked, continuing to interrogate the sheriff. Ava felt her cheeks flush in embarrassment at Corinne's forthrightness.

"Yes, ma'am," the deputy spoke up. "Them three are as thick as thieves. Have been since they were knee-high to a grasshopper."

"Strange that he never mentioned them . . ." Corinne began.

"Well, I am sure he wasn't out with them last night," Ava said. "I had him here working on the preparations for his betrothed's arrival. He went to bed at half past nine."

"All right, then," the sheriff said. "We'll leave you to it, but tell Elijah I'd like him to call me when he gets a moment. We're gonna see if we can track down any of the Sleigers' other buddies, but I should be back at the station around four or so."

"I'll let him know, Sheriff."

"Ladies," he responded and, with a wave of his hand, sent his deputy scurrying back to the patrol car. The deputy got into the driver's seat and started up the car as soon as the sheriff was inside, nodding to them once before heading down the drive.

Ava looked back at Corinne. "Let's get you settled, then."

SEVEN

"Looks like Raylene has been filled with the spirit again," Rigby said, pointing toward the courthouse steps as they pulled to a stop at Conroy's only traffic signal, a flashing red light at the intersection of Main and Confederate Streets. Bell's eyes followed in the direction of the deputy's gesture, as Rigby stepped on the gas. "Guess that means the mayor is gonna get an earful from her again."

"And we're gonna get an earful from him." Bell looked back over his shoulder and rapped his knuckles on the dashboard. "Stop the car and let me out." Rigby flashed him a confused look, but did as he was told. "I need to talk to her about those end-of-the-world letters, and the vandalism that's been popping up. I suspect the old girl's behind it or knows who is. 'Sides, I want to talk to her about her boy anyway." Bell opened the door and swung his long legs out. He stepped out, pulling down the brim of his hat to shield his eyes from the bright sunlight that had come breaking over the city hall's polished brass dome.

"Raylene," he called, though the woman went on preaching. "Raylene, you hear me, don't act like you don't."

She turned to look at him, lowering the Bible she held in her left hand, and lifting the cigarette in her right hand to her lips. She drew a long drag, then puffed out the smoke. "'Call to me and I will answer you, and will tell you great and hidden things that you have not known.' That's Jeremiah 33:3, Sheriff."

"I'm sure it is," Bell said, crossing the sidewalk and the grass it bordered in a straight line toward the steps. "Ain't no one knows her scripture like you do."

She smiled at him, showing her rotten, nicotine-stained teeth, more than a few missing. Bell took in the sight of her. He knew for a fact that he was her senior by two or three years, but with her saggy jowls, deeply lined face, and her stringy, dirty gray hair that she wore long and parted down the center, she could've passed as his mother, or certainly the grandmother of her real son, Merle. In spite of his underage smoking and his ducktail haircut, Merle was a decent enough boy who'd begun working as a dishwasher at the diner around six months back. Only problem was even now he was about eighteen months too young to drop out legally. "School's been asking after your boy. County truant officer's bound to come knocking on your door soon."

She shifted her stance over her wide hips, as if she were bracing herself to be tackled. "Let him come knockin'," Raylene said and lifted the Good Book up to Heaven. "We gonna be with the Lord by the time he gets to the door anyhow. The angel done told me."

When it came right down to it, Merle wasn't causing him any grief, so what the hell. Merle had to eat, and Bell was pretty damned sure his daddy hadn't left him any money when he drank himself to death. He'd leave it be for now, at least until and unless he got called in on it. There were still the other matters.

He placed his right leg on two concrete steps higher than the left and leaned in, pulling a small notepad from his pocket and flipping a couple of pages. "Tell me, Raylene, just what does Proverbs 23:2 say?"

She tossed her cigarette to the steps and crushed it beneath her heel, then held the cover of the Bible up to her temple, like she was preparing to perform some kind of magic act. "'And put a knife to thy throat, if thou be a man given to appetite.'" She lowered the book and glared down at him.

He drew his leg down a step so he could stand up straight. "Seems that someone saw fit to paint the reference to that verse on the side of Bill Bledsoe's house." He looked back at his pad. "Exodus 20:14 showed up on the side of Dotty Turndot's house, but she saw that it got painted over right quick. Paint was all nice and dry by the time Tom got home from his business trip." He held up his hand. "I got that one. 'Thou shalt not commit adultery.'" He closed the pad and returned it to his shirt pocket. "So tell, me, Raylene, is it just a coincidence that you have these verses right on the tip of your tongue, or have you anointed yourself our local prophet?"

Raylene stuffed her Bible under one arm, then bending over, riffled through her bag, pulling out a pack of Camels and a lighter. She shook the packet until a tip of a cigarette popped out, then she took it between her teeth, and bent to drop the packet back into her purse. She flicked the wheel on her lighter until it flamed, then she cupped her hands around it and the cigarette. Bell watched as puffs of blue smoke built up a healthy cloud around her face. She lowered her hand, and flicked closed the cap of her lighter, dropping it into her bag, without bending. She clutched her Bible again, this time in her right, and with her left, she pulled the cigarette from between her lips, gesturing with its burning tip.

"Well, no, sir, I ain't anointed myself nothing. A greater power than myself has chosen me. And it ain't no coincidence that I have those or any other of God's words on the tip of my tongue. 'Then said I, Woe is me! for I am undone; because I am a man of unclean lips, and I dwell in the midst of a people of unclean lips.' No, sir, scripture is the armor of the spirit, and I wrap myself in it. 'Therefore put on the full armor of God, so that when the day of evil comes, you may be able to stand your ground, and after you have done everything, to stand.'"

"But you did commit these acts of vandalism . . ."

"Vandalism? The word of God is vandalism?" She shook the book at him. "'In the same hour came forth fingers of a man's hand, and wrote over against the candlestick upon the plaster of the wall of the king's palace: and the king saw the part of the hand that wrote.'"

"'Thou art weighed in the balances, and art found wanting,'" Bell interrupted, determined to knock her down a peg or two by showing her she wasn't the only one who knew scripture. "Knowing what the Good Book says doesn't necessarily qualify you to act as judge."

She lowered the book and smiled at him as if he'd just told a joke. "No, I am happy that I am nobody's judge." She nodded. "Yes, Sheriff, I shared the words of God. The angel, I done told you, she comes to me." Raylene's eyes lost their focus. "She's such a beautiful thing. Blue like the heavens themselves." She dropped her cigarette, and it fell, rolling down the steps. Raylene took no notice of her loss. She turned her gaze to his face. "She knows everyone's sins, all of them. And she's told me to announce them all. Warn these poor weak sinners that they're running out of time. These are the last days. The angel of death has come to Conroy, Sheriff. She's passing through right now, and there's only one way to make sure she's gonna pass you by."

"Exodus 12:22," he said thinking of the letters that had been sent to just about every church in the county. "You saying this angel wants folk to paint their doorways with blood."

"That's right, Sheriff. 'And ye shall take a bunch of hyssop, and dip it in the blood that is in the bason, and strike the lintel and the two side posts with the blood that is in the bason; and none of you shall go out at the door of his house until the morning.' I got down on my knees before her. I pleaded with her, just like Abraham pleaded for Sodom. She swore to me, she'd accept this as a sign of a person's righteousness. She wouldn't raise her hand against those who honor her by keeping this pact."

Bell wasn't easily frightened, but something about her intensity spooked him. He went backward down the two steps he'd climbed toward her. "All right, Raylene. I'm telling you, you need to knock it off. Stop harassing people, or I'm gonna have to lock you up. Merle ain't gonna like seeing his mama behind bars."

"My boy, he understands . . ."

"Well, I don't, and I'm the law around here. This is your last warning, Raylene. Cut this nonsense out, and find somewhere else to do your preaching. The mayor, he doesn't like having you hanging out here. Keep this nonsense up and you'll find yourself standing before the real judge in these parts."

"I ain't worried about none of you," she said, shaking her head, almost like she was trying to wake herself from a dream. "'For we wrestle not against flesh and blood, but against principalities, against powers, against the rulers of the darkness of this world, against spiritual wickedness in high places.'"

"Go home, Raylene." He pushed the brim of his hat back and then pointed at her. "Get yourself home, and get that boy of yours back in school, you hear me?" He turned his back on her and took the widest strides he could without looking like he was running away.

"'But I say unto you,'" she called out after him. "'That every idle word that men shall speak, they shall give account thereof in the day of judgment.' That day's comin' quicker than any of you fools around here think."

EIGHT

Corinne could remove shrapnel, stitch up a wound, and perform a thousand and one other acts to save a life. Her future mother-in-law had not taken any of these talents into account when judging Corinne on her, at best, rudimentary cooking skills. Ava hadn't exactly banished her from the kitchen, but she'd relegated her to performing the most basic of tasks. Luckily, her skill with a scalpel helped her make short work of peeling five pounds of potatoes, and her experience with removing stitches served her well when it came to prepping string beans. They worked in near silence; Ava's cautious welcome seemed to have curdled as quickly as cream with lemon juice.

Corinne had expected a barrage of questions about her past, her family, and how she had come to choose a career rather than immediately settling down. But Ava didn't ask her about any of this. In fact, Ava hadn't shown even the slightest bit of curiosity regarding the woman her only son was soon to marry. Corinne decided to break the ice. "How did you and Elijah's father come to meet?"

Ava stopped rolling piecrust and gave her a shocked, almost angry look—her eyes open wide, her eyebrows pinched together. Her lips parted, then zipped back together into a tight, thin line. She gripped the rolling pin with such fervor that her knuckles whitened and started to attack the pastry. "That was so long ago, I hardly see as how it matters now." She dusted her hands once more with flour and whipped the dough off the pastry board, parachuting it into the pie tin. "I don't know what it is like in San Francisco, but I think you will find that folk around here don't take kindly to being asked personal questions."

"I'm sorry." Corrine startled in her chair. "I didn't mean to pry. I was just trying to get to know you better." Though she knew she had put her foot in it somehow, she couldn't begin to understand how. "I thought you might enjoy reminiscing . . ."

"Young lady," Ava said with a tone of exasperation, "you will learn that in these parts, if someone wants you to know something, you won't need to ask. They will share it with you when they are good and ready. And we don't get to know people overnight either. We take our time to build relationships. You're marrying my son. That means you will be sticking around for a while. There is no rush for us to become better acquainted."

"Perhaps I should go unpack," Corinne said. Ava answered her with a curt nod toward the exit.

Corinne made her way out to the sleeping porch. She retrieved her suitcases from the floor and sat them on the larger of the two beds that dominated the space. The family had stationed a battered pine chifferobe up against the wall that separated the interior of the house from the porch. She surmised that it had been moved here for her temporary use, as it effectively blocked the kitchen window behind it. Roman shades had been hung above the screened openings to offer her privacy. Or perhaps they'd been put up without her modesty in mind; they seemed to be a permanent fixture. Regardless, they were rolled up now, affording Corinne a good view of her future-in-laws' property. The modest, white two-story frame house itself had been built on an unimpressive hill, but the surrounding countryside was pleasing to the eye. The field behind the house descended at a gentle slope to a body of water too small to be called a lake, but much larger than what Corinne would have considered a pond. Her clothes clung close to her skin in the humid air, and she longed to strip down and dive headlong beneath the surface of the crystalline water. Perhaps Elijah would take her there after he'd finished with the day's work.

To the right, on the opposite end of the vista, Corinne spotted the barn. It had been left to weather, unpainted except for a spot where she could, when squinting, make out the words "Dunne's Dairy." The words themselves had faded with age and peeled in the bright sunlight that beat down on the barn, leaving them more of a memory than an extant marker.

She opened the smaller of her two cases first. At the top of the case was the two-piece white silk dress she had purchased for the wedding that was to take place tomorrow evening immediately following a special prayer service in their honor at the Dunnes' church. The dress was sleeveless, with a simple V-cut that gave character to the scoop neck. She had intended to wear it this way for the nuptials, but another nurse, who was from Atlanta, had warned her that the sleeveless cut might be considered too daring for Mississippi. The bolero jacket that had come with the shift was her insurance policy. She unfolded both pieces and hung them in the chifferobe. Returning to the case, she removed a velvet drawstring bag, the original contents of which had long since been forgotten. Now it served to hold her Walther PPK pistol with its well-fed magazine. She'd traveled cross-country without a man's protection, an act that might itself be perceived as an invitation by a certain type of man. Corinne would never let herself be forced again, no matter what she had to do to protect herself. She pulled open one of the chifferobe drawers and pushed the gun to the back of it, using her neatly refolded underwear to camouflage the weapon.

Corinne pushed the drawer, but it wouldn't close completely. She tugged it out and flattened its contents, making sure that nothing was catching, and tried again. It still refused to close all the way. She realized something must have fallen behind the drawer, so she took it in both hands and carefully slid it off its runner. She knelt down on the floor and reached into the recess, feeling blindly until her fingers encountered a piece of card stock. She grasped the paper and retrieved it. It was a photograph, creased roughly down the center from its time behind the drawer. Corinne smoothed it open. Even marred as it was by the fold in the paper, the face that stared back at her was bewitching. A young woman with black hair and large obsidian eyes, but the palest of skin. Her Gallic, heart-shaped face held a small, straight nose and beckoning cupid lips. Corinne could have stared at this face forever, but she was repulsed by the sensations she felt rising up within herself. Her hand trembled, and the photo tumbled to the floor. She reached down to snatch it up. "Love, Ruby" had been signed in a careless script on the photo's reverse. Corinne reflected that girls who looked like this didn't need to worry about their penmanship.

Elijah had never mentioned a girl named Ruby. In fact, he had been adamant that there was no one waiting for him stateside. The word "love" danced before Corinne's eyes. What had the beauty been feeling when she scrawled it? Did the word signify a casual affection or a deeper emotion? Had it been intended for the Dunne family as a unit or Elijah alone? She decided to take the photograph to Ava and explain how she'd found it. How it had come to be damaged. But she couldn't resist flipping it over, if only to study this Ruby's features once more. Without reflecting on her actions, she returned the drawer to its runner and hid the photo beneath a stack of underwear, with the velvet bag. She closed the drawer.

Outside, she recognized Elijah's voice, even though she was unable to make out his words. She hurried to the window, zeroing in on its source. Two men had exited the barn, and they were taking turns pumping water so that each could wash his hands, arms, and face. Ablutions complete, the men looked up at the house and started toward it.

Caught up in the sentiments conveyed by six months' worth of love letters, Corinne surprised herself with her own enthusiasm. She bounded out the screen door and ran in the direction from which the men were coming. She had expected for Elijah to run as well, meeting her halfway to sweep her up in his arms, but he continued toward her with an unhurried pace. How foolish. As she should know better than anyone, his wound had ensured he'd never run again. She had come within ten yards of the men when she stopped in her tracks, questioning her own senses.

Of the two men coming toward her, neither was the Elijah Dunne she remembered. Even after eliminating the second man due to his age, Corinne could not convince herself that the man who'd proposed to her a mere six months earlier was the other fellow standing before her. She took a few measured steps in his direction, hoping her impression might change after a closer perusal. The younger of the two was unshaven, a thick blond beard hiding the lower portion of his face. His hair was unkempt, badly in need of cutting. His body had thickened, the middle filling out two, maybe three inches, the V-shape of his torso turning into a barrel. It was both Elijah and not Elijah; the man who stood a mere few feet in front of her was a fattened, feral version of her fiancé.

"Corinne," he said, extending his hand, palm facing inward. The reality of the situation began to tumble in on her. The letters they had written each other over the last several months had been full of such warmth, but she'd really only known the man for less than six months . . . and that had been more than six months ago and seven thousand miles away. Now she stood here before him in a world even more alien than the battleground where they'd met, not quite believing that this was happening—that this was her future husband—and he was greeting her with a handshake. She held out her own; he gave it a quick pump and released it.

"This her?" his father asked, nodding in Corinne's direction, as if she weren't worth addressing.

"Yes, sir," Elijah said.

Mr. Dunne looked her over. He disregarded her eyes, instead taking in her breasts, the width of her hips. Corinne felt like she was being appraised for purchase as livestock rather than being welcomed into the family. "All right, then. Let's not keep your mother waiting." The older man turned and, without a word of greeting, began trudging toward the house.

Corinne's mouth trembled and her jaw fell open. "No, sir," Elijah responded, but now that the old man was facing the other direction, he winked at Corinne and planted a quick kiss on her cheek. The relief that washed over her was so complete that a small gasp escaped her. "Give 'em some time. You'll get used to them."

"What if I don't?" Corinne whispered.

"Well, they can't live forever." A lopsided smile curled his lips, and small crinkles formed around his eyes.

There, Corinne thought to herself. *There he is.*

NINE

Elijah followed a few steps behind his soon-to-be bride, watching her square and sturdy hips move up and down like pistons as she mounted the slight incline leading to the house. He'd hoped that seeing each other in the flesh would do something to fan the embers of their affection for each other, but she'd barely seemed to recognize him. In Korea they'd been a couple; here they were strangers. Or maybe it was only his own guilt over betraying her that made him imagine things?

He'd enlisted in the army in the hopes of returning a hero or not returning at all, but the army in its infinite wisdom decided he would best serve the cause if indentured to kitchen patrol duty, feeding the workers who staffed the olive-drab circus tent Uncle Sam chose to call a "hospital." The greater part of his foreign deployment had seen him peeling potatoes and carrying refuse out to the garbage pit dug on the far end of camp. It was on one of these trips when a sniper caught him in the leg. He was lucky that a more essential body part hadn't been destroyed. His buddy, who'd been a few steps ahead of him, hadn't been as lucky.

He and Corinne had met some months before in the mess hall, just after she'd transferred in from another MASH unit. He'd spooned a cooling glop of chipped beef in gravy onto her plate, and the look of resignation in her eyes at the sight of it caused him to laugh. It was the first honest laugh he'd enjoyed in a very long time. Their eyes met, and her lips curled into a shy smile. And that was it. That was the moment when he began to think he might just survive losing Ruby.

But then, not long after he returned home, he learned he might not have lost Ruby after all. The Judge's men had found her and brought her home.

The things folks told him had happened, the things that drove him to leave Conroy, to leave Ruby—she swore they never happened. He'd listened to the wrong voices, believed the wrong people. If only she hadn't been so beautiful—too beautiful for him. She had so much life and spark to her. He, on the other hand, was such a dullard. He'd believed from the start that sooner or later she'd tire of him and move on, and when he heard what people were saying, well, he believed that was exactly what had happened. Both he and Ruby ended up paying for his lack of faith. He went off to Korea to get his leg shot up, and broke her heart in the process.

Then she ran off to California with Dylan Sawyer, the pretty boy from a grade behind them. She and Dylan had only been friends, though, and had gone their separate ways within weeks of reaching Hollywood. She swore it, and he believed her.

It was almost too much to bear when she started to fade away before his eyes, losing more strength each day, his hope withering along with her body. Ultimately, he could do nothing to save her. It happened so quickly, before he could even summon the courage to write to Corinne and tell her not to come. A twinge of conscience told him he should have written anyway. Explained everything and let her decide if she'd still have him. But his courage had failed him. Corinne had become his only light in an endless black tunnel.

The crunch of his boots on the water-starved east Mississippi grass pulled him back to the present moment. Yes, his loyalty had wavered, but he'd never fail Corinne again. Ruby was gone now, and a few paces before him walked his future. Their relationship would never know the razor-edged passion he'd felt for his first love, perhaps his only true love, but he'd do all he could to help resurrect the easy camaraderie he and Corinne had known before. Still, he caught himself praying it wouldn't be Ruby's face he saw when it came time to lie with Corinne.

She glanced back over her shoulder at him, and he did his best to muster a reassuring smile.

TEN

Marjorie's thighs rubbed against each other as she climbed the steps that led to Mrs. Sawyer's front door. That old sun seemed to burn hotter than it used to, frying her to a crisp in no time anymore. Sweat formed dark circles under her arms, and her underpants began to ride up and bunch. She stopped midclimb, balancing a cake carrier on her right hand and tugging at the back of her skirt with the left. The cake nearly toppled, causing her heart to thump and putting an end to her private rendition of "I'm Walking Behind You," a song she hoped would remind Dylan of her whenever he heard it play on the radio.

She righted her burden and padded up the last three steps onto the wide gray porch that wrapped around the Sawyer house's front and sides. As she scooted deeper into the shade of the porch's overhang, a flash of a well-worn fantasy hit her, the one where Dylan returned to Conroy, broken by the big city and ready to settle down once and for all. With her. She played this dream over in her mind so often, if it had been a record, the groove would have been scraped smooth.

She had another dream, though, a better one. Rather than failing in Hollywood, Dylan would shine as its brightest star. She would head over to The Strand Theater to catch his debut, and as she stood beneath the marquee admiring his name, or whatever his name would be once they made him famous, a big shiny black car would pull up alongside her. The back window would lower, and Dylan would lean out. There'd be no words. There would be no need for words. He'd smile, then sweep her away with him out to California, without even stopping so she could pack. He'd buy her all new clothes once they made it to Hollywood. She imagined the buzz at the phone company and her supervisor's face when she called in—long distance—to quit.

But the weeks turned to months, and one year became two. Marjorie was no fool. She'd realized it was time to grow more realistic and let this latter dream slide. If Dylan were going to be a star, he'd have made it by now. She'd returned to rehearsing the more realistic scenario of welcoming the weary prodigal's return, a choreographed soporific that carried her off each night. Hollywood hadn't appreciated Dylan the way it should have, but the ending would still be happy, because she'd be here waiting for him. Yes, she would welcome him home with open arms and an open heart.

Then her thoughts veered without warning toward the woman who'd seduced him away in the first place. A familiar hurt rose, and she forced it back down. She had not welcomed Ruby when her supposed friend returned. It was unforgivable that Ruby, the girl who already had everything, would steal Dylan from her and lead him so far from home, so far from her and his mother who loved and pined for him.

She could feel her heart breaking all over, hot tears threatening to whelm the dam she'd built to block the pain of the betrayal. She imagined stuffing the fear and hurt into a box, no, a small coffin, a miniature of the casket Ruby had been laid in.

No, she had not welcomed Ruby home. Nor did she go to Ruby's funeral, although she had ventured out to the cemetery to watch Ruby's casket be locked away in the Lowell family crypt. Delmar Blount had noticed her standing at the edge of the scraggly pines that formed the graveyard's eastern border and sidled up beside her. "Tramp the dirt down hard, boys," he said, his words followed by a bitter laugh. "Make sure the bitch is good and buried." Silently, he offered her a cigarette, but the gleam in his eyes warned her the smoke would come with a price. The price of something she was saving for Dylan.

She shook her head and focused on the sea of mourners. A lot of them were the Judge's hired people, but there were a heck of a lot more regular townspeople than she would've expected to see. They all milled around, their attention focused either on the Judge himself or on the six pallbearers who bore the casket. "They aren't burying her like that. She's going into the mausoleum there, with her mama," she said and pointed at the Lowell family crypt.

"That's a damned shame," Delmar said. "I'd been looking forward to thinking about the worms eating her." He took a puff. "Reckon that Sawyer boy is gone, too. Course if he ain't, he's pretty much dead to Conroy anyway." She turned on him, ready to denounce his foolish thoughts, but he carried on. "If he ever sets foot around here again the Judge will skin that pretty face off him like an apple peel."

"The Judge is a good man," she countered. "He knows this all was Ruby's doing. He'd never lay the blame at an innocent man's feet."

Delmar's eyes widened, and his lips curled up in a look of amusement. He started to speak, but didn't, instead drawing another puff of his cigarette. He shook his head and slid back off through the pines. "Go on, then," she'd whispered. "Get on out of here and take your nonsense talk with you."

She had remained in place, though, keeping vigil until long after the crowd had taken off, and even after the sexton locked the gate to the mausoleum, giving it a good shake to make sure it was sealed. He must have questioned himself, though, because a few minutes later, an old man she recognized as Charlie Aarons came around to check it again. She fought off the urge to try the gate herself, wondering if a charmed third attempt, like in a fairy tale, would cause it to spring open. Instead, she swatted at the mosquitoes that had set on her, and took advantage of the failing light to pick her way around the graveyard and head home.

She tried to find the forgiveness Reverend Miller at Five Point Methodist preached about. It had been a bit over two months now since Ruby had been sealed away, but Marjorie's sentiments toward her still hadn't softened, not one whit. Maybe the problem was that Miller offered only the Methodist flavor of forgiveness. Marjorie had been raised Baptist. She'd only switched over to the Methodists since Mrs. Sawyer was the organist at Five Point.

No, the milk of Christian kindness had failed to irrigate her soul; Marjorie remained glad Ruby had died. It would make it easier for Dylan to come home, now that he wouldn't have to suffer a living reminder of his moral lapse.

A small thrill ran through her. Wouldn't it be wonderful if he chose today, his birthday, to come home to them? She spared a moment to let the image play in her mind's eye; then a bead of sweat rolled down her spine and pulled her back to the white house's wide gray porch. She balled up her left hand into a fist and rapped on the Sawyers' hunter-green trim.

ELEVEN

"Do come in, dear," Francis Sawyer said as she took in the perspiring mess of a woman on the other side of the screen door. Majorie's peroxided blonde curls were matted against her forehead, her round cheeks flushed red all the way down to her downy double chin. Francis used her left hand to force the door to open, its spring screeching out in protest at the unwanted pressure.

At first Francis had found the woman a bother, showing up at her door every two or three days to inquire after Dylan, but soon she realized that Marjorie was the only other person on the earth who cared for the well-being of her beautiful boy. As the days went along, blurring one into the next, their shared vigil for Dylan's safe return began to outweigh Francis's concern for the woman's obviously delusional nature.

"I brought a cake," Marjorie said, an earnest smile on her lips. "So we can celebrate Dylan's birthday."

Francis did her best to feign surprise. "That's very thoughtful of you." It had been Dylan's birthday—his real one—the first time loneliness drove Francis to welcome this woman into her home. That day her sense of loss led her to take Marjorie upstairs, to show her Dylan's empty closet, let her touch the pillow where Dylan had laid his head. Now Marjorie brought a cake with her each and every visit; in her mind every day was Dylan's birthday.

Francis watched the sad, dumpy creature shuffle over the threshold. That the woman could function well enough in her position as telephone operator seemed a miracle, considering how she seemed to spend her nonworking hours floating through some kind of dream world, a dream world that centered on Dylan.

Oh, it was true that Dylan had befriended Marjorie; both he and Ruby seemed to enjoy spending time with the old-maid telephone operator, but more than once Francis had overheard the two young folk laughing over Marjorie's perceived romance with her son. Marjorie had to be twelve, perhaps fifteen years older than Dylan, even though she swore her age was eighteen. Francis had made Marjorie's acquaintance three years ago, and by Marjorie's reckoning, she was still eighteen. Francis stifled a sigh as she acknowledged that in Marjorie's mind she would always be eighteen, just as it would always be Dylan's birthday.

As was her habit, Marjorie stopped to consider the family photos Francis kept on the wall. But this was the first time she'd ever made a comment. "Mr. Sawyer was so handsome when he was young. A lot like Dylan." She turned back to Francis. "Do you think Dylan will go bald like Mr. Sawyer did?"

"Oh, I wouldn't think so," Francis replied. "That kind of thing comes from the mother's side, and all the men in my family have beautiful heads of hair." Marjorie offered a bland, relieved smile at the assurance.

Francis followed as Marjorie took the lead to the kitchen. Marjorie stopped and looked back at her. "Buttercream frosting," she beamed. "His favorite."

"It certainly is," Francis responded with a smile. It wasn't. If it were, Francis, as his mother, would have known. The boy'd never had much of a sweet tooth, which, considering that he had inherited his father's delicate health, was probably for the best. Still, what harm could it cause to let Marjorie believe? Francis smiled and forced herself not to focus on the dark hairs that formed a light mustache on the other woman's upper lip. Marjorie turned and shuffled into the kitchen, the thick damp wad of her undergarments showing plainly beneath the graying white of her cotton skirt.

Perhaps it was cruel on her part to feed Marjorie's delusions—her hinted at, but never fully voiced belief that shortly after his homecoming, Dylan would take her as his wife. That was a worry for tomorrow, not today.

For more than a year, it had only been companionship and empathy that kept Francis opening her door to Marjorie. Then around two months back, something extraordinary happened. At first Francis thought Marjorie had finally slid past confused and straight into full-on crazy, as she watched Marjorie's face change before her very eyes, the muscles tensing and her regard taking on a sharpened clarity that usually lacked in this habitual sleepwalker's eyes. Then Marjorie began speaking, her voice transformed, growing deeper, raspier. Francis stared in amazement as the spirit of an Indian guide spoke through the plump bottle blonde. Francis would never have believed it, had the next voice not been that of her own dear Clarence, who spoke of things only her husband could have remembered. Then, after proving himself to her, he shared what he, from the realm of spirit, could glean about their son's well-being.

Now Francis lived for Marjorie's visits, hoping and praying that after a few minutes of exchanging pleasantries, Marjorie's head would tilt back, and her mouth would open to announce Little Feather's arrival. Francis knew it was wrong. The Bible made it clear a good Christian shouldn't ever make an attempt to speak with the dead. But she hadn't made the attempt to speak with them. No, they had chosen to speak to her through Marjorie. Perhaps it was Marjorie's weak grasp on reality that allowed the spirits to use her?

Marjorie placed the cake on the counter, and found her away to the drawer where Francis kept the knives. Francis took a seat at the table, contemplating the degree of comfort this strange woman seemed to feel in her house. Undoubtedly in Majorie's mind, this was already her home, and Francis her mother-in-law. Francis folded her hands, resting them on the table. "Just a small piece for me, dear."

TWELVE

Ruby's new life didn't come with a guide, so experimentation had been necessary, learning all the rules of this new existence by trial and error. Early on she found that if she could capture her prey's gaze, she could mesmerize them, compel them to act against their own best interest—even elicit the invitation that allowed her to enter their home. As she grew stronger, she learned how to control someone nearby, even if the subject couldn't see her. But still her control only lasted while she was in direct contact with them. One taste of her blood, though, and that made everything different. Once she was in them, she could feel them, control them, like puppets.

With animals, control came even easier, and in the first days of her new life, she'd taken no little pleasure in forcing them to behave in ways their natural instincts should have prohibited. She thought of the tiny red fox whose heart had beaten oh so fast as she compelled it to stand and face down the headlights of an oncoming car. It had been both a whim and an exercise of a godlike power over the beast that she let it flee mere moments before the car's tires crushed it. It was a disappointment that the beast forgot its mortal terror almost as soon as the danger passed. Such a pardon should have merited worship, but the fox slinked off into the night, forgetting its deliverance along with its fear. Now, Ruby rarely wasted her time with animals.

Ruby passed through the deserted Cooper house's kitchen, with its sagging floor, and opened the door leading to the cellar. "Mama's coming," she called as she began to descend the steps, the floorboards creaking, even under her light step.

The space was windowless, and the house's filtered green light failed to make it any farther into the cellar than to illuminate the top two stairs. It didn't matter, though. Ruby no longer needed light to see, as the thing she'd been joined with had no need for eyes. It had come from a place where light had never existed, summoned from an eternal darkness by means of magic, a magic Ruby had once believed only to be a bit of theatre put on by tired charlatans vying to appear more outré in their perversions than the average Hollywood freak. The tireless movement of the force within her, the thing that shared her body and was privy to her every thought, stood as a mute witness to just how wrong she'd been in this supposition. She stepped from the last warped stair onto the cellar's dirt floor, and turned.

Wooden shelves lined the cellar's southern wall. A petrified potato, wrapped in newsprint, and so hard and black that Ruby had at first mistaken it as a stone, testified to the shelves' original use as storage for seed potatoes. Now these shelves were empty, except for a hacksaw and the head of a hobo that Ruby herself had placed there. Ruby smiled and wiggled a finger at it as its eyes followed her movements.

She had taken the man, infected him with her own blood, took his mortal life, so that he could be born again. Then she forced him to dismantle himself piece by piece, whittling himself down to where he could neither feed, fight, nor flee. She had taken over the task herself only when it had become a true impossibility for the hobo to carry on by himself.

The head had lasted weeks now in its current state, and she suspected survival could go on indefinitely. She could only imagine the pain of feeling the hunger, but being incapable of feeding. She was no fool. She realized that if she could so easily control the people she'd turned, there might just be someone out there who could handle her the same way. She'd good and done made up her mind never to set foot near California again just in case.

She reached out and tousled the head's dirty blond curls. She had found this bum's unwashed face the most pleasing of all those she'd taken, his features reminding her somewhat of Dylan. This vague and watered-down resemblance was why she'd chosen to keep him around. What had started out as an experiment had turned into a kind of pet.

Its mouth opened, and Ruby snatched her hand back out of the way of the snapping of its long canines. Ruby laughed and flicked its nose with her thumb and middle finger. "Is that any way to treat your mama?" Ruby smiled, thinking how much her pet must hate her. She took extreme satisfaction in the outcome of this particular experiment, having learned how far this form of existence could be stretched. The head on the shelf: she would grant it peace, one day, once she'd grown tired of toying with it. She'd burn it in the woodstove in the living room, or maybe leave it outside, unprotected, so the rays of the sun could find it. It struck her that she hadn't considered the effect a bullet between its eyes might have. Perhaps she'd do a bit of target practice before putting it out to burn.

Ruby had never felt so in control of anything in her life.

The hobo hadn't been her only project, only her most extreme to date. For weeks now, she'd been experimenting on the penniless nomads unlucky enough to disembark near Conroy, so that she could learn the strength and weaknesses of her kind, not only as a means of self-preservation, but as a way of devising a perfect punishment. These strangers, she reasoned, were the best source of test subjects for the same reasons they made the best supper.

Like some kind of fairy-tale injunction, three exposures to her blood were required to bring about the change. It took different lengths of time, she'd learned, for different people to wake. Some took days, others mere hours. Her own rising, she had come to realize, had been affected by what those who'd infected her had done to slow her change; Ruby's hand trailed up to her breast where the last of the sigils they'd carved had only just begun to fade.

Fire, she'd learned, kindled or brought by the sun, was possibly the only way to completely destroy her kind. Outside of fire, most injuries would heal themselves, though some were permanent. Destroying the heart ruined the body, rendering it immobile, incapable of rising and seeking prey. Still, even in a broken body, a strong enough will might be able to draw the prey to it. The body might not rise, but it could still find means to feed. Ruby wondered how many times her kind had been left in this state—conscious, but crippled—calling out with a seductive will to passersby.

She wondered about her near embalming. Would the act of embalming have brought her true death? Would draining her blood have removed the being who'd become one with her, or did the connection between them run deeper? She would have to experiment with one she had changed and find out. She'd promised Merle she would change him, and she intended to keep her promise. Things would soon be different around here, and she'd no longer need to skulk in the shadows, taking whatever fate delivered to her. Soon, she could pick and choose. The boy should prove a satisfactory subject when the time came.

In the meantime, she had two new pets.

She'd fed the Sleiger boys once. Just as she had commanded, they sat silent in the corner, their backs against the cellar wall. They'd be sensitive to direct sunlight now, and might need an invitation before entering someone's house. An observant witness might take note of an occasional blue fleck glinting in their eyes, but for the most part they'd be able to carry out tasks for her.

"So tell me," she said crossing to stand before them. "What do you boys know about explosives?"

THIRTEEN

"Ripped him clean open, Sheriff. Gizzard to gonads," Whitey Vaughn said, and spat tobacco out onto the parched earth next to the sheet-covered lump. A trail of juice dripped down his chin, and he pulled a dirty handkerchief from the pocket of his overalls to dab at the sticky brown spittle.

When Bell first got the call from Whitey, he'd assumed the farmer had lost more livestock. More than a few animals in the area had suffered strange injuries over the last couple of months. Most of the wounds weren't deadly, at least not at first. Then, a couple of weeks back, Whitey had found one of his calves with its throat ripped out. A few days later, a chicken farmer had awakened to a coop full of nothing but blood and feathers. Now this . . .

"My boy found him on his way back out to the milk barn," Whitey said. "I probably walked right past him this morning, but I missed him in the dark."

Sheriff Bell nodded at the farmer, then squatted down and threw back the bloodstained sheet that covered Dowd Johnson's body. He grimaced and turned away. "I'll need to speak to your son."

"Course, but he's still out in the fields. Got a late start, what with . . ." The old man gestured to the battered body. "Who do you reckon did this?"

Bell stood and gave the old man a stern look. "Looks more like the work of a 'what' than a 'who,' wouldn't you say?"

"No, sir," Whitey replied and spat to the side. "Sure, that's what I thought when I found the calf, but take a closer look at the bits that are missing."

The sheriff reached down and tugged the sheet completely off the body. As he did so, he noticed that a patch, a red circle with a white cross in its center, had been sewn on the once-white fabric. Bell recognized it instantly. He didn't participate as an active member of the Klan, but he was not without sympathy toward its cause. The sheriff felt the farmer's eyes on him. "You keep quiet about this," he said, tapping his index finger on the patch, "you hear?"

"Course, Sheriff." The farmer looked past Bell at Dowd's gutted remains. "They took his heart, see?"

Bell looked over the bridge of his nose at the body. Even though the corpse had been covered, the sun overhead was doing a fine job of baking it. The rank scent wafting up from beneath the sheet was as repulsive to him as it was attractive to the swarm of flies that were rushing in to sample the meat. He forced himself to focus on the job at hand. "Still looks like the work of a wild animal to me."

"Ever do any butchering, Sheriff?"

Bell answered Whitey's question with one of his own, "What does that have to do with anything?"

"Well, sir, I can tell you that this here"—he pointed to the body—"didn't happen on my land. Butcherin' is messy work. There ain't enough blood around the body for the killing to have happened here."

"So the animal killed him a bit off, then dragged the body over here."

"That would have left a trail. Now my eyes ain't what they used to be, but I don't see no trail."

It was Bell's turn to point to the body. "Look. He wasn't slit open, he was ripped open. I'm telling you, Whitey, this was the work of an animal."

"Think so? Take a look in his mouth."

Bell squatted down once more and pulled out the new-fangled ballpoint pen his wife had given him for their anniversary. He inserted the tip of it between Dowd's lips and opened them to find Dowd's manhood looking back at him instead of the man's tongue. In spite of himself, Bell rocked back and sucked in air. He wondered if this might have been the work of Frank Mason and Bayard Bloom. Had Dowd done crossed the Judge?

He bit the inside of his cheek and shook his head in answer to his own question. It was too messy for Frank and not quite artistic enough in its brutality for Bayard, who probably would have considered this display too obvious. Besides, the Judge always gave Bell a heads-up before ordering any of his extracurricular executions. It gave him time to round up a suitable scapegoat. Of course, the Judge had been absent lately.

"His mouth was hanging open when I got here, which is how I knew what was in there," the farmer said, answering a question Bell hadn't yet thought to pose.

"And you left it in there like that?"

"What was I s'posed to do with it? 'Sides, I figured you'd've insisted an animal had done the killing, 'less you saw this for yerself."

"Yeah," the sheriff said. He stood and flung the pen off into the weeds—gift or no gift, he no longer wanted it anywhere near him. "You figured right."

"It had started falling out, so I used a stick to push it back in," Whitey said. "Weren't no easy job getting his yap closed, but I wanted it to stay put."

Bell stared at the farmer, not sure what to say.

"Trying to do my civic duty, Sheriff," Whitey said and nodded. "That's all."

"Sheriff Bell," Fred Rigby, his deputy, called out from over near the tree line. His voice broke like he'd just that moment hit puberty. "We got something over here, too."

The sheriff took his time getting to the deputy. Just past noon, and he was already sweating like a bald donkey's ass. Of course, the worst heat of the day had yet to come. *I'm getting too old for this*, Bell thought silently, even though he wasn't sure if he meant the heat or the job or the sight of Dowd Johnson's bloody giblets baking in the red clay field. He drew up near Rigby, who was kneeling on the ground and heaving.

"Ah, pull it together, boy," the sheriff said, circling around in the direction opposite of his assistant's breakfast. There, right where the grass and weeds gave way to a line of scraggly pines, lay a decapitated head, hairy side up.

"It's a head," Rigby coughed out, using the sleeve of his uniform to wipe his mouth.

"Yep. I can see that," Bell replied. "Roll it on over so we can see whose." The deputy shot a look up at the sheriff, his lip quivering. "For God's sake, you pansy." Bell leaned over to grab the head by its hair, but thought better of it. Standing up straight, he rolled it over with the sole of his shoe. Rigby fell over backward and scurried away like a crab from the upturned face. He made it to his feet, but then stood frozen, staring down into the head's open eyes. "If you are through with pissing yourself," Bell said, recognizing Bob McKee's face, "you can start beating the bush to see if you can find the rest of ole Bob here."

Bell decided he could make his own life a whole heck of a lot easier if he called Frank Mason to confirm this wasn't some of his or his buddy Bayard's handiwork. He turned back to the farmer, who had followed him to the tree line. "Mind if I use your telephone?"

FOURTEEN

"It's for you," Nola called to Frank from behind the bar. "Looks like folks think this is your office."

Truth was, Frank had come to feel more at home in this window-less, whitewashed concrete block bunker of a bar than he did anywhere else. No signs, no windows, three and a half miles down a dead-end dirt road, the bar was hidden well enough that the fine upstanding people of Conroy wouldn't call upon the Judge to shut down the only watering hole in this damned dry county. Everyone in the know called the bar "Nola's Place," but Nola herself didn't own it. She only ran it. Nope, this fine establishment belonged to Judge Lowell himself. Only a handful of people knew that, though, Frank being one of them.

Frank fingered the dart he was holding, annoyed at the interruption of his practice. "Give it to him," he said, nodding toward Bayard, who was sitting at the bar making love to a glass of sour mash bourbon.

Frank and Bayard had grown up together, but you'd never guess it. Even though he was barely thirty, Bayard looked like an old man now—all that remained of his coppery hair was a few unsightly tufts over his ears. He always looked tired; the puffy bags that bulged beneath his eyes forced them into a tight squint and enhanced Bayard's resemblance to a pig even more than the flesh that lapped over his belt buckle. Frank felt disgust for the way his short, balding partner hung over his stool in every direction. Seeming to feel the weight of Frank's eyes, Bayard turned to face him and peered at him down his purple-veined nose with bloodshot blue eyes.

Nola shook her head. "Sorry, sugar, they're asking for you."

"Who is it?" Frank asked, but her only response was to raise her eyebrows and thrust the receiver in his direction. Nola was well past her prime. Probably old enough to be his mother. But she was still well put together, and she was all woman. Ratted bleached blonde hair tumbled around her shoulders—her cuffs and collar didn't match at all, but Frank didn't mind—and smudgy bright red lipstick stained the cigarette dangling from her lips.

Frank didn't have a taste for Sunday school teachers, so Nola and her hardened look suited him just fine. Besides, her age made it possible for him to have her anytime he wanted without a rubber, and that was real nice. Today, though, he was thinking it might be nicer to give her something other than that cigarette to rub her lipstick off on. He felt himself stiffening at the thought.

Nola whisked the cigarette from between her lips and flicked ashes into an already-full tray. "Come on, don't keep your boyfriend waiting," she said. Nola had gotten real cocky with him since he'd finally started slipping it to her, but he didn't really mind that either. He liked some fire in his women.

He threw the dart he'd been holding, landing it dead in the bull's-eye. Quick. Clean. Efficient. Just the way he liked to deliver. He ran a hand through his thick black hair and headed for the bar. As he took the receiver from Nola, he grasped her hand around it, forcing her to look into his eyes. He held on until he saw the flash he wanted to see, the spark that told him Nola wanted exactly what he had to offer. Then he loosened his grip, and she let the receiver slide into his fingers.

Frank held the phone up to his ear. "Frank Mason," he said as his free hand moved to lay claim to the pack of cigarettes Nola had left on the bar. He pulled one out and nodded to Nola for a light.

"Frank," the voice on the other end said. "This is Sheriff Bell. I'm out here at Whitey Vaughn's place." There was a moment's silence. Frank suspected it meant Bell was worried someone might be listening in on the farmer's party line. "Listen. I was just . . . I just ran into a couple of local boys, Dowd Johnson and Bob McKee." Another pause. "I was wondering if maybe you or Bayard might have met with them in a professional capacity."

Professional capacity. Frank nearly laughed, but wiped the smile from his face as he took a puff from his cigarette. Bell was well aware of his profession. He and Bayard worked for the Judge, making sure his sideline businesses ran smoothly. They collected debts and kept agitators in line, occasionally taking them out when the need presented itself. Of course he knew Dowd and Bob. Everyone around these parts knew everybody. But no, they hadn't had "professional" dealings with the boys in question.

"No, sir, can't say that we've ever had dealings with those gentlemen," Frank said automatically, then cast a wary glance at Bayard, who had abandoned his drink and sat at the bar sharpening his knife's blade against a whetstone. They usually handled all their "work" together, but Bayard did have his hobbies. "Hold on. I'll see if they're Bayard's buddies." He rapped his knuckles on the bar to draw Bayard's attention. His dull blue eyes met Frank's, but he never broke the rhythm of the striking of steel against flint.

"Dowd Johnson, Bob McKee. You been going out on your own again?" Frank asked him. There was no need to go into further detail. Bayard would understand that his partner was asking if he had killed the two. Or worse, played with them, then killed them.

Bayard shook his head, then returned his attention to his blade, turning it so that the bar's artificial light glinted off its razor edge.

"Nope, Sheriff. We haven't seen 'em."

"You sure about that?" The sheriff's voice crackled as it came down the wire.

"Yes, sir." Frank took a draw on his cigarette. The click in his ear told him Bell had hung up. Shrugging, he returned the receiver to its cradle.

"Trouble?" Nola asked, reaching out for the bottle of bourbon Bayard had been hoarding. In a flash, Bayard plunged his knife's blade into the bar, slicing the air between his bottle and Nola's hand. He did it without speaking a word. "Jesus, Frank. Will you do something with him?" She huddled back against the cabinet behind her, wrapping her arms around herself.

"Bayard," Frank called his name in a calm, even voice. "Put that thing away." Bayard looked at him through narrowed, resentful eyes, but he pulled the blade from the wooden surface and returned it to its leather carrier.

Bayard needed violence like crops needed rain. Normally there were plenty of opportunities for that capacity to be channeled into work, but lately the Judge hadn't had much of a head for business. The Judge was letting his fields go fallow, and Bayard was wilting along with them. Frank didn't know what to do about the Judge, but he was going to have to take Bayard out to run him, like a good hunting dog. Maybe a trip over to the colored side of town would give him a chance to blow off some steam.

"It ain't been the same since we brung her back," Bayard said. They'd had this conversation nearly every day since delivering Ruby to the Judge. "We should've killed her right where we found her." He grasped the neck of his bottle and flung it to the concrete floor, shattering glass and wasting good whiskey. "Those people out there. They done something to her. And now she's going to do it to us."

"Clean that up," Frank said to Nola. He pointed at Bayard, "And you, shut it." Frank reached behind the bar and grabbed himself a fresh bottle of bourbon. Maybe enough booze would keep him from thinking about what he'd seen in California. The bourbon burned on its way down, but it didn't burn brightly enough to keep the memories of what'd happened three months ago from resurfacing.

◆ ◆ ◆

To Frank, the Los Angeles Union Passenger Terminal looked more like a fancy church than it did a train station. Marble floors and big rounded doorways. Huge chandeliers. Bayard turned gray at first sight, casting uneasy glances around the place. He looked like he'd do just about anything to climb back on the train and return to Conroy. But although the fancy station gave Bayard the jitters, Frank had to practically pull him out of the air-conditioned cave and into the searing sunlight. Once outside, the building's exterior did little to rid Frank of his impression that the terminal looked like a church. Hell, the damned place even had a kind of steeple.

As planned, Joe Crane, the private investigator whom the Judge had hired to track Ruby down, was waiting just outside the station in a white delivery truck marked "Canyon Grocers." Bayard spotted the truck first, and made a beeline for it. Frank followed a bit behind, stealing a few moments to absorb the sights and sounds of this new place. As they approached the truck, the detective, all lantern-jawed and watery eyed beneath a gray flat cap, acknowledged them with a nod.

"Toss your luggage in the back and get in," he called out, motioning with his thumb to the passenger-side door without bothering to get out from behind the steering wheel. He'd clearly recognized them right off, but Frank wasn't sure if it was due to his detective's intuition, or because the two of them looked like a couple of hicks who'd fallen off a turnip truck. Frank opened the truck's back door and put the case the Judge had loaned them inside, careful not to scuff its leather. That done, he closed the back and followed Bayard around to the side.

Bayard tore open the passenger-side door and dove in, giving Frank a frustrated look when he realized he'd be the one sitting next to the stranger. Frank slung himself in and closed the door before Bayard could complain, as he'd been doing ever since they'd left Conroy. Truth be told, Bayard was obviously scared shitless. Until the Judge had sent them on this trip to California to bring Ruby home, neither of them had been any farther west than Natchez.

Bayard acted tough, but Frank could tell he was frightened by the big city. Not Frank, though. No, he wanted to peel off his skivvies and dive right in. A group of young women approaching the truck caught his attention. He gawked out the delivery truck's open window and whistled at one dark-skinned beauty.

"You whistling at the mulattoes now?" Bayard asked. They hadn't even pulled away from the station yet, and Bayard was already trying to pick a fight. Frank felt too good to care. He turned back to Bayard and winked. "I am at that one." He laughed as he watched Bayard struggle to form an appropriate look of disgust.

Crane looked over his shoulder, then leaned a little further back to catch sight of the woman Frank had been eyeing. "Naw, she isn't a mulatto. That there's a Mexican señorita." He nearly sang the last word. "Plenty of 'em around here willing to entertain fine gentlemen such as yourselves if you're interested. I could help arrange . . ." Crane stopped talking midsentence. Bayard was a firm believer in the separation of the races, and Mexican or mulatto, the skin of these pretty young women was decidedly not white. Frank couldn't see the look on his partner's face, but he knew it must have silenced the detective.

"Your young lady is just a few miles from here," Crane said, firing up the truck and pulling out, "in one of the big houses on Sunset."

"Sunset Boulevard, like in the movie?" Frank asked, a bit too much excitement in his voice. He'd never seen anyplace famous before, and he would probably never get the chance again.

"The very same."

"The Judge ain't sent us here to be no damned tourists," Bayard snarled, rubbing a hand as if for comfort on the knife concealed at his waist.

Frank decided to let Bayard's smart comment slide and sat back, soaking in the sight of his first palm tree. Crane ignored his oafish partner, too. "You like the movies, do you?"

Frank turned to Crane. "Yeah. No crime in that, is there?"

"None at all. Like 'em just fine myself. You know, your Ruby, the house she's at doesn't belong to just any old body. It's Myrna King's place."

"Myrna King? The actress?"

"That's right. That lady takes a lot of interest in young folk. The magazines say it's what keeps her young. Seems to be working for her. I've seen her with my own eyes. She must be in her fifties, but she could easily play an ingénue if she still made movies." He stopped at a red light. "Keeps a constant flow of young courtesans running through her place."

"Courtesans?" Frank asked.

"It's a nice word for 'whore,'" Crane explained and shifted, pulling forward as the light changed.

"So Ruby's out here whoring herself," Bayard said with obvious pleasure pulsing beneath the surface of his voice.

"Yeah, her and that young man she came out here with." Crane looked over at them and nodded to confirm what he'd just said. "Handsome young fellow like that probably gets more *attention* from the gents than he does the ladies." He hit the clutch and shifted gears. "Out here it isn't that uncommon . . . the whoring, that is." He paused. "Well, I guess the other thing, too."

"So if you know where she is, why play dress-up with this truck and the uniform?" Bayard asked. "Shouldn't we just go knock on the door and tell Ruby we've come to bring her home?"

Crane gave them a sidelong glance. "I've been keeping an eye on the King house for a few days now. People always coming and going at odd hours." He looked back at the road just in time to swerve around a stopped vehicle. "Some just pop in and come right back out. Others, young folk like your Ruby, they go in and stay. I've been asking around about Myrna and her friends. Seems some years back she got herself messed up with that bunch of occultists who've up till recently been running around up in Pasadena."

"Occultist?" Frank asked. "Like an eye doctor?" He had never heard the word before.

Crane looked over and laughed. "No, not like an eye doctor. These people think they can do magic. They do sacrifices. Get up to all kinds of nonsense. Their leader, an honest-to-God rocket scientist, blew himself up a year or so ago while trying to work some kind of spell. After that, they began trickling into the city from Pasadena."

Bayard turned to Frank, his face ashen. The man was so damned superstitious, Frank worried he might just turn tail and run. "But it's all nonsense, right?" Frank asked, hoping the man's answer would help put Bayard at ease.

"Maybe. Maybe not," came Crane's unhelpful reply. "I've lived out here for quite a while now. Seen some mighty strange things."

FIFTEEN

Lucille sat at the Judge's kitchen table, her hands clutching a cooling and untasted cup of coffee, wondering if she were simply trapped in a dream too stubborn to shake. None of what she'd experienced in the last day could really have happened. Ruby was dead. Dead and buried for these last two months. Lucille knew that. She'd soloed a capella on "Amazing Grace" as Ruby's casket was slid into the crypt next to her mother. Lucille had forced a smile on her face and thanked Mrs. Blanton when the old woman commented that colored folk had the most melodic voices.

No, it was impossible. Plain and simple. But that cruel laughter she'd heard was undeniably Ruby's, and deep down she knew that if hell were going to shut its door on anyone, it would be that darkly exquisite, manipulative young woman.

Lucille had known the Judge's daughter for more than ten years now, ever since she'd taken over as the family's housekeeper, back when Ruby'd been nothing more than a mere slip of a girl. Marva, the maid Lucille had replaced, had grown too old and blind to work anymore. Lucille knew beyond a shadow of a doubt it was the only reason her predecessor had been allowed to leave the Judge's employment. On Lucille's first day, Marva met her on the Judge's front porch. Without further ado, the older woman rolled up her sleeve to expose a burn scar extending from her wrist to her elbow. "Mind yourself around the little one," she said before shuffling back into the house.

Since then, there had been plenty of opportunities for Lucille to witness Ruby's cruelty firsthand, and she'd borne the brunt of it herself more than once. At first, Lucille tried to feel for Ruby, to sympathize for the pain being motherless must have caused the girl, but sympathy could only stretch so far before snapping. Ruby proved to be the most unkind, greedy, and covetous child Lucille had ever met. Lucille could not begin to understand what had happened to twist the girl's soul into such an unfeeling knot.

Many times Lucille had been forced to step in and protect children who'd been strong-armed into joining Ruby for playtime. Ruby's sole source of happiness seemed to be toying with people, humiliating them, ruining anything that made them feel good about themselves. What she couldn't steal, she'd destroy. Lucille would never escape the image of that poor Blake girl, clasping her hand on her cheek, blood spilling through her fingers. It had been Ruby's twelfth birthday party, and someone said the Blake girl was almost as pretty as Ruby herself. The girl would always have an ugly scar.

As Ruby grew, her methods of torture took on a greater refinement. While Ruby the girl had enjoyed weaving lies to land others in trouble, Ruby the young adult preferred learning secrets and using them to keep those around her in line. God help the soul whose sin Miss Ruby uncovered. Eventually Lucille decided to stay the hell out of her way.

Then, when she was nearing eighteen, Ruby seemed to transform overnight. She fell in love with that Dunne boy, Elijah, who was stupid or crazy enough to love her back. The affair came out of nowhere. The two had known each other all their lives; just all of a sudden it was like Ruby finally took notice of the boy she'd been happy to ignore till then. For a brief while, it looked for sure like the two were heading for the altar, but in the end it didn't last long. Right about the time Lucille received the letter informing her of her husband Jesse's brave sacrifice, Elijah left to play soldier in the same conflict. In no time at all, Ruby took to disappearing and hanging out with the boy who ended up running off to California with her. Lucille had seen Ruby's disappearance as a great mercy, and she would feel very little shame in admitting she regretted that the Judge's investigator had ever hunted Ruby down. It would've been better for everyone if she'd stayed gone, or, failing that, had stayed dead.

Because Lucille knew Ruby was back. Perhaps more than anything, what convinced her of that fact was the way those men had accused her son of a theft the boy hadn't committed. Setting up her playmates had been one of Ruby's well-worn pranks. More than one of Ruby's unfortunate young patsies had faced a furious switching after the disappearance of a prized object from the Judge's house. Right about the time the child was able to move again without bleeding, the missing knickknack would suddenly reappear in its customary place. The kids involved knew better than to say a word to anyone.

Just as little Ruby framed her friends for her own amusement, the resurrected Ruby had somehow stitched Willy up as a thief to entice Dowd and his buddies to group together where Ruby could take them out with a single strike. Why Ruby had wanted to harm these men, Lucille had no idea, but she did feel sure that her son had been used as bait. In some twisted way, Lucille felt certain Ruby had meant it as a way of honoring her, like a cat bringing a dead bird to his owner's doorstep.

At least now both her children had escaped, headed north where Lucille prayed they'd stand a chance for a life better than the one their mother would know here.

SIXTEEN

Mrs. Dunne had entrusted Corinne with the after-lunch washing up while she did laundry. Corinne had just finished the chore when she heard a car horn bleat out a tentative beep. She dried her hands and walked down the dark hall to the front door, watching through the glass as the black-and-white Hornet pulled down the long drive, sending the crunching gravel scattering like shrapnel even though the car proceeded at a careful pace. *The sheriff's car.* She opened the door and headed out onto the front porch. The Hornet pulled to a stop, and the man she recognized as the deputy killed the engine. The sheriff spat out the open window, but then flung open the door, arduously extricating himself from the car as if he'd aged a hundred years since he'd dropped by earlier that morning. The deputy did not move.

"Sheriff," Corinne said.

"Ma'am." The officer touched the tip of his hat curtly.

"I'm afraid you've just missed Elijah." Corinne registered the annoyance on the man's face in his lowered brow and twitching mustache. "He headed back into the fields, but he knows to call you at four," she added quickly to dispel the sheriff's frustration, "like you wanted."

"Yeah, I reckon that is what I had asked, but there have been some new *developments*, and I can't wait till this afternoon."

"I'll be glad to go find him for you." She took a step or two back and opened the screen door. "Would you and your deputy like to come in and wait for him? We have some of Mrs. Dunne's peach pie left, and I'll brew up some coffee if you'd like."

He took off his hat and used his sleeve to wipe the sweat from his brow. "Cold water would be just fine," he said, then climbed the steps up to the porch.

"And your deputy?"

"He's feeling a bit green around the gills right now, ma'am. We'd best leave him right where he is."

Before opening the main door, Corinne flashed a quick look out at the deputy, who certainly seemed out of sorts. She stepped into the hall, marveling once again at how dark it was with all the shades pulled down to ward off the growing heat. For a moment she missed San Francisco's seemingly never-ending cool sunshine. He shut the door behind them. "This way," she said, immediately feeling self-conscious about her choice of words. She was the stranger here. The sheriff might have been to this house many times for all she knew.

A few feet down the hall, she turned left and stepped into the kitchen. Ava stood there at the sink. All the dishes Corinne had washed had been returned to soapy water, and her future mother-in-law had started the process all over again. She yanked one of the plates out of the suds, rubbing it as if she were out to wipe away original sin. "I fear you are woefully lacking in the domestic arts," Ava said without turning, her voice cold. The sheriff cleared his throat, and she spun around, nearly dropping the plate to the floor. Her disposition turned to reconstituted sunshine in an instant. "Sheriff," she said, a smile pulling her lips taut. Rather than backing that smile up, her eyes darted to Corinne.

"The manners of these young people," she said, shaking her head, keeping those lips pulled up at the corners all the while. "You shouldn't have bothered coming, Sheriff. My son is planning on calling your office this afternoon, like you asked."

"Yes, so the young lady here has informed me. I'm afraid it can no longer wait."

"The sheriff would like some water," Corinne said, readying herself to duck if Ava sent the plate she held hurtling toward her. "And I told him about your excellent pie as well."

Ava dropped the plate into a large metal bucket filled with clear water, then went to the cupboard and removed a glass, filling it with water from the pitcher she kept in the refrigerator. She handed it to the sheriff, who downed it in a single draught. Ava held the pitcher up and raised her eyebrows, silently asking their visitor if he cared for more. He waved his right hand, shaking his head. *Why are they so afraid of using words?* Corinne wondered as the sheriff handed the glass back to Ava and took a seat at the kitchen table.

"I'll go find Elijah," Corinne said.

"After you do, perhaps you can help me hang the wash on the line?" Ava's tone left no room for doubt that her words were not a request. She was clearly determined to keep Corinne from learning whatever news the sheriff had to convey.

"Of course," Corinne replied. "As soon as my fiancé and I have finished hearing what the sheriff needs with us." As she turned her back, she heard the sheriff snort out a laugh.

SEVENTEEN

"Yankee?" Bell asked, as he watched Ava's face slowly regain its color.

"As good as. From California."

"Elijah will have his work cut out for him with that one." Bell couldn't help but compare the mousey-looking Corinne to the sultry Ruby. Even though the women came in very different packages, they seemed to possess the same type of fire, the same steel backbone. "Your son has a taste for headstrong women."

Ava nodded her head, her eyes narrowing and the corners of her mouth turning down. "That he does. When I learned of Corinne, I had hoped . . . well, I'd hoped for a very different type of daughter-in-law. The girl thinks she knows it all and has the right to stick her nose where it doesn't belong."

"Just remember she's Elijah's job to handle, not yours."

"That may be, but the sooner he takes a belt to her bare hide and puts her in her place . . ."

"Well, that ain't likely to happen until after the honeymoon," Bell said, giving Ava a knowing smile. "Once the heat's out of him, he'll soon decide he's had enough of her stubborn ways. I've seen it a dozen times. There he is now." The sheriff pointed out the door that opened to the sleeping porch. Elijah's face had appeared through the screen of the outer door. He hesitated a moment before coming onto the porch; the way his head and shoulders bobbed on the other side of the screen implied he was scraping earth off his boots.

"Afternoon, Sheriff," Elijah said as he entered the kitchen, Corinne dogging him a few paces behind.

"Afternoon," Bell replied, looking at the boy from head to toe, appraising him not as a young man he'd watched grow, but as a possible suspect. There was a trace of worry in the boy's blue eyes—they were focused intently on him, the right one squinting a bit more than the left—but Bell could detect no guilt, no guile. The boy's broad square shoulders were tense, pulled back enough to show that he suspected he might be in trouble, but his overall manner spoke of innocence.

"What can I do for you, Sheriff?" Elijah asked. Bell motioned to the chair across the table from his own, and the young man pulled it out and sat.

Corinne hovered behind Elijah for a few moments before deciding to take the seat next to him. In spite of the grim nature of his visit, Bell had to smile at the look on Ava's face. But he had no interest in drawing the woman's ire. "Miss . . ." he began, but couldn't put his finger on the girl's family name.

"Ford," Corinne filled in the blank for him.

Bell ran his hand over his moustache, noticing that the hairs felt somehow wirier than they used to. "Miss Ford, I am afraid I've come to discuss some rather unpleasant occurrences with your fiancé."

Corinne looked Bell dead in the eye. "I've just returned from spending over two years in a war zone. I doubt if anything you're planning to relate could be worse than what I've already experienced. I'm soon to be Elijah's wife. That means whether good, bad, or *unpleasant*, I'm here to support him." The girl was mighty full of herself, but Bell couldn't help but like her.

At first Ava blanched, but she had turned nearly purple by the time she managed to form words. "Corinne, the sheriff is telling you that this is the business of men. You need to come with me."

"No," Elijah said, reaching out and taking Corinne's hand. "I want her to stay."

Ava's eyes widened in surprise, but she said nothing. She just tilted her head to the side and tossed one final dark glance at her future daughter-in-law. When Corinne held her ground, Ava untied her apron and folded it neatly before leaving it on the counter. "I'll be out back if you men need anything," she said and exited the kitchen, passing through the sleeping porch and out the back door.

Bell had wasted enough time on Dunne family squabbles. He dove straight in. "When was the last time you saw your buddy Dowd or either of the Sleiger boys?"

Elijah slumped in his chair and ran his hand back through his hair first, then down his beard. "Last weekend, as I reckon. Why? They in trouble?"

Bell thought about how best to answer that question. He considered the likelihood that this meek young fellow could have ripped the entrails out of a man he'd been friends with since practically birth. Not at all, he decided. "I'm afraid I got some real bad news for you, son." Elijah lowered his head, but kept his eyes locked on Bell's. The boy was bracing himself. Bell decided to deliver the news without the graphic details. "I'm afraid we found Dowd Johnson and Bob McKee's bodies this morning. Sorry, son. Your friends are dead. We ain't got a fix yet on Wayne and Walter's whereabouts, but they both seem to be missing."

"Dowd and Bob are dead?" Elijah asked, obviously trying to reconcile the word with his friends' names. Everyone in these parts knew the Dunne boy had served in Korea, but dealing with death at home, where it wasn't expected, was a different matter. Corinne tightened her grip on Elijah's hand.

Bell nodded his response. "I do have to tell you that the killings were particularly brutal. Given the shape Bob and Dowd were in, things don't look good for the Sleigers either. I wish I could spare you from this truth, but I have to ask you if you know who might have wanted to kill your buddies, and do it in an ugly way." Elijah said nothing. He lowered his eyes to the table and shook his head. "Maybe they crossed some moonshiners or *interfered* with the wrong man's girl?"

"Gangsters, perhaps?" Corinne wondered aloud. She seemed surprised by the sound of her own voice. "I've heard," she addressed Bell, "that they can be extremely brutal. They do it to make a point to others."

"Ma'am, this is Conroy, not Chicago. Or even Savannah, for that matter." It was more of a knee-jerk reaction, though—the woman had a point. Whoever had killed the men had left their bodies as a warning, a way of marking their territory. Bell knew damned well there were plenty of gangsters in Conroy, but up till now they'd all been held tight under the Judge's thumb. He believed Frank and Bayard hadn't been involved, but he found himself wondering if some upstart thugs were flexing their muscles. Taking advantage of the Judge's bereavement to try and wrest away the reins of his operations. Bell was long overdue to pay the Judge a visit.

The phone rang in the hallway. Elijah didn't move. His face was frozen, his eyes burning into his own clenched fingers. Bell and Corinne exchanged a look, both uncertain as to whether Corinne had earned the right to answer. Corinne paused a moment, but then patted Elijah's shoulder and followed the ringing out of the room.

Bell watched the boy as his face cracked and his lips began to tremble. "I ain't the same man I was before I went to Korea, sir," he said looking up at Bell. "I see things different now. Corinne, she don't know about the things I used to get up to with Dowd. I'd like to keep it that way."

"Sheriff?" Corinne's voice interrupted before he could respond to Elijah. "The phone is for you."

Bell acknowledged the young man's request with a nod. He passed Corinne in the hall on his way to the telephone table. He lifted the receiver from the table and answered, "Bell here."

"Sheriff, this is Reverend Dean Miller from Five Point Methodist. Your office said I might find you there." There was a pause on the line.

"And found me you have, Reverend Miller. What can I do for you?"

There were a few more moments of silence. "Well, sir," Miller finally said. "I got something here at the church I need you to take a look at."

"I'm rather busy at the moment; can you be more specific about what this *something* is?"

A pause on the line, then, "It's a body, Sheriff. I don't know whose. There ain't no head. And it's . . ."

"Yes?" Bell prompted, losing patience.

"It's tied to the steeple."

EIGHTEEN

Last night, it had proven slippery work using Bob's own intestines to lash his body to the Methodist steeple, but Ruby felt she owed it to the bride and groom to help decorate for the wedding. Now as she stood in the dim green light of the Cooper kitchen, using the hand pump to flush water over her fingers in an attempt to clean the rest of Bob from beneath her nails, she wondered if her efforts had yet been appreciated.

The couple would probably feel she'd already done too much for them, but still, this show of affection was merely the beginning. Ruby had been making plans from the second she'd learned Elijah was to wed.

Corinne had no friends here, so Ruby herself would serve as the maid of honor. It seemed the least she could do.

Ruby loved tradition, at least when it came to weddings. For the bride, something old, something new, something borrowed, something blue. Between Corinne and herself, they had all four tokens covered. Corinne, she was new, at least new to Conroy. Ruby herself was Elijah's old fiancée, the one he was now pretending had never existed. She looked down at her cornflower-tinged hand; she had the blue part covered as well. And Corinne, well, the bride was living on borrowed time.

But what about the groom? Ruby couldn't bear the thought of overlooking Elijah. The finest tradition for the groom was the shivaree. Such a pretty-sounding word, for such a raucous affair. Stealing the groom away, to the accompaniment of the clanging of pots and pans, shrieks and bells, horns and whistles. Without a doubt, Elijah's buddies had made plans to kidnap him after the wedding, and drop him at least a half night's walk away from where his bride's tender and quivering womanhood awaited.

Since she'd shredded Elijah's two best friends, Ruby would also need to stand in as best man. Elijah needn't worry; if he married this new woman, Ruby would see to it that he had his shivaree, and it would be a much grander event than anything poor old Dowd or Bobby could have ever dreamed of pulling off.

Ruby would wait. Give Elijah a chance to walk away from this wedding. If he called it off, if he showed that he belonged to her, she would take him to live with her forever. Let him reign beside her in the new world she was going to build right here in Conroy. But if he pledged his troth to Corinne, Ruby would still take him; she would take him apart, and take her own sweet time doing so.

Ruby felt overcome by a burning desire to meet this Corinne, to see up close the woman who could have so easily erased her memory from Elijah's heart. She decided that tonight, right after stopping in to see her daddy, she'd pay Corinne a visit, maybe even give the woman a chance to save herself by leaving Conroy and heading back where she belonged. But it wasn't mere curiosity or some deep-seated sense of fair play that prompted Ruby's decision. It was a realization that when it comes right down to it, killing strangers isn't nearly as much fun as killing the people you know. Their acquaintance would be brief, but Ruby wanted to get to know Elijah's ladylove, at least a little, before Ruby ripped out her throat.

NINETEEN

Elijah nodded when Sheriff Bell popped his head back into the kitchen and told them he had to leave; then he focused on his own hands, wishing to God Almighty he could think of a way to make all this go away. A cold sweat broke out over him, and the room around him seemed to darken. He felt sick to his stomach, and he stood quickly and pushed past Corinne, out of the kitchen, out through the sleeping porch, falling to the earth on his hands and knees and dry heaving until his chest hurt.

Corinne followed on his heels, lowering herself so that she could drape her arm over his shoulders. Elijah reached back and pushed her arm away, standing and stumbling off to where his dad's truck sat. He ignored Corinne's calls as he flung the truck door open and hopped in.

A part of his brain protested. He knew what he was doing to her was wrong, but he also knew she would want him to talk, and talk and talk and talk. Like somehow yammering about any of this would fix it. He caught a glimpse of her standing in the yard and looking all helpless as he peeled away.

He shot down the drive and onto the road, no other destination in mind than *away*. He drove around, most likely in expanding circles, his hands cramping on the wheel. Somehow he lost track of direction in this area where he'd lived the better part of his life, and ended up a bit south of town, where the train tracks swung in sharply away from the river and crossed over the road before turning back north. When the bumpy and rutted lane leading to the Cooper house showed up on his right, bringing with it memories of happier days, he pulled off the paved road without thinking twice.

The old Cooper place sat two miles down a deserted red dirt road, and he sped up enough for his tires to kick up some of that copper clay onto his fenders. The house, which had been empty for longer than Elijah had been alive, sagged on its foundation. Once it had sheltered a family, but now it only played host to cottonmouth snakes and Saturday-night teenagers looking for a place to do the things they'd deny ever having done, come Sunday morning. Outside of the well-trampled front porch and the poorly hung door, kudzu had nearly swallowed the old house now, one of its few remaining bubble-glass windowpanes winking at the dying sun from behind the vine's heavy lashes.

He killed the engine and sat for some time, might've been a minute, might have been an hour, his eyes tracing the weave of the twining vine. Finally he swung open the door and slid his boots to the dry ground. He slammed the truck door shut, and strode up the rickety steps to the porch, trying to remember the good times he'd had here and shut the rest of it out.

Elijah, Dowd, the Sleiger brothers, and Bobby—hell, even old Rigby before he got his badge—used to come out here to drink. They'd swing by Delmar Blount's place for a jar of his corn liquor, then find their way to this house's slanting porch. They'd bring girls out here, too, then scare them with ghost stories to get them to cuddle closer. One well-timed owl hoot could be credited for Elijah losing his cherry, stretched out with Kay Grimes on an army surplus sleeping bag in the back of his dad's truck.

The plank steps bowed with too much play to be safe, but he climbed them anyway, each one groaning then sighing as they bore and then were relieved of his weight. He approached the door and tugged on the knob. It was, of course, unlocked, but it had shifted in the frame so that it stuck. He concentrated his anger, and gave the knob a hard shove. The door vibrated as it came open. He stepped inside.

The room, in spite of the sweltering heat and humidity outside, was surprisingly cool, no doubt thanks to the vines that might one day rip the house apart. He couldn't imagine why, but someone had gone to the trouble to board up the front room's window. The light that pierced the open door seemed to be swallowed by shadow, somehow not managing to make it more than a foot or two beyond the threshold. The light that did make it into the room did so through the filter of the kudzu leaves, leaving it dim and tinted an eerie green. He drew in a breath of the dry, dusty air. It smelled different than he remembered. There was a resinous odor, not quite like pine sap, not quite like the scent that would waft from his mother's cedar chest. It was like both, but neither. Like the two crossed with the smell of a warm vinyl record.

He walked over to the abandoned potbellied stove that stood in the far corner. When they used to come out here, sometimes they'd hide a jar of shine or a bottle of whiskey inside. He knelt and opened the door, staring in at the empty grate. No luck. Least not today. He ran his hand over his face and stood, coming to attention as a thudding sound resounded on the floor upstairs. For the briefest of moments, he wondered whether the derelict place might be haunted after all.

Probably just a fat squirrel or some other animal hopping around. If it stayed up there and left him alone, he'd stay down here and return the favor. The place wasn't haunted. Any ghosts around this old house now, Elijah had brought with him. He cast one final glance around the room, then returned to the porch, pulling the door closed with as much vehemence as it took to yank it open.

The floorboards squeaked as he turned around, sounding for all the world like they were asking him where he'd been all this time. He'd spent a good part of his teenage years right here on this very porch.

Memories of those days, really not that long ago, passed through his mind. Layer over layer of his past crowded in on each other. So many twilight hours spent here passing the jar, talking about the world and what they believed should be their place in it. Shame crawled up from the small of his back, passing between his shoulder blades and reaching up to tickle his scalp. A lot of what they got up to—a lot of what they had planned sprawled out across this porch's warped boards—he knew now was wrong. Hell, he knew it then, too. They'd hurt people. Good people. Just because they'd been born different. Dowd used to run on at the mouth about the natural order, the rightful position of the white man at the top of the ladder of races. Elijah had never really believed any of it himself, but he went along with it anyway. Maybe someone had finally fought back. Maybe Dowd and Bob had earned their end.

Still, Dowd and Bob were dead. Walter and Wayne—the sheriff felt odds were good they were dead, too. And then there was Ruby. These men he had been so close to. The girl he'd loved. All these people who'd gotten themselves caught up in the same bundle of lies that had sent him running off to get himself shot in Korea.

Dowd had sworn to him, sworn, that Ruby had come to him. Like a bitch in heat, he said. And he'd had her. So had Bob.

Elijah had beaten the hell out of Dowd, despite the difference in their size. Bob had stood back at first, seeming confident that Dowd could hold Elijah off. But Elijah had never felt such rage in his life. It had been like everything anyone had ever done to make him feel bad, to feel weak, boiled up all at once. By the time Bob joined in, trying to restrain him, Elijah had pretty much taken the bigger guy down. Elijah got a few good licks in on Bob, too, before leaving the pair to patch their wounds and their pride.

He'd gone straight to Ruby's, straight to the Judge's house, but Ruby wouldn't see him. The maid, Lucille, met him at the door, placing a firm hand on his chest when he tried to push past. "She said she don't want to see you," Lucille said, pleading with her eyes. "You just go on home now, sir. You don't want the Judge to hear about you showing up like this, and if you force your way in here, I ain't gonna have no choice but to tell him."

He didn't resist her surprisingly strong backward force, but he still called out. "Ruby! Come talk with me, girl. I don't believe them. I don't." No response came, though he was sure she must have heard. He waited, craning his neck trying to see into the hall. His heart began pounding, breaking. Doubt crept in. He didn't have any money. Not the kind that Ruby should find herself marrying into. He was handsome, by Conroy's standards, but he knew anywhere else Ruby's beauty would place her far out of his reach. He knew the stories about her. How sadistic she could be. But he had never believed them. Now he wondered.

Had their time together been nothing more than a cruel and heartless prank? She'd ignored him for years while they were growing up. He might as well have been invisible to her. Then all of a sudden, she sought him out. Then they were together, and he was in love. He'd never let himself wonder what had turned her attention toward him, but he sure spent plenty of time going over why she broke his heart. Had she tired of him? Had she given herself to Dowd and Bob? Had she lain with his friends just to drive him away? "Ruby, please," he had said, his voice no longer loud enough for anyone other than the black maid to hear. "Come tell me it ain't true."

He didn't resist when Lucille pressed a bit harder, causing him to take a complete step back over the threshold. Before she closed the door, he caught an odd look in Lucille's eyes, one that combined sympathy and caution and the sharpest of hatred all in one glance. In that moment, when his pain had made him human, he realized that she knew him for what he was, a weak and cowardly boy who needed to believe the color of his skin made him superior, 'cause he knew deep down he had nothing else. If his whiteness didn't lift him above others, he was at the bottom. And so he left. He left his buddies. He left his family. He left Ruby. And he went into the army hoping to prove to himself he was somebody, or to die trying. In the end, he'd done neither. Getting shot by a sniper at the side of a garbage ditch hardly made him a hero.

He came home, a gimp in his leg and a promise from a girl he liked a lot, a woman he was really fond of. He didn't love her, though. Not really. Not like he had loved Ruby. So he resigned himself to limping through what was left of his life, with Corinne by his side, a woman he respected, until his clock stopped ticking, and he could move on to whatever came after this life. He hoped it would be nothing. For him, Heaven would be nothing.

He'd resigned himself to the future open before him. But not long after he'd made it back to Conroy, the Judge tracked Ruby down in California and had her brought home. She wasn't well. Not at all. But she was home, and the Judge sent along a message that she was asking to see him, if he was willing to come.

If he was willing.

He nearly flew to the Judge's door. This time Lucille had welcomed him, and she continued to welcome him every day after that.

What Dowd and Bob had said, it was all a lie. She had been too ashamed to face him for fear he'd believe them, even a little bit. For a while there, it seemed like they might find a way to start anew. That's what she wanted. She swore it was so.

Her health varied greatly day-to-day. Sometimes the things she'd talk about seemed crazy, but McAvoy reminded him that she might still be imagining things due to her illness. Elijah suspected it might have had something, too, to do with the drugs she'd taken in Hollywood, and the doc was too kind to rub anybody's nose in it. But on the whole it seemed like she was getting better; then she took a sudden, unexpected turn for the worse . . . and died.

That night while Ruby lay cold at the funeral parlor, Elijah went home and read the pile of unopened letters from Corinne that had been collecting in a Phillies Perfecto box. He knew he should write her back, tell all that had happened. Give her the opportunity to rethink the commitment she had made to him. A commitment that on his part he had broken. Instead, he set the six preceding weeks aside. Treated them like they were a dream, something that never happened. And he responded to Corinne's latest letter, just as if they hadn't.

Elijah scanned the tops of the trees surrounding the slanting house, letting his eyes rest on the point where the blue of the sky touched the green of the highest point. He would take all this. Everything he was feeling. About his women. About his friends. He'd lock it up and put it away. Just do the best he could from this point on.

The position of the sun told him it was getting late. He needed to get home and do the milking. Elijah allowed himself one last moment before heading back. He closed his eyes and drew a deep breath, surprised to realize the unfamiliar scent he'd noticed earlier seemed to be growing stronger. He opened his eyes and trod down the steps, retreating quickly when this time the second one down cracked beneath him.

He stopped in the yard, casting a backward glance at the old place. It was funny, really. Although it lay miles away by road, as the crow flies the cemetery where Ruby lay was only maybe an eighth of a mile away, dead west in the direction of the sinking sun.

TWENTY

Even though he couldn't bear the light of day, the Judge hated it when the evening shadows started to descend upon his room. When Ruby died, he'd thought the darkness was the worst thing that could happen to him. Now he knew better. He prayed she'd rest in peace tonight, but he knew it was not to be. He could feel her stirring, even before the last of the sun's rays had bent around the horizon. She was waking. Thinking of him. She'd come for him again, just as soon as the shadows outweighed the light.

He'd pretended to the old doctor that he believed his daughter only returned to him in nightmares, but that wasn't so. She'd visited him every night since her burial. For a while, the signs had been subtle—her distinctive scent, a strange flicker against the shadowed wall—sensations he could deny, figments he could ignore. But these impressions of Ruby's presence had grown stronger with time. Then, last week he saw her, saw her with his own two eyes. And she spoke to him, pleading with him to invite her in. He'd thought her visit a dream at first, then, feeling her cool touch, he began to consider the possibility that he might be losing his mind. But once she began feeding from him, he knew what Ruby had become.

Back when he and her mother had started dating, they'd gone to just about every movie Hollywood had churned out. Maybe the blame could be laid at her mother's feet. Ruby had inherited her love for both the silver screen and the macabre. The Judge couldn't have given a good goddamn about either. He had just been hoping to do a little spooning before dropping his date home at the end of the night.

A chilling spicy scent that reminded him of myrrh—sickly sweet, but still somehow woody and medicinal—told him that Ruby was on her way. He grasped at the bedclothes, pulling them to his chin. A tentative scratching, which he refused to acknowledge, on his door. His eyes pierced the shadows, taking in the sight of a luminous mist as it insinuated itself through the space between the door and its frame. He watched as the knob turned and the door squeaked open. The mist billowed into the room now, as thick as the fog from the mill, and his daughter's animated corpse came riding in on the ethereal wave.

She floated a yard or so above him, her long hair cascading down, nearly touching his pillow. The Judge closed his eyes and held his trembling hands up, trying to shield himself from the phantasm, praying that his flesh would not meet with her coldness. "Daughter, I wish you'd leave me be. Let your father rest."

"Oh, Daddy, I know how you feel," she whispered, reaching down and running her fingers through his graying mane. "I do." She leaned in and purred into his ear. "I felt the same way every night you came to me, pressing your flesh against mine. Smelling of just enough bourbon that come morning you could tell yourself nothing had happened, and even if it had, you weren't really responsible."

He clenched the edge of his covers with tight white knuckles as hot tears forced their way through his tightly closed eyes. "I was weak. I know that. I admit it. I'd do anything to undo the damage I've done."

A wail came from between his grinding teeth. "I'm sorry. I'm sorry. My God, I am so sorry."

"That is quite a show of contrition, Daddy, but if you're trying to throw yourself on the mercy of the court, I gotta warn you, I am fresh out of forgiveness."

Ovid opened his eyes, though he hated the sight of her, this thing his daughter had become. Her moonlight-blue skin, the burning cerulean of her pupil-less eyes and the light they cast on him.

"Leave me," the Judge commanded, trying to take control of this living nightmare. "Go back to the hell that bred you."

"But I already have, Daddy," she said, her voice like wind through dry grass. "That's why I'm here."

TWENTY-ONE

The dour faces of Ruby's ancestors challenged her approach. The dressing table where they sat strained under the silver and gold framed images of those who'd come before her, those who had long since turned to nothing more than dust and sour memories. There were no pictures of her in the collection; all of them predated her mother's death, so Ruby had always reckoned it was her mother who'd assembled the photos there.

Ruby glanced in the mirror, past her own flickering reflection, at her father as he lay rasping and shaking in his bloodstained sheets. Did the Judge hold on to the photos because he truly felt some form of affection for the people depicted, or did he just care so little as to never have them removed? No, more than likely they'd remained in place as a testament to his own origins, witnesses to his own greatness, betrayers of his own vanity.

The portraits were all more or less familiar to her; she'd seen them many times during her life. One of them, though, had always fascinated her. This one she'd memorized by heart. A much younger version of the Judge sat in a paper crescent moon next to a woman—the woman wearing the only smile recorded by any of the photos there—she'd always been told was her mama. Ruby had to take this assertion on faith; nothing had ever stirred within her as she looked at the pale and lovely young face that stared back at her. Nothing in her heart had ever said, "This is your mother." And if she'd hadn't felt this quickening before, she knew she'd never feel it now.

Ruby bore absolutely no physical resemblance to the woman. She shared neither her coloring, nor the kindness she had always imagined she could see in her eyes. Ruby doubted she shared any of the woman's moral or emotional traits either. No, Ruby was her father's daughter, through and through. Her face carried his fine features, and she knew also his sharp and merciless regard. It was almost as if she, like Athena, had sprung from her father's brow, or at least as if her mother had been nothing more than an incubator, leaving no mark of her own on Ruby.

It struck Ruby as inevitable that the Judge should have ended up destroying this fair and seemingly joyful creature. Ruby only regretted that she'd been his accomplice in the act. Maybe things would have been different, better, had the woman not died giving birth. Then again, perhaps it was a mercy to the woman that she'd died never knowing the depravity her husband was capable of. At least Ruby hoped this was the case. Regardless, Ruby's mother hadn't needed to spend her years pretending to be ignorant of the Judge's crimes committed both in the world and under his very roof.

She'd never learn of Ruby's own crimes, or the thing that she'd become.

Ruby paused, lifting the portrait to examine it, but the metal irritated her skin, stinging like a paper cut. Ruby dropped the photo on the table, relieved when it landed lying facedown. She paused and focused again on her own flittering image in the glass. Every so many seconds, it would resolve into a seemingly normal reflection, the face she'd always known, though her complexion showed a strange silvery blue. Then the reflection would blur, as if she were moving quickly, though she stood perfectly still. Ruby intuited that the thing inside her, the force she'd been bound to, came from a blind realm. Her quivering reflection testified to either its attempt to shield itself, or light's own attempt to reject it.

She closed her eyes and let her mind drift. She knew she and her father were not alone in the house; Lucille crouched fearfully in her mama's old sewing room. Ruby could feel her fear, smell it like a magnolia flower on a warm afternoon, and although she had no intention of harming the servant, the scent of her fear brought pleasure to the thing inside her, a rich warm dessert to the feast of her father's blood.

At first she'd loathed the sensation of it moving within her, but she'd come to accept it. No, cherish it. Those who had bound it to her thought they were punishing her. They could never begin to understand the great gift they'd given her. Her mind drifted back to the moment when she lay, nearly lost to the opium she'd so willingly accepted from the great Myrna King's own hand. She found herself lying on a gurney that had been covered with a type of silk. She remembered it had been black, embroidered with symbols in crimson.

"You wanted to know our secrets. Now, my dear, you shall have your way," King had said, leaning over her. A man approached them, and only then had Ruby realized they weren't alone. No, the gurney stood at the center of a circle of men and women. Ruby was beyond the ability to count them, but she sensed they were numerous. She cast her eyes around, her head lolling. Sleep, oblivion, warm and wondrous, called to her. No, she couldn't count them, but the glimpses that registered in her mind informed her that they were all young, and oh, so very beautiful.

Those gathered round them began drawing closer, tightening the circle around her in a synchronized yet lurching movement, too ungainly and awkward to be thought of as dance. The reedy whine of a high-pitched flute sounded in opposition to their movements, the rhythm of its atonal moan out of time with their steps. Had Ruby's senses not been dulled by drug, she probably would have laughed at the sight of them; it was just all so overly dramatic, so Hollywood.

They began singing, or maybe chanting, the melody nothing more than a repetition of three discordant notes that seemed to share no relation to the tune played by the piper. The utterances they made were ugly, guttural, sounding more like the cries of a tortured beast than a proper language, but the repetition of these sounds told her that they must have been words that held meaning. A man's face appeared before her, a cruel lopsided smile on his lips, and then drifted back. Another, this time a woman she knew from one of Myrna's parties. She'd fetched her drinks and lit her cigarettes, laughed at her jokes, and even bore the brunt of a few of them in the hope of ingratiating herself.

The woman's face receded, replaced by that of another man, one she recognized, a financier, she'd been told, to whom she'd offered herself at another of Myrna's parties only the week before. She'd hoped to find herself a spot in his entourage, worm her way into his circle of wealthy acquaintances, and discover which of them might demonstrate behaviors in private that they'd pay to keep secret. His gaze had passed quickly over her without attempting even the most superficial appraisal of her form or features and settled on Dylan, who'd approached, carrying a mound of cocaine on a small silver tray. The financier watched as Dylan cut the mound into lines and snorted two of them. Dylan held the tray out to him, but the man only set it aside and took Dylan's hand, leading him away into the mad throng of guests. Ruby had instantly begun to calculate ways to catch the men alone, in a well-lit room, with a camera in her hand. The financier should've led to a fat payday, but then Dylan had up and disappeared without a word.

The financier's face gave way to another, then another, of whom she'd begun to collect bits and pieces of information, tidbits that might prove effective in either befriending or blackmailing them. Others were strangers, people she'd never seen before even at Myrna's parties, but she sensed they held something in common with the others she did recognize—the same cool, unsympathetic expression. As the thought registered in her clouded mind, Ruby realized for the first time that this was more than a theatrical performance. These people intended to kill her. Still, the opium she'd smoked left her feeling distant and removed. In a dim and claustrophobic corner of her mind, a part of her was screaming, but the rest of her remained aloof, watching on with a nearly clinical dispassion.

"You won't feel a thing," King had said, as she slid the needle of a syringe beneath her skin. Ruby had never liked needles. Only real addicts did. She tried to draw her arm back. "Now don't be a child. This, my dear, is your chance to become something greater than yourself. No longer just a darling backwoods hayseed hoping to make it here in Tinsel Town. No more a simple schemer, preying on the weaknesses of others." She held up the syringe, and the man took it from her. "No, my dear, you are to be a gateway, an opening through which something much greater than yourself will come.

"Now this bit, you'll feel," Myrna said as rough hands forced Ruby up into a near-sitting position; others pulled her head back. She choked as another woman, with cruel black eyes lined with kohl and long, straight dark hair parted down the center, poured a liquid, a metallic taste, down her throat. She forced Ruby's mouth closed, and massaged her throat in a downward motion. But Ruby had felt something. The burning cold.

It had been at her fifth birthday party that she'd first experienced this type of sensation. Impatient to taste the ice cream Marva was making, she'd touched the side of the ice cream maker's metal cylinder, chilled to below freezing by rock salt and ice.

The cold burned, shocking and fascinating her in the same instant. She'd felt compelled to experiment, so she grabbed a girl's hand—what was her name, Missy?—and held her soft pink palm against it until the girl cried out. Ruby wasn't sure why she'd done it. She'd just wanted to see what it would feel like—both for herself and for her playmate. To experience the effect the surprising source of pain would have on the girl, and how she herself would feel as the one who forced the suffering on her. In the end, she felt nothing, not even when Missy slapped her with her free hand. Missy's attempt at revenge had been half-hearted at best. The Judge witnessed the slap, and dragged the child outside, giving her several rough shakes along the way. Ruby seemed to remember that her little friend's parents moved away sometime afterward; at least she couldn't remember ever spending time with Missy after that.

For the first time in years, she thought of the nearly forgotten girl at her birthday party, and as she looked into Myrna King's eyes, she finally understood how it must feel to be the one taking pleasure in another's pain. She whined through gritted teeth, the numbing effect of the opium not strong enough to alleviate the sensation of being frozen and burned alive, at the same time and from the inside out. The hands propping her up then lowered her in a single rough drop, her head bouncing as it banged against the table.

"Careful, careful," she heard Myrna say to the others. "This is a delicate operation here. We don't want to damage the portal." Then Myrna's smooth and perfect face appeared over her, framed by blonde ringlets. "Great and ancient magic is passing through you now, my dear, magic first harnessed and forgotten long before the pyramids were planted on Giza." She reached around her neck and unhooked the clasp of the necklace she'd been wearing, allowing it to dangle before Ruby's upturned eyes. At first Ruby thought it was a cross, the kind the Catholics she'd met in California seemed so fond of wearing, but then she noticed the hoop shape at its top. The tip of the thing appeared sharp, a tiny golden blade.

"Life. Eternal," she said, then laughed, "or at least a hell of a lot longer than any of us could ever expect otherwise. You're about to house the source of it." She dropped the necklace on Ruby's breast, and let her finger run along her clavicle, up the sensitive skin of her neck to the side of her windpipe. "All that mummification nonsense the Egyptians got up to. It stemmed from the folk memory of the practices a debased priesthood forgot. Still what has been forgotten can be rediscovered, my dear." She paused. "But let's forget ancient history and focus on the now.

Do you feel it awakening in you? Yes?" Ruby felt unable to move, even to blink her eyes in response. "You must be so frightened. Or at least you should be. We welcome the force into you by infecting your blood. It will take three times, just like in a fairy tale, to seal the charm." She leaned over Ruby and placed a kiss on her lips. "But you'll be no Sleeping Beauty. You'll be aware. Trapped in there as your own life force fades. But we'll be out here working to manage your transition, keep you alive as long as possible so to expand your period of usefulness. These sigils will help with that," Myrna said as she let her hand slide back down Ruby's breastbone to the rounded cross pendant she'd dropped there. Myrna lifted it and pressed its sharp tip into the skin of Ruby's breast. The pain was enough to drive away the last of the opiate fog. Ruby bucked upward, raising her arm to fight.

"Secure her," Myrna said in a flat, almost-bored voice. Ruby felt her arm being pulled back with nearly enough force to dislocate her shoulder. She fell back, trying to kick her legs or strike out with her other arm, but before that impulse could be realized, thick leather straps and cuffs were fastened around her limbs and tightened. Another strap was pulled over her legs near the knees, and two men, one of them the financier, moved to pull another over her chest. "No, not there. It will be in my way," Myrna said. "Use your hands." The two men leaned over her, using their weight to pin Ruby's shoulders down as Myrna began carving out bits of her flesh.

"Don't worry, my dear," Myrna said, nearly cooing her words, "I will take it on as my personal duty to make sure that this experience lasts as long as it possibly can before we finally dispatch you to whatever hell is awaiting you."

◆ ◆ ◆

The Judge moaned, pulling Ruby's mind from California back to Conroy. Ruby turned toward the sound, and as her eyes focused on the old man before her, she wondered if that wasn't exactly what had happened. Maybe this was her hell.

Her father's eyes were open and fixed on her, foolishly still seeming to be begging her for mercy, but in Ruby's stilled heart, there was no mercy to be found. "Can't forget the best part now, can we, Daddy?" She let herself ride on a wave of magic to his side, never taking her eyes off him as she opened the drawer of his nightstand. She pulled out the bottle of colloidal silver, and unscrewed its lid.

"Open wide, Daddy." He shook his head, trying to resist, but he couldn't. The days of his ability to refuse her ended when she first forced him to taste her blood. After that, she was the mistress of his will. His lips slid open, as his eyes widened in fearful anguish. She tilted the bottle over his mouth and poured, fascinated by the popping sound as the silver burned his tongue and then his throat. "Swallow," she commanded as he choked on the burning liquid. He did as she told him, leaving her to savor every moment of his pain. She waited until his body stopped spasming, until his last whining moan silenced itself. She ran her finger along his quivering jawline. "Might as well finish this bottle up, no?"

TWENTY-TWO

Night fell quickly over the Dunne farm. The mass of trees to the west was just tall enough to block out the setting sun, so the sky seemed magically to shift from pink to plum to black in mere minutes once the sun had been hidden away. Corinne sat on the Dunnes' porch, rocking calmly on the porch swing, pushing herself back and forth with the tip of her right shoe, the movement absentminded, unconsciously synchronized to a choir of croaking frogs. The Dunnes knew she was waiting there for their son to return, but they hadn't offered to turn on a light, and with the way Ava reacted to simple questions, Corinne was a bit wary of making a full-on request, let alone risking committing the crime of turning it on herself. Just as well, Corinne told herself; the porch light would only attract bugs.

She focused on the stars she could make out beyond the porch's overhang, wondering if any of them might grant power to her wishes, but knowing she'd long since given up on wishing. This was to be her new life, a chance to put the past behind her. She'd hoped to find a family here, one to make up for the one she'd never really had. She tried to be optimistic, chalk the bad first impression up to nerves, but it looked like the Dunnes were going to be just as much a disappointment as the family she'd been born into. And what about Elijah himself? Was he, too, bound to be another letdown?

The Elijah she'd known in Korea had been so gentle, so thoughtful. There, an ocean away, he'd been a spinner of simple, wholesome dreams. A home, a family, companionship. They'd sat together beneath these same stars, holding hands. The words they'd shared were warm, early imaginations of what their life together could be. The silences between them, for there were many, were comfortable, intimate, a wall built around them, unlike the hostile taciturnity of the Dunne household, a wall that kept them apart. Still, Elijah seemed to feel comfortable in this environment, though she couldn't for the life of her imagine the man she'd known overseas being so. Was the man she'd come to marry some kind of quisling, or had she just filled in the blanks herself, turning him into a man she could feel safe with? So odd that she'd find happiness with Elijah in a war zone, but that a single day in this backwater town could threaten their relationship.

Corinne felt as if she'd found herself in a play with a whole team of characters she'd never heard of. She pushed the thought of the beautiful Ruby aside. The woman was probably a cousin, or even just a friend of the family. Corinne comforted herself with her certainty that if Ruby had any interest in Elijah, Elijah would never have chosen Corinne over her. No, they faced real issues; Corinne was not going to entertain petty schoolgirl insecurities now. These friends of Elijah whom she'd never heard one word about until they'd been found slaughtered. The old doctor on the train had warned her that his friends were the rowdy type. Still she couldn't help but feel the type of behavior that gets your headless body strapped to a church steeple must have gone beyond boisterous.

Corinne had experienced enough of this kind of man, all whiskey sweat, and wadded, losing racing forms. Physical strength used to intimidate, to overpower.

The scent of gunpowder rose to her memory. All right, she, too, had secrets she would probably never share, but there were thousands of miles between her and the skeletons she harbored.

A flicker in the trees, the beams of headlights pulling around the corner. She held up her arm to shield her eyes, relieved to see that it was the Dunnes' truck pulling up the drive. Gravel crunched beneath the tires, the sound prodding Corinne to rise. The swing groaned as she abandoned it and headed across the porch. She waited at the top step, until the sight of the truck door opening spurred her on. She wanted a moment to get Elijah alone. To speak with him privately before his parents could cut him off from her.

The dry grass crunched beneath her feet. The air was still. The world around her, lit only by a spray of blue stars and the bright sliver of a new moon, seemed somehow dreamlike. Elijah climbed out of the truck cab, and closed the door behind him. He came around the front of the truck to meet her, stopping and looking down on her with tender eyes. Was his forehead creased with worry, or were the lines witnesses to his regret? He tilted his head, leaning in toward her. His lips found her. A gentle kiss that spoke of his caring. His beard tickled her, but she didn't mind. His kiss had broken the evil spell that had fallen on her. Corinne felt her shoulders relax, and she went up on her toes, leaning into him. His arms tightened on her, tentatively at first, but then almost as if he were clinging to her for dear life.

He pulled back, but his calloused fingers touched her cheek, then cradled her jawline with great tenderness. Corinne watched silently as he struggled to find the words. "I'm sorry." His voice broke as he spoke to her. He coughed. "I'm sorry." He leaned down and placed a kiss on the top of her head, then another on her forehead. "What I did. Leaving you here like that. That isn't me. Or at least I don't want it to be me." He tilted up her chin so that their eyes met. "Things will be different from now on. I promise. I just . . ."

"You just learned of the murders of very dear friends." Corinne found herself making his excuses for him. She was so desperate for what he was saying to be true. For everything to be all right. For him to be the man she'd come to care for. For coming to Conroy not to have been a gross mistake. "Don't shut me out," she said. "I'm going to be your wife, Elijah. Your helpmeet. Let me share your burdens."

As he nodded, his hand released her and fell to his side. "I want that. I do. I just don't know where to start." He began to turn away, but she reached out and caught ahold of his hand. He stopped, but still he looked away, seeming incapable of meeting her eye to eye. "Sometimes lately I feel like I'm two different people. There's the man you know. The man I want to be. Then there's the guy I used to be before I left here. A guy I don't like very much. I came back here thinking he was gone, but he was just waiting here for me to get back. He's here. Haunting me, like some kind of ghost."

"Tell me about him," she said, realizing that she was now clasping the hand she'd been holding between both of hers, tugging on him, unconsciously trying to lead him away from the house, away from his parents. She'd like nothing better than if she could coax him back into the truck, and get him to drive off again, only this time taking her with him.

He would not be budged. He shook his head. "No." His voice came out harsh, then softened. "No. I'm ashamed. I'm afraid of seeing the way you'll look at me if I tell you."

"All right, then. Tell me about your friends. This Dowd and Bobby." She felt a tremor pass through him as she said their names. "They weren't good men, were they?"

"If I tell you about them, I'm telling you about me. All the things they done. All the things they're guilty of, I'm guilty, too. I've done the same things they did."

Corinne took a step closer, slipping her arm around his waist and leaning her head against his chest. "No. You're different. You knew whatever it was you fellows were getting up to wasn't for you. You got out. You served your country. You received an honorable discharge and a Purple Heart . . ."

"For being shot by a sniper while carrying garbage to a pit."

"For being an honorable soldier who was wounded doing his part in the war effort." She leaned back so she could see his face. "There are always going to be people who want to tear you down, minimize the good you've done in this world. Don't let yourself be one of them." She lowered her head, trying to decide whether she really needed to know the details of Elijah's past, or if it would be easier to help him be the man he wanted to be by letting the secrets die. She made her choice and looked up to meet his gaze. "Okay. I don't need to know. I don't care who these men were. I don't care what type of things you used to do together. That version of you. The man you want to leave behind. I want to help you leave him and his crimes, real or imagined, in the past. I want to help you be the Elijah I know. The Elijah I came halfway round the world to marry."

Elijah's gaze drifted up and away from her, as the yard behind them was illuminated by the sudden flaring of the porch light. Corinne glanced over her shoulder to see her soon-to-be mother-in-law standing in the doorway. "You two need to come on inside now," Mrs. Dunne called to them. "I've held supper all I plan to." Ava turned and walked away, but she left the door standing open.

Corinne turned back to Elijah, whose attention had once again focused on her. "I appreciate what you're saying. I do," he said. "And I want what you want." He pulled her in for a quick hug before releasing her. "I just worry he might not be put down so easy." Elijah took her hand and led her toward the house. Even before they crossed the threshold, Corinne could feel an angry pair of eyes settle on them.

"Come on now, get cleaned up," Mrs. Dunne snapped at them.

Corinne didn't know what she would be facing when it came to helping Elijah put his past behind him. And tonight, she couldn't even begin to imagine that she'd ever feel at home in this strange place. But if their marriage were going to succeed, Corinne was sure of one thing: she and Elijah were going to have to work out alternative living arrangements.

TWENTY-THREE

McAvoy took a swig of his bourbon and water. He wasn't a drinking man by habit, but his afternoon with the Judge had left him on edge. Though the Judge's medical problem appeared to be some form of anemia, guilt was what had consumed Ovid. Guilt and anger and the disappointment of finally learning he really wasn't God after all. Ovid had spent two years and heaven only knew how many thousands of dollars locating Ruby after she left home. Watching his daughter die only weeks after getting her back had derailed the man.

McAvoy thought back to a day, eight, maybe nine years ago? A cold February morning. A heavy frost had descended on the town, painting it a shimmering white, and a yellow sun hung in a cloudless gentian blue sky. God had built that day for beauty, but man had found a way to mar it.

The Judge showed up at his surgery with Ruby in tow, the girl wearing a coat that was far too light for the cold snap that had hit Conroy. How old was she then? Thirteen? Fourteen? She was such a petite thing, he might have thought her younger, but there was no childlike exuberance in the way she carried herself. She came through the door, all hunched over and crumpled in on herself, her father following, on his face a look that spoke more of embarrassment than worry.

McAvoy led them into his consulting room and motioned for Ruby to take a chair. "What seems to be the trouble?" he asked, expecting any number of the usual ailments. He pulled his stethoscope around his neck and reached over to grab a tongue depressor.

Ovid snatched off the hat he'd been wearing, holding it with a white-knuckled hand. "She's been vomiting. She isn't bleeding," he said, almost in a whisper, his dark eyes pleading with the doctor.

"*Not* bleeding?" McAvoy asked, not registering the full import of the situation at first. "Oh," he said after a moment. "How long has this been the case? How long since your last 'visit'?"

The girl looked up at him with reddened, terrified eyes. "A month or so now. Maybe two."

"Is there a young man in your life?" McAvoy asked. The girl trembled. She looked at her father, then her eyes darted up to the doctor before returning to the floor.

"Yes, sir," the child responded again, just staring down at her scuffed shoes this time. McAvoy sighed. He knew she was lying.

Looking back now, McAvoy knew that *this* was the first moment he'd failed her. He should have found a way to help. He should have taken her away from the Judge then and there.

Ovid leaned in toward the doctor, a worry line forming between his eyebrows. "You can fix this, can't you?"

"We can send her away. Tell everyone she's gone to boarding school up north, maybe Europe. The Catholics aren't good for much else, but they do have facilities set up where she can give birth. They'll see to it that the child's basic needs are met, until it can be adopted or is old enough to cope on its own."

"No." Ovid began trembling, shaking even more than his daughter had done. "I cannot live with the thought of *it* out there. Alive. I am asking you to *fix* this. Not only for my sake, but for the sake of my father's memory. Or have you forgotten your friendship with him?"

"I have forgotten nothing," McAvoy said, a sudden anger causing his pulse to pound in his ears. That Ovid would turn him into an accomplice to his own sins infuriated him. Ruby fell forward out of the chair and at their feet. McAvoy knelt down and felt for her pulse. She was a strong, healthy girl. All of this had just proven too much for her young system. "Help me get her up." The two of them picked up the birdlike girl without difficulty and lifted her onto an exam table.

The Judge ran both hands, fingers linked, over his head. "Will you do it? Will you fix this for me?"

McAvoy nodded, a weariness entering him that he hadn't to this day been able to shake. "I will *fix* this, as you say, but let me warn you now, Ovid. Never again." Ovid's shoulders collapsed as he breathed a heavy sigh. The doctor looked Ovid over from head to toe, sickened by the relief that had flooded over the man's face. "Shall I make sure the need for this type of procedure can never arise again?"

McAvoy watched as Ovid considered the possibility. At first his eyes opened wider, as if the doctor had presented the solution to a particularly vexing problem, but then his face went slack. "No." He shook his head. "She's my only hope of having a lineage. Leave her intact."

"I wasn't talking about her," McAvoy said, his voice cold. "I was talking about castrating the worthless bastard who done this to her." They looked each other in the eye as an understanding passed between them.

The doctor and the Judge had never spoken of the unpleasantness again. He'd told himself that the understanding they shared was enough to protect Ruby. Truth be told, he had no idea. Truth be told, he hadn't wanted to know.

A tapping at the window startled the old doctor, pulling him back to the present. He saw Lucille on the other side of the glass. "Damned fool of a woman," he thought, angry that she had alarmed him, as he waved her around to the front entrance. She hesitated, but then went to the front of the house.

He opened the door to find her fidgeting. "I am sorry for disturbing you, Doctor. I rung the bell at the back of the house, but you didn't seem to hear me."

The bell had stopped working months before. He'd never gotten around to having the darn thing fixed. Lucille looked over her shoulder. "It's the Judge, sir. I've been checking in on him, every hour, like you told me. But he's had a bad turn. I think you had better come." She tossed another look behind her. "Quick, sir, please?"

TWENTY-FOUR

Corinne felt grateful for the privacy the sleeping porch afforded her. It gave her shelter, without making her feel as if she were truly under the Dunnes' roof. She extinguished her light and rolled up the Roman blinds, watching through the screen as fireflies punctuated the darkness. A stillness enveloped the whole scene; the only sounds were the chorus of the croaking frogs and rattling grasshoppers. Corinne's prayer for a breeze went unheeded.

She focused on the sharp slice of new moon, a poor source of light, but a familiar companion all the same. The same moon had followed Corinne from San Francisco to Korea and now to Conroy; it watched over her almost as closely as Elijah's parents had been surveying the young couple. Ava had a strong sense of propriety, so she insisted that the two be chaperoned at all times until the wedding. Elijah had set up a cot in the barn because she'd claimed it wasn't proper for the two of them to sleep under the same roof until they had the blessing of the good Lord to do so. It broke Corinne's heart to think of him out there alone, trying to come to terms with the news of his friends' violent deaths. Corinne considered the wisdom of sneaking across the fields to the barn to join Elijah on his cot. She heaved a sigh. Without a doubt, Ava was sitting upstairs near her own window, keeping a lookout to prevent just such an encounter.

Corinne's eyes scanned right to left from the barn, running along the timberline before stopping where the moon reflected off the pond. She had learned over a nearly wordless lunch that the water ran cold because it was spring fed, and that it was much deeper than the surface area would lead one to believe. The heat of the day hadn't surrendered with the light that had brought it. She longed to dip beneath the water, to feel herself breaking its surface before her body started to bob up and down in its cool liquid embrace.

"Corinne." The sound of her name carried over the field to her, almost as if the grass itself had called to her. "Join me, Corinne." The voice seemed to come from within her own mind. Unfamiliar, feminine, irresistible, as if it were touching her in places she kept hidden even from herself. "Join me."

Corinne saw a movement down by the edge of the water. A naked paleness, so white that it shone nearly blue in the moonlight. "I shouldn't," Corinne whispered in response to the summons, but her hand was already pressing against the screen door. It let out a low plaintive cry as she pushed it open and insinuated herself into the gap. It was too early and hot for dew, so the dry grass scraped against the bottoms of Corinne's bare feet.

Silently she descended toward the water. The pale figure before her left the shore and submerged itself in the water. Several seconds passed, and Corinne stood frozen in place. In the woman's absence, Corinne felt that a spell had been broken, that her own better sense had been returned to her. She nearly turned and ran back to the house, but in that same moment, the woman broke the surface, water cascading off her black hair, down her opalescent breasts. She had been under water for what seemed like an eternity, but when she rose, she didn't gasp for air as Corinne surely would have needed to. She stood there, beautiful, still, composed, like a granite statue. Her head tilted to the right and she looked up with eyes shining as blue as the hottest edge of a gas flame.

"It's you," Corinne said, recognizing the heart-shaped face and delicate features of the woman in the photo. The photo with which she had been unable to part. "Ruby."

A smile formed on Ruby's lips. "Of course it's me, darlin'. Who else would it be?" The extreme oddness of the moment nearly broke through to Corinne, but she felt as inescapably drawn to the pond as a hooked fish being reeled in to dry land. "The water is so, so nice, Corinne. So refreshing. Join me." Ruby held out her hands and took a few graceful steps toward Corinne, but it wasn't necessary. Without intending to, Corinne had already begun her own course toward the water, which was a sharp contrast to the warm night air. Weeds tugged at her ankles, making their weak attempt to stop her progress, but nothing would stop her, could stop her, from becoming one with the light shining in Ruby's eyes.

Growing wet, Corinne's gown at first clung to her legs, but then billowed up around her hips as she was drawn deeper into the water. Ruby held her arms out wide in welcome. Soon Corinne could no longer touch bottom; the mucky floor fell clean away, and she found herself treading water. How could Ruby be standing there so stationary? Corinne was an excellent swimmer, but as treading lost its efficacy, she shifted into an awkward dog paddle, unwilling to look away from what awaited her. She drew up close to Ruby, who reached out and pulled her into an embrace. Stabilizing Corinne with one arm, Ruby caressed her face with her free hand, her long cold fingers sliding along her captive's cheek, down the side of her neck, then across her shoulder.

"He's never gonna love you. Not really," Ruby said. "Not like he loved me, so if you know what's good for you, you'll get out of Conroy and head on home." She leaned in and placed her lips near Corinne's, so near they almost touched. "Take this as your only warning." Pressure began to build behind Ruby's touch and, before Corinne could process what was happening, both hands were pinning her shoulders, forcing her head underwater.

Corinne struggled against the downward pressure, surprised when her head easily broke through the water. No one was holding her; she was alone. She gasped in the night air and fought her way back to shore.

TWENTY-FIVE

Lucille had waited in the old sewing room with the door shut tight, sitting on a footstool, not daring to move, barely daring to breathe. The feeling in the house reminded her of when she was a small girl, swimming in the pond with her brother. He held her underwater without the intention of harming her, but he'd kept her there for too long, nearly drowning her. She'd never been able to forget the pounding in her ears, the burning in her lungs in the moment before he finally pulled her back above the surface. And just as her depleted lungs had welcomed the sweet air, she felt a relief every bit as precious sweep over the house. She knew in her heart what it meant: Ruby had left.

Still cautious, she'd made her way back to the Judge's bedside, forcing her hand over her mouth to stifle a shriek. He was completely naked except for the sheen of his own blood. A loose flap of skin hung nearly torn from his thigh and, revealing a similar gouge that had been torn into his neck, his head was thrown back over a blood-soaked pillow. Still, he lived. His eyes pleaded with her, his quivering hand lifted as if to reach out for her, but she stepped back, moving beyond his reach.

That was when she ran from the house, not stopping until she reached the doctor's residence.

Lucille let Dr. McAvoy lead the way to her employer's room. She suspected the Judge would be long dead by now, and she'd seen enough death to last her a lifetime. When she went to check on him earlier, she'd immediately realized *he wasn't alone.* The house's atmosphere changed within moments, feeling unnaturally heavy. Whispers were floating down from the Judge's room, whispers that sounded an awful lot like Ruby's voice. Lucille had witnessed Ruby's handiwork the previous night by the light of that burning cross, so she knew better than to interrupt. A part of Lucille's conscience pecked at her now—she should have done something, should have tried helping the old man. But no, whatever had happened in that room was simply the Judge's own sins coming home to roost.

She followed Dr. McAvoy as he moved stiffly up the stairs, weaving a little. Lucille could smell the alcohol on him. Well, maybe that would help him get through what was coming. She watched as he hesitated outside the Judge's door.

"Ovid?" he called. "It's me." There was no response. He crossed the threshold and entered the room. Lucille followed a few steps behind, but she didn't want to take even a single step into that room. Even from the partially eclipsed view afforded from the doorway, she could see that the bedding was soaked through with blood. Lucille knew it would fall to her to clean up, but she would not, could not while the Judge was lying there. Had death closed his eyes, or had they stayed open, glassy and wide in terror?

The doctor bent over the Judge and pressed his fingers against his wrist. It was at that moment the Judge gasped in air, his hand shooting out to catch McAvoy's.

Lucille failed to suppress a startled caw. Until that moment, she'd felt certain the Judge had passed on.

The doctor looked at her, his face ashen, his jaw quivering. "Lucille, find some brandy. Or some whiskey, rum. Whatever the Judge keeps on hand. And don't even try pretending that this is a dry Baptist house."

Lucille fled downstairs and found her way to the Judge's office. She entered, but not before flipping the switch that illuminated the large overhead chandelier the Judge rarely used. The tantalus chest stood in the far corner, behind the Judge's desk. She tried to lift the lid, but she wasn't surprised to discover the Judge kept it locked. She attacked the desk itself, intending to look for the key to the tantalus in its drawers, but they, too, had been secured. Finally she spotted the Judge's letter opener sitting on the desktop, and used it to jimmy the chest open. She'd probably end up paying for the repair if the Judge lived.

Unlike the Judge, Lucille didn't imbibe, even though the events of the past day and night were threatening to drive her to it. She didn't know what the bottles contained, so she grabbed two of the four and one of the tumblers the Judge kept near the chest. She stiffened her spine and made her way back upstairs.

"I got your alcohol," Lucille said from the hall, not wanting to return to the Judge's side.

"Well, bring it in here, woman," Dr. McAvoy snapped.

Lucille obeyed, but her aversion to entering the room was so strong, it felt like she was dragging a ball and chain along with her. She knew deep down that the fetter was her own better sense. She handed the glass to McAvoy and held the bottles up before him. "The rum," he said, and when Lucille hesitated, the annoyed doctor reached out and yanked away the bottle that contained the clearer of the two liquids. Lucille took several steps backward and set the unwanted bottle on the small table near the door. She hovered near the exit as she watched the doctor pull out the stopper and pour a good amount of the liquor into the tumbler. He held it out to the Judge, but the wounded man didn't even have the strength to rise.

"Give us a hand here, Lucille," McAvoy ordered.

It took every bit of her resolve not to turn and flee. She took cautious steps toward the bed, moving to the side opposite McAvoy. She forced herself to reach out and put her hand behind the Judge's shoulders. She flinched at the sight of his neck. It was still bloodied, but there was no longer any wound there. Her eyes shot down to the Judge's ravaged thigh, but the flap of flesh had closed and healed, leaving not even a sign that the skin had been broken. Lucille had seen the damage done to the Judge, and now it was as if it had never been. There was no longer any room for denying that some unnatural magic had come to Conroy.

A cry began to build in her throat, but she swallowed hard. She wasn't going to let on that she knew anything. Besides, even if she did tell the doctor what was going on here, he'd never believe her. Probably wouldn't even take the time to hear her out. He'd just think she was another high-strung female. She let the muffled cry turn into a silent prayer, even though she wasn't quite sure what she should ask the good Lord to do about this. Besides, the sting of having lost her husband and now her babies made her wonder if God even gave a damn about anything going on below him anyway. A cynical thought, but it felt justified.

Lucille slid her hands beneath a still-white part of the twisted bedsheet. She tried not to make contact with his skin, but even through the cotton barrier, she could feel his clamminess. She used gentle force to help him rise, and the doctor held the rum to his blue lips. The Judge took a deep draught, but immediately began to cough.

"What happened here, Lucille? There's a lot of bruising, but no wounds to account for the amount of blood here. I've never seen a plain illness cause this degree of blood loss."

"I don't know, sir," Lucille lied.

McAvoy set the glass on the night table and took the Judge's wrist again to check his pulse. He glanced at his watch, but then turned his full attention to Lucille, seeming to be awaiting a different answer. He moved his hand toward the Judge's neck, but the Judge whimpered and pulled back with a start, pressing his weight against Lucille's already trembling hands.

Lucille nearly dropped the Judge back on his pillow. She felt her body go cold and begin to tremble. Her knees weakened, so she reached out and grasped the headboard to keep from collapsing.

"Pull yourself together, woman," McAvoy said, flashing an angry glance at her. He refilled the Judge's glass with more rum and handed it to her. "Drink this."

Lucille held her palm up to the doctor as she struggled to form words. "Thank you, sir, but I don't imbibe."

McAvoy pushed the glass toward her. "It's medicinal. Drink it. I need you to help me, not faint."

Lucille's hand shook as she took the glass from him. She held it to her lips, then let the fiery liquid slide down her throat. The rum lent strength to her spine, and after a moment she released the headboard. McAvoy nodded and turned his attention back to the patient. "There's blood on the bedding, but no obvious injury." The way he spoke told Lucille that the old man was speaking to himself, trying to suss out what had happened. "Ovid," he said, focusing on the Judge, "I think we should get you to the hospital in Tupelo."

"No," the Judge spat out—his first word since Ruby's attack. He exhausted himself shaking his head, and began wheezing.

McAvoy nodded. "You take it easy there, son." The doctor's eyes flitted up to Lucille. "Help me clean him up. Pull the chair closer, so we can shift him into it. Then go find some clean sheets." Lucille did as she had been commanded. She assumed she'd have to bear the greater part of the Judge's weight, but he came up off the bed much more easily than she'd expected. Once he had been moved, Dr. McAvoy held the Judge by the shoulders to make sure he didn't tumble out of the chair. Lucille did her best not to stare at the sight of the Judge pinned in that armchair. Just two months back, he'd glowed with health. His eyes may have glistened with cruelty, but they had been clear and sharp. His hair had been black like a raven's feathers, like the soul that lived within him. Now he was a waste of a man. He looked so old and dried up.

These ain't never gonna come clean, Lucille thought to herself as she tore the fouled sheets from the bed. She carried them from the room, letting them drop to the floor of the linen closet, and pulled out a fresh pair of sheets and a thick blanket. The blanket would cover any blood-stains left on the mattress. It would keep the doctor from telling her to flip it, and having to find a way to balance the weight of the mattress without letting any of the bloody mess covering it rub off on her. She carried her burden back to the room, moving quickly to cover the mattress and dress the bed with the clean, ironed sheets. The pillows and cases had been completely ruined, so she snatched them up and turned on her heel to find replacements.

She made it to the closet in no time, but she took her time finding her way back, feeling for all the world like her legs had turned to lead. To her surprise, McAvoy met her in the hall. The door to the Judge's room had been closed and the doctor stood before it, like he was standing guard.

"I'll take him these," Lucille said raising the pillows.

"Wait," the doctor said, blocking her way. "You realize your employer is seriously ill?"

"Yes, sir. I can see he's doing real poorly."

The doctor licked his lips. "Yes, poorly." He squinted. "He should be in the hospital, but you know how stubborn the Judge is."

"It's more than stubbornness. There are folk around these parts who'd like nothing better to see him in this state," Lucille said, instantly regretting her words. "I'm sorry, sir, I shouldn't be speaking out of turn about the Judge."

"No, Lucille, you are right. The Judge cannot afford to appear weak. He's got too many enemies who would be quick to take advantage of it. Given how long you've worked for Ovid, you are certainly aware of that."

Lucille judged it best to hold her peace. She kept quiet, clutching the pillows to her chest as she waited for him to speak.

The doctor continued, "But I have to ask myself, what could be at the root of the Judge's illness? Sure, he took Ruby's passing hard—I'll be honest, a whole hell of a lot harder than I thought he had—and grief can do a lot of harm to a man, but I managed to get a little bit of a look at him. I could tell he has been coughing up blood."

Against her better instincts, Lucille spoke up. "Could be cancer," she said. "Man from my church, he had the lung cancer, and he coughed up blood."

"Yes, you are correct. Coughing up blood is a symptom of lung cancer. So are fatigue and headaches. Poor Ovid has complained of those, too. But something doesn't sit right with me about all this. This could be cancer, or it could be something else entirely. The kind of something a body could arrange."

"I don't understand."

"You know the Judge has enemies. Like you said, making the Judge look weak would do harm enough. A person wouldn't even need to kill him outright. Maybe someone has been giving him something to make him this way. A bit in his food, his drink. Someone wishing the Judge harm might just pay a pretty penny to get what they want."

"There's no way that's happening, sir. Least not at home. I do all the cooking for the Judge." Lucille realized too late this was the point he'd been making all along.

"Of course you do. You take real good care of him. That's what's got me wondering why you didn't come to me when Ovid fell sick."

"You know he told me not to."

"But you got better sense than that, Lucille. You have eyes in your head; you must have known the man might well be dying. I have to wonder, Lucille—you came in and saw the Judge was in distress, but you took the time to walk over to my house rather than call. Why is that?"

Truth was she had wanted to get out of the house before Ruby could return. She found a quick answer. "I was afraid news might get out if I called. The Judge has a private line, but I didn't know if you were still on a party line. I was afraid somebody might be listening in."

McAvoy nodded, seeming to accept her excuse. Then the doctor ran his hand over his mouth, holding it beneath his chin. "How are your children doing?"

She paused, uncertain where this was heading. "They're just fine, sir. Thank you."

The doctor tilted his head back, a wry smile forming on his lips. "Well, that's the funny thing. I heard you sent your children away to visit family up north. Maybe you were thinking about joining them? Of course, we both know there is no way that could happen. Ovid always says you'll leave him over his dead body. We both know how true that is, don't we? If Ovid doesn't get better, and real soon, I may just have to bring Sheriff Bell in to consider matters." He paused, she gathered, to make sure his words had fully registered with her. "Now, I don't for a moment believe you're capable of poisoning the Judge. Not really. But I can tell you know a hell of a lot more than what you're telling me."

A burst of anger shot up her spine. She stood tall and dropped the pillows to the floor. Had he already tried and convicted her, or did he just know the sheriff would be too lazy to try and find out the truth when there was such a convenient scapegoat at hand? "I got nothing to do with any of this. I came upstairs to check on him, just like you told me to, and I found him this way." She pointed at him, her hand shaking. That she had come up here at all tonight was the doctor's fault.

McAvoy grabbed her wrist, bending it with more pressure than she would have thought him capable of mustering. "Now, you listen up. I don't really think you have anything to do with Ovid's state, but I am not a fool. There is something you are not telling me. If Ovid passes, I will cut him open, and if I don't find his lungs eaten up with cancer, I will go to the sheriff and spin him the kind of story that will make sure you swing. Unless you start talking. Now."

With her free hand, she pried the old man's fingers from her wrist, then took a step back. "I heard voices. I heard the Judge, and I heard a woman . . ."

McAvoy looked at her through narrowed eyes. "You recognized the voice?"

Lucille knew that once she spoke the words, she'd never be able to take them back. "Yes, sir. It was Miss Ruby."

The doctor lunged at her, and Lucille jumped back, fearing he would strike her. Instead he stopped and fell back against the closed door. He started to speak, then stopped. Finally he said, "Woman, you must have taken leave of your senses."

"You may just be right about that, Doctor, but I know what I heard. The Judge, he and Miss Ruby were talking. He was begging her. Pleading with her to leave him be."

"You heard someone in there harassing your employer, and you didn't step in to help him?"

"No, sir. I heard Miss Ruby in there with her father, and sir, I ain't ashamed to tell you I was too afraid to open the door. I done seen . . ." She was about to tell him what she had witnessed in her own yard, but she stopped herself. It was bad enough to risk being on the hook for the Judge's death. She didn't need anything else laid at her doorstep.

The Judge had made sure she could never escape Conroy by public transport, but Lucille began to wonder if she should just start walking. If she kept off the main roads and hid during the day and walked by night, maybe she could get to where she wasn't recognized, where she wasn't thought of as the Judge's chattel. Of course, in the event that the Judge didn't make it, her flight would be read as her confession, and that would spell her end. Even if she weren't officially convicted and hung on the gallows, she knew she'd end up swinging from a tree limb. Lord knew, one ride to the pearly gates worked just as well as the other. No. She needed to sit tight for now. If the Judge died, and she managed not to get blamed for it, she'd join her children. It was the only plan that made sense. After all, if she fled and the Judge *didn't* die, he'd hunt her down and have her brought back as surely as he'd done with Ruby.

"You saw what?" the doctor pressed her, pulling her out of her thoughts.

"I done seen Miss Ruby being put in that crypt next to her mama. I knew they ain't no way she could be in this house. Not really. But she was. I didn't just hear her voice; I *felt* that it was her."

"What do you mean, you felt it?"

Lucille drew her arms in around herself. She felt trapped in this airless space. She wanted to fling open a window or, better yet, leave this hall, this house, leave Conroy altogether. "When Miss Ruby came back from Los Angeles, you and the Judge, you thought she was sick. But she didn't come home sick. She came home *wrong.*"

The doctor stepped toward her again, this time with less violence, but still with determination. "I don't have time for your Negro superstitions." Lucille was more than happy for him to believe she was suffering from delusions if it meant he no longer held her under suspicion. He shepherded her down the hall and toward the stairs. "I need to use the phone. Don't worry"—he held up his hand to fend off an objection she had no intention of making—"I will speak in veiled terms of the situation. You go put on some coffee."

"Yes, sir," she said, relieved to have a task that didn't require her to be near the Judge.

"And Lucille . . ."

"Yes, sir?"

"Whatever it is you're thinking, you need to keep it to yourself. Don't go sharing your nonsensical ideas with anyone else, and don't you go getting the other coloreds worked up about any of this either. From now on, you do as I tell you, and that might just help me forget how guilty you look right now, hear?"

Lucille nodded. "I'll get that coffee."

TWENTY-SIX

Corinne sat at the edge of the water for what felt like hours. She stared into the depths, doing her best to convince herself she had been dreaming, that her first day in Conroy had been too much for her, that she had sleepwalked into the water and had been awakened by its cold currents. Deep down, she knew that was bullshit. She had spent years in a war zone without suffering any hallucinations, but the only two alternatives she could come up with were that she had gone mad or the woman from the photo truly had called her out for a starlight swim before disappearing into thin air. Corinne felt another chill and wrapped her arms around herself, doing her best to rub the goose pimples from her flesh. Her damp and muddied gown clung to her like a second skin. She forced herself to her feet, then took a few stumbling steps toward the sleeping porch. She would get inside and change. Rinse the mud out of her gown in the sink.

Suddenly, the darkness was pierced by the porch's light being turned on.

The screen door squeaked open, and Ava stepped out and stood beneath the light, the brightness of which reflected off the white lace cap she wore over her hair rollers. Her pink robe glowed like the dawn. She scanned the field with one hand over her eyes, the other resting on her hip. Corinne fought the urge to turn and run before Ava spotted her, but it was too late by the time the thought occurred to her. She had already been spotted. Ava stomped out from under her hundred-watt halo into the shadows. "Good Lord, girl, what is wrong with you?"

"I just wanted to cool off," she said, but even though Ava's face was now obscured by darkness, she could tell the woman's expression had grown even more sour. She knew Ava would launch into a lecture, so she tried to cut her off. "I only meant to dip my feet in the pond, but I slipped."

Ava started to speak, but then shook her head. "Get on inside and clean yourself up. Dr. McAvoy needs your help. Clay's gone to fetch Elijah out of the barn. He'll drive you into town once he's up." Ava headed back toward the light without another word.

"Wait." Corinne hurried forward and grasped Ava's forearm. The older woman froze, her eyes delivering a withering glance to the spot where Corinne's flesh connected with her own. Corinne felt a nearly physical shock from the venom in her soon-to-be mother-in-law's eyes. She pulled her hand back. Ava's angry eyes rose to meet hers. "Dr. McAvoy wants my help? Why?"

"It seems you make quite the first impression. On the menfolk, at least. He has requested your help in caring for a patient. A special patient." Ava scanned her up and down. "If he saw you like this, he might question the wisdom of that." Then she tugged the screen door open and let the spring slam it shut in Corinne's face.

Without stopping to consider the dismissive gesture, Corinne pulled it open, and hurled herself over the threshold. She wouldn't dream of refusing to help care for someone in need, but the odd hour of the request, combined with the fact she had spoken only briefly to the doctor on the train, raised a lot of questions. "Who is this patient? Why me? Why not a local nurse?" she asked in quick succession. Ava turned to face her, her eyes hard. Her expression showed Corinne that she considered her questions, or perhaps any question, impertinent.

"I don't know for sure. The doctor wasn't forthcoming with details, but as you're to be taken to the Lowell house, I think it's safe to assume the patient is Judge Lowell, the most important man in these parts. As to why Dr. McAvoy would ask for you rather than a woman with good sense, I'm sure that is a question the doctor will be asking himself in an hour or two." Ava reached for the knob of the door leading into the kitchen.

"Why do you hate me?" Corinne heard the question spill out before she could prevent her tongue from asking it. "Is it the woman in the photo? The beautiful girl with the dark eyes? Ruby. Did you want Elijah to marry her?"

Ava looked back over her shoulder, her eyes wide. Her lips parted, but then cinched shut. She turned away, twisting the doorknob a couple of times before opening the door. "That girl is dead," she finally said without looking back. Her voice changed, sounding weaker, perhaps defeated. Something about the way she spoke told Corinne all she needed to know. "But no, I would not have chosen her for my son . . . And I do not hate you." The words came out in a near whisper, as delicate as a spider's web. "Now get changed. Elijah will be ready soon." She paused. "I'll put on some coffee." She pulled the door shut behind her.

Corinne lowered the Roman blinds, relying on the light seeping in from behind the chifferobe and the blinds covering the porch light to change from her wet gown. She wished she had time for a hot bath or, better yet, a shower, to wash away the pond water and the clinging remnants of the already distant nightmare. She opened a drawer and tugged out clean underwear. Before she closed it, she slid her hand into it and found her pistol. Corinne felt safer with its velvet-swathed metal beneath her fingertips. Logic told her that she would have no need for the firearm tonight—after all, she had sensed that McAvoy was harmless, avuncular even. The circumstances of his request for her to help nurse the ill—or was it wounded?—judge felt odd, but there was no need to see this as anything more than an emergency situation that called for her nursing skills. Conroy was a small town in a mostly rural area, so perhaps she was just the closest nurse. Yes, logic told her she would have no need for the gun. Still, instinct insinuated that she might.

She told herself she was being foolish. She had come to live among these people, to become one of them, and the surest way to inclusion was not to carry around a firearm to use against them. She took the gun and returned it to the drawer.

Her angry subconscious caused hot prickles to dance along her skin, but it admitted defeat and bargained with her to at least transfer the roll of bills she had stashed next to the gun into her bra. She had heard others refer to this instinct as "fight or flight." An inappropriate response in this situation, perhaps—no, certainly—but something chewed on her gut, and her gut had carried her through Korea and her own family war zone prior to that. Again she considered taking the gun. Instead she fastened her bra and stuffed the soft purse filled with bills inside the left cup.

"You about ready?" Elijah's voice startled her. She spun around and took in his silhouette, which the porch light had cast on the blinds. For a moment, she was tempted to raise the blinds and show herself to him. Would the sight bring fire to his eyes, or would it cause him to turn away and yearn for the beautiful Ruby? Corinne reached out, felt the fabric of the blinds beneath her fingertips.

The door to the kitchen banged open to reveal Ava with a steaming cup of coffee in hand. "Not just yet," Corinne replied, quickly stepping into a modest, button-front blue dress, not too terribly different in style from what a lot of stateside nurses wore as a uniform.

"Thank you," she said, stepping to the door that led from the porch into the kitchen and accepting the coffee from Ava.

Ava lifted her head and addressed her son's shadow. "Dr. McAvoy called ahead. The ferry is waiting for you." She turned to Corinne. "Don't dawdle."

TWENTY-SEVEN

The glow of a kerosene lamp cast a halo on the grimy table where Charlie Aarons sat shirtless, sweaty, and hunched over, one arthritic hand rubbing the other that was cramped around the latest addition to his collection of French postcards. These were the queens of his three-room, no-electricity, no-plumbing castle. It was hours until dawn, and he should be asleep on the thin feather mattress he called a bed, but Charlie's body ached too much to let him sleep, no matter how many times he tipped the Mason jar to his lips. Charlie made his living doing odd jobs, mostly for the Dunne family who lived across the field, barely a mile as the crow flies, but his only sure source of income was what he made working for the funeral home out by the river's bend. Tonight, his arms and shoulders and back ached from the digging it had taken to plant Joe Gentry. His manhood ached from the fantasies fed by the dirty pictures that were now spread out before him. Grave digging was a young man's work; rutting between a woman's thighs was a young man's pleasure. Charlie had long since stopped being a young man, but he forced his body to work like one. In revenge, his body remembered the needs no woman was willing to satisfy.

Charlie shook a cramp from his hand, letting the whore's photo fall as he did. It landed on top of the others. Yesterday, the picture had been new. Exciting. Her clean-scrubbed face and innocent expression had fueled his fantasies. In his mind, he'd taken her in just about every way a man could have a woman. Now her tired eyes mocked him. She was just another dirty whore lying in a pack of them.

But in the end, they were all dirty whores, every single last daughter of Eve. God had put them on earth to serve men. To please men. Charlie was a man, but still they looked on him like he was nothing more than trash. Even the waitress at the diner, the one with the wide, pockmarked face whom he thought of as "Bucktoothed Betty," though he knew Betty wasn't her real name. He took another sip of the moonshine, the smell of the corn liquor like sweet, hot garbage in his nostrils as he struggled to remember her name. It failed to come to him, but what the hell, it didn't really matter what she called herself. To him, she'd always be Bucktoothed Betty.

Betty would linger around the tables of the other men she served, leaning in toward her customers, inviting them to reach out and place their clean, smooth hands on her, maybe on the small of her back, or if she was lucky, lower. But she always took her time finding *his* table, and hurried away as soon as she laid his coffee and eggs before him. She tried never to look at him, and when it could not be avoided, she focused on the cataract that clouded his bad eye. Still, his good eye undressed her until she stood before him as naked as any of the women who splayed their legs on his postcards.

Another sip of liquor turned his mind from the waitress to that smart-mouthed girl he'd delivered out to the Dunne farm. He remembered her name, which had been drilled into his mind by Mrs. Dunne. A beauty compared to Betty, but still a plain girl when he considered her against the naked French girls looking up at him from his table. Even so, that Corinne was a healthy girl, a girl with a sturdy frame. The kind of woman who could struggle up against a man's weight, not just lie pinned beneath it. Still, after Ruby, she was a step down for young Elijah.

Charlie felt himself stiffening at the thought of Ruby. She'd been so beautiful. So proud. She never would have considered giving herself to him in life, but in death she'd looked so sweet and cool and willing. He'd gotten to see what she had to offer, all right. As he dressed her, he even got to let his hand run along her breast, down her stomach, clean down to just above her secret place. The Judge would have hanged him if he'd even suspected the thought had entered Charlie's head, but Charlie would've liked to hike her skirt right back up and mount her before he laid her out in her shiny steel coffin. If he could've found more than a moment alone with her, he might've done just that.

As the fantasy insinuated itself in his mind, Charlie's breath grew heavier, and he pushed his hand against the tabletop to force himself up. His hand shook as he dimmed the lamp's flame, extinguishing it. Light, dark, it didn't matter to his eyes, not when his vision was blurred with need. It was the need itself that called for darkness, that cried to be hidden. His gnarled fingers struggled with the buckle of his belt. He tugged the leather strap from its loops and swung it with such ferocity that it cut through the air with a whistle. The metal buckle swooped down and bit into his skin. A sharp intake of breath. He let the sting linger, then swung the strap against his back again and again.

Sweat formed on his brow, then his chest as the rhythm of the strap and the pain carried him away, raising welts, which were the price of his pleasure. His left hand lowered itself beneath the band of his trousers. At his own touch, he gritted his teeth and raised his head. Through his narrowed eyes, he saw a face on the other side of the window, watching, mirroring his own pleasure. Charlie quickly freed his hand and fell back from the table.

"What are you?" Anger overtook him. Anger at having been caught, at having been interrupted after he had already paid his price. "Watching a man like that? Some kind of pervert?" His passion was washed away by a hot flash of shame. His heart felt like it would explode. In the next instant, he realized the face must have been his own reflection, and he very nearly smiled until he noticed the blue light that shone from the other's eyes. Then the blue light was gone, and the face along with it. Charlie took a few careful steps toward the window, drawing near the glass. He leaned forward, his stomach pressing into the sink's cold porcelain, his hand grasping hold of the manual pump that fed water into it. The windowpane suddenly shattered inward, and Charlie fell backward onto the floor, raising his arm to shelter his eyes from the shards of glass. When he looked up at the broken window, he saw that it had been smashed by the force of his own dog's muzzle. The dog, Tic, pulled back, then lunged again, weakening the wood between the panes.

"Ask me in." A woman's voice, a familiar voice, came from the dog's mouth. Tic then growled and backed away.

"What the hell?" Charlie asked no one in particular, as he struggled to place the voice. Somebody was fucking with him. This had to be some kind of damned joke. He'd seen a man talking with a doll in his lap at that vaudeville show in Tupelo. This was the same trick, nothing more.

Tic made another angry lunge at the window, and Charlie twisted around on the floor, pushing up to his knees. This time the animal made its way through, but a broken pane nearly severed its right front leg as it tumbled to the floor. Unable to stand, the beast wailed in agony, but then it began to drag itself across the kitchen floor, growling and snapping. Charlie whipped at it with his belt, but the dog caught the strap in its mouth midair and yanked it from his hand. Charlie pushed himself back in quick and jagged movements until he felt the pain of the welts on his back make contact with the wall. He couldn't risk taking his eyes off the dog, so he moved sideways, feeling behind himself until he found the open threshold leading to the main room.

Tic strained and tried again to stand, but the floor was wet and slippery from the dog's own blood, so much blood that Charlie wondered how it could still be alive. Something, a quiet voice at the back of his own mind, told him that the dog wasn't really alive. Tic whined as he continued his slow slide toward Charlie, not from pain but from the frustration of not being able to reach his prey. Tic's head turned at an angle. "Ask me in," the voice said once more. The dog's eyes shone blue with the same haunted, fiery hate Charlie had seen in the eyes of the watcher from the window, then Tic's head fell flat.

Charlie's bare feet pumped against the kitchen floor as he forced his way through the doorway. He carried on, moving backward, crossing the whole of his main room, stopping only when his back thumped against the wood of his front door. He reached back over his shoulder, feeling around until he found the brass doorknob. He was almost ready to turn it, to open the door and make a run for his truck, when he heard a woman's laughter coming from its other side. He froze as a banging began, fists pounding, shaking the door. The pounding stopped, only to be replaced by something worse: the scratching of desperate—no, hungry—animals. A whining he well knew, the sound of another one of his dogs. It was the bitch, Tac. She was young and willful. He'd had to take a strap to her more than once, and he knew the sound she made when she was scared. But this time she wasn't scared of him.

His own whimpering reached his ears, and he hated himself for it.

A pane of the window in his front room shattered, and a hot breeze blew through. "Open the door, Charlie," the woman's voice called through the opening. Charlie forced his eyes closed so that he could concentrate. He *knew* this voice. But it was impossible.

Charlie's breath came in hard gasps now, and his heart was pounding like it wanted out of his chest. He fought until he could remember how to make a sound. "You done had your fun now," he said, his voice breaking. "Get on out of here. Go on," he called out as loud as his failing lungs would let him. "Get on home now."

Again he heard the woman's shrill laughter. "One last chance, Charlie," she said. "Ask me in, and I might let you keep your balls." His mind tried to deny what his gut knew—who *she* was—but his body couldn't. He pissed himself. His whimpers grew to sobs.

The door began to shake again behind him, causing his sweaty palm to lose its grasp of the knob. Now he could hear the howling of both his remaining dogs behind the door, feel each jarring of the wood as they took turns slamming their weight into it and clawing it. He spun around, calculating the distance back to the kitchen. He knew the woods around this place better than anyone. Could he get out the back and make it past the tree line? The front door was weakening, a bulge forming behind his back, and it wouldn't be long before his animals broke through . . . and turned on him. He forced himself into a crouching position, then rose to his feet. The dogs seemed to have stopped their assault, but then the door burst out of its frame, large splinters scattering across the room.

His dogs, Tac and Toe, padded through the ruined door, each stopping a few feet before him, waiting obediently for their mistress's command. "You should've asked me in, Charlie." Her voice came from the bitch's muzzle. "I might have gone easier on you then." Now her voice came out of the remaining male. "I might have let you serve me."

Then, just beyond the splintered opening that had once held his front door, he saw Ruby, her eyes beckoning to him, erasing any fear, any thought of resisting. He shuddered at the sight, not in fear, but in desire. For the briefest of moments there was no sound, only stillness.

Quicker than his eyes could register the movement, Ruby pulled back, away from the opening, away from his house. She stopped when she reached the middle of the field, nearly glowing in the darkness. He stood and walked to the gaping opening of the door so he could get a better look at her. She was beautiful, perfect. She wasn't a whore like all the others. For the first time in his life, Charlie knew what it felt like to be in love. He took a deep breath, a sense of peace rising up in him. Then the dogs fell on him, snarling, biting, knocking him down. The bitch sunk her teeth into his leg, gushing blood all over the denim of his pants. The young male took his other leg. They spun him around and pulled him facedown from the house and onto the porch. His face banged again and again and again against the concrete steps, knocking out the few front teeth he had. Blood filled his mouth as the dogs dragged him away from any hope of safety and into the woods.

TWENTY-EIGHT

Frank had polished off the bottle pretty much on his own, but the alcohol wasn't working. True, it had dulled his senses and messed with his memory, but what was forgotten and what was remembered didn't follow Frank's preference. He had made his way from Nola's bar to her bed without remembering how, but for the life of him, he couldn't shake the memory of that trip he and Bayard had made to retrieve Ruby. Eyes open, eyes closed, his thoughts kept returning to a day best forgotten.

They had made their way from the train station and traveled miles down the straight then winding Sunset Boulevard. "There it is," Crane, the detective, had said right before pulling his fake delivery truck into the drive leading to Myrna King's house. "Keep low," Crane ordered, but Frank couldn't help but lean out the window to take it all in. The house was huge, with a rough white plaster exterior. It had one of those red tile roofs, the likes of which he'd never seen before arriving in California. Naked lady statues and bright flowers lined the drive, and he knew without looking there had to be a pool in back. This was exactly the kind of place where a movie star should live. This was exactly the kind of place Frank would have liked for himself.

Frank knew he was a good-looking guy. Definitely for Conroy. But he was also as handsome as many of the faces that ended up on the big screen. For a moment, Frank let himself imagine letting Bayard take Ruby home on his own. Staying here in Hollywood, maybe seeing if he could make it in the movies.

Crane killed the engine, and, with it, Frank's daydream. "I've got a box of groceries in the back. I'll take it around to the delivery entrance. See if they'll let me in. If so, I'll try to find an excuse to get further into the house. Figure out the lay of the place and see if I can spot your Ruby." He swung his door open. "Stay here, and stay out of sight."

"How long you gonna be?" Bayard asked, his voice thinner and more high-pitched than usual.

"As long as it takes," Crane responded, but then stopped, as if he'd suddenly thought of something. "You both armed?"

Frank patted his coat, and Bayard said, "Of course," like it was the dumbest question in the world.

Crane ignored Bayard's tone. "If I'm not out in fifteen, you come in after me." He shut the driver's door and opened the back of truck.

"You sure you want to work it this way?" Frank called back over his shoulder in a hushed but audible voice. "Maybe we should just push our way in and pull her out?"

"No. Let me take a look first." He leaned over Frank and Bayard's borrowed suitcase and lifted up the box of groceries. He slammed the door closed, and began whistling as he carried the box toward the delivery entrance of the house.

Frank looked at his watch. Fifteen minutes.

"I don't like this," Bayard said. "He said these people are witches."

"No," Frank said, trying to keep his partner calm. "He said they're 'occultists.' And they aren't very good ones or their boss wouldn't have blown himself up. There's nothing to worry about. These are just plain regular people. Crazier than shithouse rats maybe, but still nothing to be alarmed about. Nothing this"—he flipped open his jacket to reveal his holster—"won't take care of."

Bayard's face relaxed, but the dark circles under his watery blue eyes were a reminder that he hadn't felt at ease since leaving Conroy. "What about the boy? Do we take him back, too, if we find him, or do we kill him?"

"The Judge ain't said nothing about the boy," Frank continued. "He only said he wants us to bring Ruby home. And this ain't Conroy. If you get your sorry ass thrown into jail out here for hurting the boy, ain't gonna be much the Judge can do to help us. And we will have failed the Judge by not bringing Ruby home."

Bayard's jaw moved side to side as he considered Frank's words. "How much longer?"

"Fourteen minutes," Frank said, shaking his wristwatch, then holding it up to his ear to make sure the damned thing was still running. He lowered his wrist and began tracking the curves of one of the statues with his eyes. Bayard shifted in his seat, clearly impatient to get in and get the job done. He opened his mouth to say something when the sound of a gunshot caused them both to startle and stare at each other.

Frank flung his door open, ran to the front of the house, and tried to open the massive handle, only to find it locked. Always the slower of the two, Bayard only reached the door as Frank was releasing the handle. "You go that way"—Frank pointed right—"and meet me at the back." After glancing around to see if anyone was headed in their direction, he tore around the house's left. He arrived at the back to find the door to the service entrance wide open. He moved toward it with caution, keeping close to the wall and ducking as he passed a window. He slid up near the open entrance as Bayard came puffing and red faced around the corner. Frank held up his hand to signal that they should move forward with caution.

Leading the way, Frank peered through the door, which opened into a large kitchen. There was no movement, no sign of life. He rounded the doorway with his back toward the jamb. He stopped short when he noticed the box Crane had been carrying. It had been flung to the floor, its contents scattered in a nearly straight line toward the far side of the room, but there was no sign of Crane himself. Bayard arrived at the entrance, nearly stumbling over the threshold and into the room. He'd already drawn his gun, and in his other hand he held his favorite knife, the one with the serrated blade. Frank nodded toward the door at the far side of the kitchen, and made his way across the room with the softest steps his leather-soled shoes allowed. Bayard plodded heavily behind him, causing Frank to turn and hold his finger up to his lips. His partner clearly didn't understand, so he pointed down at Bayard's feet and mimicked taking a step.

The sound of a woman's laughter rang out all around them like a pealing bell. "Really," a voice came from a darkened corner, "you two are positively delightful. Now put away your toys." She pointed at Bayard's weapons, and watched until he obeyed.

Frank squinted to make out the figure he'd somehow missed. He instantly recognized her from the matinees he'd seen as a boy. It was Myrna King herself. She laughed again, gliding with a practiced grace across the floor and toward the open door. "If you wanted an autograph, there are easier ways to go about it than breaking and entering."

"We didn't break nothing, lady," Bayard said, a quiver in his voice. He gave Frank a look that begged him to figure out what was happening, to take the lead.

"Perhaps not," Myrna said, closing the door and turning the lock with a pronounced click. "But you did enter." She stopped and struck a dramatic pose. "'Welcome to my house! Enter freely and of your own free will,'" she said looking at them with expectation in her eyes. She tilted her head to the side, and in spite of the uneasiness Frank felt gnawing at his guts, he liked what he saw when he looked at her. Crane was right. She looked a hell of a lot better than a woman her age had any right to look. She had a waist he could put his hands around, and her bottom reminded Frank of a sweet, ripe peach. She had tits for days, and they still hung high and perky. Her blue eyes sparkled. Her curly blonde hair felt softly around her face. More than that, though, this lady had class. She gave her curls a slight shake. "No?" she asked, seemingly disappointed by their failure to react. "Okay, not the literary type, I see. How may I help you gentlemen?"

"We heard a shot . . ." Bayard began.

"So dramatic you two are. You heard the neighbor's auto backfiring." She waved her hand as if to dismiss his worry. "One of those odd little foreign jobs. That still doesn't explain why you're here."

"We're looking for a friend," Frank said, but she responded only by raising her eyebrows. "The guy who brought in those." He pointed at the groceries strewn across the floor.

"Oh," she said, her perfect lips curving into a smile. "The delivery fellow. I've never known a delivery man to travel with an entourage before." She batted her eyelashes at Frank. "I'm afraid he took a spill coming in, twisted his ankle or something." She crossed the room to the door that led from the kitchen deeper into the house. She placed her hand against it, then looked back over her shoulder at them. "Come through, come through," she said, smiling widely. "Your friend is inside getting patched up." When neither of the men moved, she held the door for them, her smile growing wider. "Come."

Frank took a few furtive steps toward her, then recovered his normal self-assuredness. A new and exciting fantasy began to stir within his imagination. He returned her smile and glanced back at Bayard. "You heard the lady," he said, following her as he spoke. Soon the sound of Bayard's heavy footfalls echoed behind them.

Frank found himself walking a tad closer to her than perhaps he should. Her perfume, a spicy, almost too-sweet scent, made him lean in even closer, drawing his breaths slowly, as if to breathe her in. Myrna noticed, but she didn't seem to mind. She kept glancing over her shoulder at him. "You smell real good," Frank said, feeling foolish as soon as the words escaped him. "Your perfume," he backpedaled.

She paused. "Are you a religious man?" Her eyes seemed to mock him, but he didn't care. "Catholic perhaps?"

"No, ma'am."

"I only ask as I've been told the scent is reminiscent of the incense of which they are so fond. Myrrh, to be precise. The papists evidently burn it by the pound." She paused as if in thought. "Of course, the resin was used long before the church was born. The ancient Egyptians associated its scent with immortality. But then again, what did the ancient Egyptians know? Sure, they built the pyramids, but they also married their own sisters." She smiled again, her eyes narrowing seductively. "Would it surprise you if I told you I don't wear perfume?" She turned and continued down the marble-floored hallway that seemed even longer than the great hall of the cathedral-like station where they'd arrived. He felt like they'd been walking for several minutes, even though he knew it couldn't be true. The walls were lined on both sides with mirrors in golden frames. Frank was sure it was just his imagination, but it seemed his hostess's reflection blurred in each of them, almost like she was vibrating as she passed. He cast a glance back at Bayard, lumpy and sweating through his suit, but in fine focus. The reflection of Bayard's eyes, skittish and uncertain, met his own. The way the mirrors were situated across from each other reflected the three of them into what seemed an eternity.

Just when Frank was about to ask how much farther the hall could possibly reach, she stopped before a door and placed her hand on its oversized knob. "If you two will just wait in here, I'll go see what's become of your friend."

She pushed open the door, motioning with her free hand that they should enter. Frank stepped over the threshold into the room, which was presided over by a long, curving sofa, covered in white fabric. He turned back to see their hostess carrying on down the hall in the opposite direction from which they'd just come.

His focus returned to the room. Before the sofa sat a low round table that echoed the shape of one of the couch's inward bends. A chandelier—not a dangly one like the one he'd noticed in the train station, but rounded like a puffed-out dandelion—hung in the center of the room. There were three large windows, but each had been covered in curtains of heavy gold fabric. This place sure as hell beat the two-room apartment he kept in Conroy, and it didn't stink of pulpwood either. It smelled like her. The whole place carried her scent, a scent, Frank realized, he could grow to like very much. Bayard entered the room, and the door closed with a loud clack behind him, as if it had been slammed shut by an unseen hand.

"What the hell is wrong with you?" his partner asked, the reek of his musky sweat breaking through Frank's intoxication. "I'm going to take a look around, see if I can find Ruby and get us out of this place."

Frank nodded slowly, and licked his dry lips. He no longer felt so sure he wanted to leave.

TWENTY-NINE

War had accustomed Corinne to the colors of injury, disease, and death, but there was something about the sight of Judge Lowell's pallor and his rasping breath that caused the skin of her arms to prickle. She hesitated before taking his wrist, the way she might before touching a slug. Silently cursing her own cowardice, she forced herself to place her fingers against the man's wrist, then focused her eyes on her trusty wristwatch—the one gift she'd bought for herself upon completing her nurse's training—and counted. "His pulse is still thready, Doctor." *Hypovolemia*—the term crossed her mind, a lack of blood. But it was a condition, not a diagnosis.

The Judge needed to be treated in the hospital; any fool could see he wouldn't survive for long without a transfusion, but Dr. McAvoy was adamantly opposed to moving him.

The doctor struggled to pull an armchair closer to the bed, then sat in it and looked up at Corinne. "I know you are worried that I am just a country sawbones, filled with all kinds of antiquated ideas." The doctor's large blue eyes watered behind the thick lenses of his glasses. "Don't worry, though, I'm not just some bumpkin." He took a deep breath and removed those glasses, pretending to use his handkerchief to clean the lenses, but quickly dabbing his eyes in the process. "Come daylight, I'll drive over to the hospital in Tupelo. They got one of them blood centers there. I'll take a sample of Ovid's blood to get it typed, and bring back what we need to replenish the blood he's lost. I'll see to it that he gets the good, proper, modern care he needs, but we will have to provide that care for him here, in his home."

Rather than taking Muhammad to the mountain, McAvoy seemed intent on bringing the mountain to Muhammad. "But wouldn't it be better to take him there now? I know how to drive if you are worried about seeing . . ."

"You don't understand, Miss Ford," he interrupted her. He didn't sound angry, just weary. "We can't let people know how poorly Ovid is doing. He's an important man around these parts," he said, speaking slowly, as if he were responding to an inquisitive child who couldn't comprehend an adult matter. "A lot of people . . . depend on him. We need to patch him up, get him back on his feet first, and then we'll worry about what comes next."

Corinne nodded a silent assent, as if she agreed with his plan of care, even though in truth it made no sense to her. Dr. McAvoy sat still for several minutes, watching over the Judge like a concerned father until his own eyes fell closed, and he, too, began soughing. An hour passed, then two. Corinne had learned to take catnaps standing up and during heavy shelling, but she couldn't bring herself to do so now. Something in all of this struck her as unwholesome, unnatural, so in spite of her weariness, she remained on high alert. But it was more than the situation with the Judge or the old doctor's odd behavior that bothered her.

Had she done the wrong thing in coming here? In spite of her earlier conversation with Elijah, the trip across the river to this house had been done in a nearly complete silence. What resolve Elijah had within him seemed to wilt beneath his parents' scornful gaze. Elijah felt like a stranger to her or, worse, an imposter of the man who'd charmed her all those many thousands of miles away.

Corinne went to the window, scanning the sky for familiar constellations. Somehow knowing where she stood in relation to the sky had always helped her center herself. If it were a winter sky, she could have easily spotted Orion by his belt, but she had to settle for the sight of Vega before picking out the five brightest stars of Cygnus that also made up the Northern Cross. She felt foolish. She hadn't even given Conroy a full twenty-four hours, but a very large part of her wanted to leave on the first morning train out. She couldn't do that to Elijah, though. He'd just lost two dear friends, maybe four. Her thoughts slowed as the instincts she was trying to suppress began hitting back.

Did she love Elijah? It struck her as an odd question to be contemplating, even in this strange place, on this far from typical night. The human race didn't used to think along those terms. Until a couple of hundred years ago or so, marriage was a practical proposition, having little or nothing to do with romance or other emotional entanglements. Now most people seemed to think it was the only aspect that mattered. Corinne had never known this intoxicating variety of love. Fondness, yes. Passion, no. She searched her heart again, hoping to find some kind of spark or fire there for her intended.

She cared for Elijah; she knew that. Or at least she cared for the man she'd met beneath the mess hall's canvas flaps. She'd believed that would be enough, but now she suspected that Elijah had known that fiery variety of love before meeting her. It was the kind of love he would never forget, and that they could never re-create together. These feelings couldn't be cultured. They sprang fully formed, or they never rose at all.

Was it crueler to leave or crueler to stay and marry him, knowing she'd be depriving him of the chance to find again what he'd lost? Or was this type of love a once-in-a-lifetime thing? She even began to wonder if she should envy Elijah. Was this romantic fervor an experience she should risk all to seek out for herself? Movies and music portrayed

romantic passion, losing one's self in the beloved, as the ultimate pleasure, the very pinnacle of human existence. But the thought of surren-
dering herself, her will, completely, even for pleasure, terrified her. Did
it make her less of a woman that she'd never gotten caught up and lost
in her emotions? She'd met plenty of men over the years, good, solid,
decent men, and a few absolute scoundrels. Was there something wrong
with her that none had ever stirred those desperate, romantic feelings
within her? She leaned against the window frame and asked the stars
for answers.

At around 3:00 a.m., the Judge startled, his eyes flying wide open.
His jaw worked silently at first, then sounds resembling the yelps of a
frightened dog rang piteously through the room. He struggled to free
himself from the bedclothes, finally managing to fling the blankets to
the floor. Corinne moved quickly to comfort him, to try and return
him to a supine position, but he lunged forward, grasping her forearms
so tightly that she couldn't help but squeal. His grip was much stronger
than any sick, middle-aged man with soft pale hands should be able
to muster. McAvoy, who was startled out of sleep by the commotion,
rushed to their side and administered the Judge a barbiturate. Judge
Lowell went limp, collapsing back on the bed, but not before he spoke
a single word: "*Ruby.*"

THIRTY

Merle presented himself naked before his mother, averting his eyes when she failed to avert her own, and focused instead on the cigarette that dangled between her lips. As she inhaled, its tip flared bright in the darkness, shining like a red star in the nearly moonless night. She grasped the cigarette in her right hand; a stream of smoke, more sensed than seen, issued from her mouth. She coughed and spat on the ground.

"It's time," she said, in those last few minutes before the dawn, motioning toward the fence with the cord of rough hemp clothesline she held in her left hand.

He nodded and walked before her, holding his hands behind himself to cover his buttocks, toward the wood rail fence that marked the property line. He felt every inch of his nakedness, other than maybe the soles of his feet, hardened as they were this time of year by going barefoot whenever he wasn't working, to save wear on his shoes. It had been hot and dry for days. Too hot for dew, even at this time of day, or maybe night. The grass crunched beneath the soles, but he barely felt the way it scratched as it bent underfoot.

"The angel"—that's how his mama insisted on referring to Ruby— "it's good she commanded this of you. You're like your daddy was, too weak to resist the lusts of the flesh." He ignored her. He'd heard her say this about his father so many times, the words had lost any meaning. He kept walking. "'For if ye live after the flesh, ye shall die:'" She raised her voice, nearly singing the words of the apostle—"'but if ye through the Spirit do mortify the deeds of the body, ye shall live.' Romans, chapter eight, verse thirteen."

His mama liked to think of Ruby as her own, but he had spotted Ruby first, on a hot full-moon night, back toward the end of July. He'd been sitting, dangling his legs out of the window of his second-floor bedroom, smoking and trying to catch any kind of breeze. He saw her, cutting across the field that separated his mama's land from the old Cooper house. She wore white, but even from a distance he could see the entire front of her gown had been stained dark.

"Wait," he'd called out to her, and she'd stopped and turned. He clambered down the stairs, waking his mama—she'd always been a light sleeper—as he did so. He rushed out the door to meet Ruby. At first his mama chased after him, tried to catch hold of him, and keep him from going out to Ruby. But then she stopped and looked out across the way to where Ruby stood.

"Yes, come in," his mama said as if she were replying to an unspoken request.

As Ruby drew near, he could see that the stain on her dress was blood. But it didn't matter. He was only sorry that it hadn't been his own blood coating her breast.

They'd been serving Ruby since that night. Helping her prepare for her great work of punishing the guilty and rewarding the faithful. Merle, she counted him among the faithful. Most folk in Conroy treated him like a punk. He'd taken so many beatings, he decided to leave school early, just to put an end to them. Ruby, she didn't care he was a pimply dropout, or that he spent his days washing dishes at the diner. He was important to her. He was a big part of her plan. She encouraged him to dream of ways to make the kids who'd tormented him pay, promising to give him all the power he'd need to turn those dreams into reality.

Ruby had never tasted his mama. Merle couldn't blame her. The thought of putting his lips against the old woman's sour skin nauseated him.

His mama loved quoting scripture, sure and certain of the righteousness of her every deed, and quick to damn all of Conroy for even the smallest of sins. When Ruby came, his mama believed she had to be an angel, and the visitation was proof positive of her own purity.

But no matter what his mama believed, none of it had anything to do with her. Ruby was no angel, no messenger for a God Merle wasn't even sure existed. No. Ruby was here. Right where you could see her. Touch her. There'd be no need for him to hope for a better world in the next life. She was going to set things right around here, starting now, and she'd chosen Merle to help her.

She'd tasted him, more than once, but it wasn't till tonight that she had shared herself with him.

Drawing near the rough rails of the fence, he hesitated. He'd grown up knowing that it wasn't his parents, but the man who owned the adjoining parcel who'd built this barrier. It had never been intended to protect him and his family; its purpose had been to keep them out. He placed one hand on the splintery top rail and stared out across the field that, this year, their neighbor had chosen to leave fallow. An unmated mockingbird began a new chorus of the song it had been singing on and off all night long. He could smell the stink from the pulp mill creeping downriver, though the fog the mill produced hardly ever carried this far down out of town.

"East is behind you," his mother's raspy voice rode over the birdsong. "Angel wants you facing east," she said, and when he didn't budge, she flicked the butt of her cigarette down by his feet. "You got to turn around." She grasped his forearm. He yanked it away. His eyes met hers. He didn't want her to touch him with her mottled and leathery hands, her nicotine-yellow fingers. Forgetting his nakedness, he fixed her with angry eyes. She looked back with a blank and bovine gaze that sharpened, her lids lowering, her brows pressing in on each other and deepening the ugly crease that split her forehead.

He hated the deep lines on her face—wrinkles that made her look more like his granny than the woman who'd birthed him. The kids at school, back before he quit going, used to taunt him about that. He hated her straggly unwashed gray hair and her yellowed snaggletooth smile. He comforted himself knowing his mama hadn't been chosen. Ruby would not share herself with his mama. Someday, soon, she'd be dead, and he would have forever to dance on the dust of her grave.

Merle's skin crawled in anticipation of his mother's touch, but to submit to Ruby's will meant, for now, doing as his mama said. He turned his back to a post, reaching behind himself and draping his arms over the upper rail. His mama began unwinding the coil of clothesline and stepped to his side. She reached behind him, and began weaving the cord around his wrists and the railing, binding him tight, more tightly than she needed to, to the fence.

She jerked the cord, causing it to bite into his skin, but he didn't complain. "That was the sin of Sodom," his mama said in a mutter that reeked of smoke and coffee, "men lusting after the angels of God. The angel, she wants to purify you. Set your soul right before the end."

No matter what his mama thought, Merle knew this wasn't any kind of punishment. It was a test of his loyalty. The final test before Ruby would take him as her own, change him forever. Change him to be like her. He would be her right hand in the new world she was building.

Minutes passed as his mama used her fingers to crochet his restraints, tying tight knot after knot into the coarse and biting fibers. "Gonna be plenty of folk around here real sorry, real soon," she said. "I warned 'em. At least I tried to. But I ain't seen a single door outside our own that has the blood."

Ruby said she found it real funny when his mama flung herself at her feet, begging her to spare the righteous souls of Conroy. Ruby said that once she changed Merle for good, she'd send him out to see if any houses had blood on their door. These would be the first he should punish.

He craned his neck in time to see his mama pull her knife from its leather sheath. He heard a snipping sound as the blade cut through the cord. She returned the knife to its case, and slid it back into the pocket of his daddy's old overalls that she'd taken to wearing after his death a few years back.

His mama squatted before him, giving him a shove so he fell backward against the fence. As he bent into the wood, the rough head of the post scraped his back—a splinter in the center rail poked him behind the knee. She unwound more of the cord, binding his calves to the lower rail. He closed his eyes, doing his best to forget his mother's presence, as she continued to make sure he was secured.

He felt a throbbing in his hands as the clothesline pinched into his wrists, slowing his blood, causing his hands to cool. Cool. Just as Ruby felt cool to the touch when she came to him last night and shared herself with him.

Before, he thought his loyalty to her couldn't have been greater, but from the first cool and coppery taste, Ruby owned him, bound him to her, even more sure than he was bound now to the fence. Even though he knew he was alone with his mother, he sensed Ruby everywhere. He could feel her inside him, watching through his eyes, hearing through his ears, as if at any moment she might even speak through his lips. Her scent, a sweet and spicy perfume that reminded him of Christmas ribbon candy, had now become his own, so that he found himself closing his eyes and breathing deep so that he could pretend she was near.

The thought of Ruby's touch caused him to begin to stiffen, a hot wall of shame collapsing on him as he heard his mama snort in disgust. His mama thought she, too, loved Ruby, but she couldn't understand. Not really. She'd never tasted Ruby. And Ruby had promised that she never would.

Ruby warned him that her blood would change him. Even this first taste would make him averse to the bright light of the sun. More than a few moments would irritate his uncovered skin. More than a few minutes would burn. An hour at dawn would feel like being scalded by hot bacon grease.

A second taste would worsen his reaction. After they'd shared the third and final communion, the sun wouldn't just redden his skin, it would light him right up, like a flare. Ruby said she wanted him to know what it felt like, to make up his mind if he wanted to become like her. He knew what she really wanted was for him to prove that he was worthy.

"Here," his mama said, her voice prompting him to open his eyes. She now stood before him. She reached into the pocket of her overalls, and fished out a short but thick leather strap. "The angel said to give you this." She held it out before him. "Open up," she said, "and bite down." He obeyed, as he always did where Ruby was concerned, accepting the bit into his mouth. "Keep you from losing your tongue."

He watched the sky shift from black to indigo to the purple of a deep and painful bruise. He felt a shiver rush through his body, feeling the approach of the dawn long before his eyes could take it in. The world fell still, then the sun dug its fingers deep into the horizon and clawed it a brilliant crimson. Moments later, the first rays landed on his pale and freckled skin, just warming it at first, but quickly gaining heat, like when the bigger guys at school used to grab his forearm and twist their hands back and forth to give him an Indian sunburn. He stood still, determined to take it, but then the light began to sear his skin like the time his mama caught him stealing from her coin purse and held the hot iron to his palm. He huffed agonized breaths through his nose, gritting his teeth so hard he thought he might bite clean through the strap of leather protecting his tongue.

He nearly surrendered, almost giving in to the urge to struggle out of the ties that held him and flee toward any source of shade, but he held his ground. He held his ground, because Ruby had asked him to. He would have gladly let himself light up like a torch and burn to ashes if the sight of his end would bring a smile to Ruby's lips.

THIRTY-ONE

A cock crow greeted the dawn. Elijah awoke to the smell of cigarette smoke and the familiar sound of his dad's rasping cough. He opened his eyes to find his father standing over his cot. "Your ma would've let you sleep in the house since the woman ain't here," Clay said before giving in to another coughing jag. He spat a glob of phlegm at the foot of Elijah's cot. The smell of whiskey working its way out through his sweat overrode the scent of smoke. His father had spent the night with the bottle again. Elijah wondered what his excuse was this time. There was always a reason, and it always had to do with Elijah or his mother.

"Yes, sir." Elijah stretched and pulled himself into a sitting position. His father was a mean drunk. The tight set of the older man's jaw, the way his heavy brow and his cheeks pinched together, turning his eyes into nothing more than dark, angry slits, told Elijah that this day, just begun, wouldn't end without violence. Usually Elijah bore the brunt of Clay's rage. "Just cooler out here, and since I had the cot set up anyway . . ." He let his words fade away. Even though the light was dim, he could still see that his father wasn't listening to him.

"The sheriff's visit has got me thinking." Clay wrapped his words around the cigarette, and took a few more drags—short shallow ones, in quick succession. He dropped the butt end to the ground, grinding it into the dirt with the heel of his heavy boot, then exhaled and spat. He took a couple of weaving steps forward. "Sometimes a man believes a wrong has been done to him, and sometimes that man feels the need to take steps to set things right, to make things even, before he can find it in himself to move on. I just want you to know I understand that."

Elijah remained silent, running his fingers through his hair, then over his lengthening beard. He could see his dad had gotten himself worked up over something, but he wasn't quite sure what. It was always best to stay silent when his father got this way, try not to provoke him, let him say his piece. He looked at his father, waiting for him to continue. They stared at each other silently for thirty seconds or so, the deep wrinkles on the older man's face pinching in even tighter than usual. Finally Clay spoke, the words coming out slurred and heated. "I'm just telling you that I understand what you've done, but it needs to stop here. You've settled the score, now you need to let it lay."

At first Elijah held his tongue, not sure what "score" his dad meant. Experience had taught him it would be best to try to diffuse the anger he sensed pulsing through Clay with a quick and humble response of "Yessir," and worry about what he'd agreed to later. But he felt his head shaking, and the words falling out before he could stop them. "Pa, I got no idea . . ."

"Don't play stupid with me, boy." The harsh growl caused Elijah to quake, even though he was now full-grown, able to take on his father if need be. "I'm talking about Dowd and Bobby. You've made your point. They had your woman. They shared that fact with you. Now they're dead, and you have another woman. It's time for you to put the past in the past."

"But I didn't have anything to do with Dowd or Bobby getting themselves killed. I swear I didn't."

The older man paced back and forth for a few moments, then stopped dead in front of his son. He reached back and swung with his left hand, backhanding Elijah so hard that stars filled the younger man's vision. Jumping to his feet, Elijah knocked the cot over. He respected the biblical injunction to honor his father, even if he didn't respect the man himself. He wouldn't raise a hand against him, but he wasn't simply going to take a beating. Those days were done. Elijah kicked backward, knocking the cot out of his way, giving him space to move should he need to fall back or feign an attack.

"Don't lie to me," Clay said. The fact that his voice had dropped to a whisper meant he was angrier than if he'd been yelling. "I ain't no fool. You got revenge, all right. Okay, I can understand that. What I don't understand is that you didn't even take your own revenge like a real man would. You got the Sleiger boys to take it for you."

"No, sir. I don't even know where they are. If I did, I would have told the sheriff. I know their ma is worried sick . . ."

"That's right, she is worried sick, 'cause she thinks her boys have let you get them messed up in something that will end with them getting their necks stretched." Clay took a step back, his shoulders relaxing. He fumbled in his shirt pocket and retrieved a nearly empty pack of Camels, then shook it until one of them poked farther from the package than the others. He took the tip between his lips and returned the pack to his pocket. That done, he pulled a box of matches from his pants and struck one. The scent of sulfur filled the air as the match's brief glare lit his face, illuminating his expression of disgust. In a second the light was snuffed, leaving the tip of his cigarette to shine like a lonely star.

"You done lost yourself two of the best friends a man could ever have," Elijah's father said, his voice a sneer. "You think it was easy for them to tell you Ruby had come whorin' after them? They weren't bragging, boy." He reached up and pulled the cigarette from between his lips. "They were warning you. Trying to get you free and clear of that bitch before you ended up marrying her. I thought you'd be grown up enough to let it slide after seeing war, but now I reckon as not. Maybe if the Judge hadn't managed to find her? If he hadn't brought her back to die?" He tapped the ash from the cigarette and licked his lips. "After you took off for Korea, I asked around. It weren't only Bobby and Dowd. There were other men who'd had her. Plenty of them." He took a deep drag. "Ruby would have let just about any man sow his seed in her. *Any* man. If you'd wedded her, you might have found yourself raising some high yellow bastard as your own. And raising somebody else's bastard ain't no life for any man."

His father's body grew taut, and he leaned in toward Elijah. "You hear me, boy? That whore of yours done spread her legs wide all around these parts before hiking her skirt up and running off to California with the fancy fellow of hers." His right eye twitched, and the right corner of his mouth pulled up into a sadistic smile. He chuckled. "She was gonna be a star, up on the screen for everyone to see. She didn't love you. You were just the best thing going for her until she could find something better."

"No, Pa. I don't believe it."

"You saying I'm a liar?"

"No, sir, I'm saying Bob and Dowd were. And any other man who said he had her."

Clay gritted the cigarette between his teeth and slapped Elijah open palmed on the ear. Then again, harder.

Elijah held up his hands to protect himself. "She told me she loved me," he said. Even in the relative darkness of the barn he could see his father's face grow a deeper shade of red. "And she promised me she had never been unfaithful to me. She didn't know why Bobby and Dowd lied about having her, but she swore they had lied about it." Elijah brushed away a tear before the sight of it could anger his father. "Thing is, Pa, I believed her. I would have taken her as my wife, Pa . . ."

"You," his father began, and boxed Elijah's right ear. "Stupid." A strike to the left. "Son." A second to the right. "Of a bitch."

Clay tried another swipe, but Elijah knocked his hand away before he could. The old man had always taken pleasure in beating him.

Humiliating him. Well, he'd allowed his father enough of that kind of satisfaction.

His father seemed to see something in his face. Something he didn't like. He took a few steps back. "Even if she had it in her to speak the truth, her mind was gone by the time the Judge brought her home. She came back here with some kind of pox. That's what killed her. The kindest thing she ever did for you was dying before she could infect you. And the kindest thing anyone ever done for you is what those friends of yours did. You owe them, boy, whether you think so or not. You want to rest easy, you want their souls to rest easy? You give them what you done denied them. When that new woman of yours births you sons, you give them your friends' names, so that they won't die forgotten. You hear me?"

"No, Pa, that ain't gonna happen. Them two sonsabitches lied," Elijah said. "As far as I'm concerned they're responsible for everything that happened to Ruby. Their lies took her away from me." He felt his fists balling up, his shoulders tensing. "I didn't kill them, but I'm sure as hell glad *someone* did, 'cause they needed killing."

His father advanced on him and swung. *No, not anymore.* Elijah's body reacted before the thought had even fully registered. He grabbed his father's fist and spun him around, twisting his arm behind his back. His father struggled for several moments until he finally stopped and went limp. "So what if they did lie to you, you worthless piece of shit? They only did it to save you."

"Save me from what, old man?"

Clay's chest began to heave, and he bent over with laughter. "To save you from bedding your own goddamned sister. Dowd and Bobby. They knew. I had to tell them."

Elijah released his father and fell back.

His dad spun back to face him, a wicked glee in his eyes. "Your mama. She was pregnant when I married her. The Judge never knew it, or at least he acted like he didn't, but you're his boy."

THIRTY-TWO

Annie Krueger's wide and oddly angled face had been ravaged by chicken pox. If she had ever found a single thing to smile about, embarrassment over a severe overbite would have prevented her from doing so. Her eyes sat too far back in her head and too closely together. A lazy right eye remained permanently turned inward to spy on its companion. Both rested on dark purple circles that never faded. With those eyes, Annie scanned the tables at the Blankenship Diner, or "Blank's," as its faithful patrons referred to it, making a special point to catalog each crease, each mole, each scar on the faces of those customers who lacked the imagination to go down the street even once in a while to eat at the drugstore's luncheon counter.

She circled the room, coffee carafe in hand, celebrating the knowledge that one day, one day soon, she was gonna kill every last single one of these bastards. Put rat poison in the coffee, in the grits, in the beans, in every spoon of slop she sat before these swine. That was the only thought that kept her going, the sole thought that kept her sane as she rose each day to meet the sun and donned one of two identical uniforms, each a pale buttercup yellow that she knew made her sallow complexion seem even more jaundiced. Black collar, four black buttons, and black stripes over the pockets made her resemble an anemic bumblebee. Pinned-back lusterless brown hair imprisoned by a black hairnet, and graying tennis shoes. This was the outfit she wore six out of each seven days of her life. There was no point in trying to look pretty. Since childhood, harsh words and avoided glances had let her know she was too far away from that goal to make her efforts anything more than worthless.

She worked here, toting plates from counter to table, from table to kitchen, from Monday through Saturday, from breakfast until the moment when Barbara Jean arrived to work the dinner shift. A nod to Barbara Jean, perhaps a mumbled word or two, then she'd return to her parents' home, where she would hand wash the scent of her sweat and the smell of bacon and onions from the buttercream dress, hanging it over the tub to drip-dry for the two days hence when she would wear it once again. Each and every evening, she'd put on her mother's old robe, and make herself a cup of tea and sit in her father's armchair, where she'd dream of the day when she would finally kill every single last one of the bastards who frequented the diner.

It had seemed an act of Providence, a prayer answered, a wish fulfilled, when a couple of years back, she'd spotted a glint from a brown glass bottle sitting in the trash behind the diner. Annie figured the rats found their way into the diner again, and the boss was trying to get rid of them quietly and on his own. Most of the label was still on the bottle, and the word "Poison" printed in red and surrounded by a red diamond, jumped out at her like a hallelujah. She'd carried it with her. Slept with it even, ever since. The only thing that surprised her was that she'd held off from using it this long.

Annie glanced over her shoulder at the clock on the wall. Seven o'clock. Eleven and a half hours before she'd pass the last customer's fouled plate back to Merle, the pimple-faced teenaged dishwasher, and walk the eight blocks east and three blocks south to arrive back home.

The house would be dark and empty when she got there. Her father had passed four years back, and her mama joined him last fall. Now, with summer ending, and the nights growing long again, Annie wished she'd hadn't tested the thallium on the cat.

"Annie." An impatient voice caught her attention. She turned and fixed her misaligned gaze on Marjorie Thompson, holding up a lipstick-stained mug. If any woman in the world could sympathize with Annie's pain and loneliness, it should be this fat, peroxided old maid, but Marjorie seemed oblivious to her own basic detestability. Annie crossed to her and filled the cup, the display of movie magazines fanned out around Marjorie's plate catching her eye: *Picturegoer*, *Screenland*, *Photoplay*, *Why*, and a few whose titles were hidden by the ones Annie could see.

"Would your friends like anything?" Annie asked, glancing down at the faces of Marlon Brando, Kirk Douglas, and Susan Hayward staring back up at her from the magazines' glossy covers. Marjorie missed her sarcasm, a look of confusion clouding her face. Annie nodded at the magazines. "Since when have you been such a movie fan?"

"I ain't," Marjorie said, reaching out with her left hand and pushing the magazines toward the table's far corner.

Their eyes locked onto each other's as Annie questioned why she had even bothered to speak to this hopeless woman. Maybe 'cause she was as near to the bottom of the pile of life as Annie herself? She let her gaze drift and started to turn.

"Can you keep a secret?" Marjorie asked in a whisper.

Annie wondered whether she should just pretend not to have heard and walk away. The clock caught her eye again. Eleven hours and twenty-seven minutes before she would hand the last soiled plate to the dishwasher. Annie could use the entertainment. She stopped midturn and looked back at Marjorie.

Marjorie, to Annie's amusement, had broken out in a sweat, the moisture darkening the hair on her upper lip, a full bead escaping the pores of her large forehead. Annie thought of the bottle of thallium she slept with beneath her pillow, that she carried now with her in her pocket. She leaned in over the table. "Sure. I can keep a secret. What you got?"

Marjorie flashed her one last guarded look, then turned away to riffle through the purse that sat next to her in the booth. *Another movie magazine,* Annie thought as Marjorie held it up to her. The words "Magic at the Macambo" jumped off the cover.

"He told me he would go there someday," Marjorie said. She held the magazine out to Annie, who sat the carafe on the table and pulled the publication from the other woman's tight, moist grasp.

Annie's eyes were nearly dazzled by the sight of the red walls and green upholstery in the cover photo. She took the magazine in both hands and held it farther down, taking the photo in fully. "Okay?" Annie said, sure Marjorie's excitement was just another example of Marjorie being Marjorie.

"Page forty-two," Marjorie said with a rapid nod. The earnest quality of her voice was almost too much for Annie to bear. Annie fought the urge to roll her eyes, and flipped through the pages until she found forty-two. Very little text, only a large photo done with one of those lenses that captures a wide space, even though the image is warped some around the edges. "Look. Right there." Marjorie leaned forward and jabbed her thick index finger near the photo's right side, an inch or so from where it ended.

Annie pulled the photo closer, and a little to the left, so she could focus on it better. She began shaking her head. "It ain't him. It ain't that Sawyer boy." She held the magazine back to Marjorie.

"No. Look again." Marjorie pushed the magazine back toward Annie. This time Annie sighed, but decided it would be easier to get away and back to her other customers if she humored Marjorie.

She tilted the magazine in so that it was better lit, but not blurred by the glare of the overhead light. She bit her lower lip, and tilted the picture back. The small face smiling back at her did indeed resemble Dylan.

And it was true he'd run off to Hollywood with Ruby, but the odds just seemed too great, that Ruby's fate would be so different from Dylan's.

"You see it, don't you?" Marjorie's voice grew more excited.

Annie didn't respond, but scanned the faces of those around the boy who might or might not be Dylan. "When was this taken?"

"The issue is from last year, so about a year ago, I guess."

No sign of Ruby in the photo, but maybe that didn't mean anything. Rumor said that the two had parted ways shortly after reaching California. Dylan, for Annie had begun to think this was indeed Conroy's prodigal son pictured, sat next to a woman, but the photo must have been taken when she was moving, as her image had been blurred. Either that, or maybe it was something to do with the lens used in taking the picture.

Marjorie reached out and snapped away the magazine. "I've been looking in every single movie star magazine ever since I found this."

Annie took a step back and reclaimed the carafe. Suddenly an unfamiliar wave of sympathy came over her. "Listen, I don't think you should be wasting your time and money on those magazines. I mean, it may be him or it may not be, but if he cared for you, he'd write."

Marjorie blanched and pushed back against the booth.

"I used to see the three of you in here. I know you think you and those two were friends, but they were only using you to pay the bill." Annie's words were falling on deaf ears, and something about that brought out her venom. "When you went to the ladies' room they sat there, right where you are sitting now, snickering. At you."

"You're lying." Marjorie slapped at the magazines with her meaty hands, trying to force them into a neat pile, but failing. "You're jealous. If they were snickering at anyone, it was you. Ruby always said you shouldn't be allowed to work around food. That your face made her lose her appetite." It was Annie's turn to flinch. "And Dylan . . ."

Annie spun on her heel before Marjorie could finish her thought, only to knock into Sheriff Bell. She rebounded off the taut muscles of his hard, lean body, the heat of this sensation nearly overriding the shame she had been running from. His blue eyes flashed at her, perhaps in surprise, maybe in annoyance. She tried to look away, but the sight of his bushy steel gray mustache held her. She wanted so badly to lean in, to press her lips against his. Feel the bristly hair tickle her nose. Feel his lips touch hers, his tongue pierce the opening of her mouth. He was older. Old enough to be her father even, but man enough to . . . Well, simply man enough.

"He called you the 'sponge face.'" Marjorie spat the words at her.

Annie flushed, somewhat from desire and somewhat from a peculiar pain caused by knowing that the sheriff had heard Marjorie's words.

Sponge face. She hastened her eyes to look away from Bell's face and focus on the checkerboard floor beneath his feet. She knew, yes, she knew she was ugly. Probably the homeliest thing the sheriff had ever laid eyes on. She couldn't bear the thought of seeing an acknowledgment of Marjorie's words reflected in his eyes. "I'm sorry, Sheriff," she said, pulling back and rushing around him. "Can I get you some coffee?"

THIRTY-THREE

"No, not here for breakfast," Bell said, and the waitress began to buzz away. "Wait. Hold on there, Annie." As the waitress turned back to him, he noticed her face had turned as red as if she'd been caught with her skirt up. He usually kept his eyes partially averted when looking at the unfortunate girl. The sight of her full-on made his mustache twitch. How could the good Lord have let a face like that come into this world? Bell wasn't sure if her look was intended as a trial for the girl herself or as a test of the Christian charity of others. Her beady, rodent eyes were tearing up. He didn't have time for any of this female nonsense. Whatever was going on between these two girls, they'd have to work out on their own. "You seen either of them Sleiger boys in here lately?"

Bell felt a bit bad asking her about the Sleigers. A lot of the men around Conroy took fun in tormenting this luckless creature, but he knew the boys were two of the worst. They often joked about whether either would ever grow desperate enough to bed Annie. "A man could turn her around and make her use those boar tusks of hers to bite the pillow," Bell himself had heard Wayne jest.

"Naw, not even then," Walter had shot back. "I still think I'd rather cut it off first."

Those words were not said to Annie's face, but loudly enough she'd have heard the exchange all the same.

Annie's face hardened, and her eyes dried like the spigot had been turned tight. "No, sir. I reckon I ain't seen the Sleigers in going on a month now." She paused. "Their mama usually packs them boys their lunch"—the words "mama" and "boys" were weighted when Annie said them—"so they don't drop by much. Not for supper either. Guess they ain't allowed out after dark."

Her obvious and understandable hatred of the brothers gave him pause. He stopped and took her in. She flinched and dropped her shoulders as he let his eyes run over her, head to toe, asking himself whether this woman was the killing kind. She folded her arms across her chest and averted her eyes. No. This woman wasn't capable of killing. And she was too much of a loner to form an alliance with someone who was. The only ally she ever seemed to have was that mangy cat that hung out in her yard. "How about Dowd Johnson? Bob McKee?"

Her eyes drifted to the floor. "Dowd. He was here the night before last. I haven't seen Bob around in a bit longer, but I'm not sure how long."

"Dowd here by himself?"

"No," Annie said, shifting uncomfortably like she wanted to fly away, or maybe she just had to pee. "Well, he came in alone. Merle's late, but you could ask him when he gets in." She nodded toward the kitchen door. "Merle was standing outside on his break. He stopped Dowd on the way in and bummed a cigarette. Dowd gave him the cigarette, but something Merle said seemed to tick Dowd off. Dowd came in and sat down alone, but then he asked for change for the phone and made a call. Sam came in after a bit and joined him, so I reckon it was Sam he called."

"Did you ask Merle what he'd said to make Dowd angry?"

Annie shook her head without even looking up at him. "No. None of my business."

"How about after Sam got here? Did you happen to hear anything they were talking about?" he asked.

At that, she seemed to become filled with fire. She shot a look at him, her eyes burning like tiny black coals. "No, Sheriff. I don't eavesdrop. That's Miss Marjorie's trick." She spun around and stomped away—as best her dirty sneakers would let her—taking shelter behind the counter. When Bell turned back, Marjorie was sitting like she had a rod shoved down her spine, glaring daggers at the waitress.

Bell knew Annie was right. Enough folk had their private affairs leaked to the public for suspicion to turn on the women who worked the switchboard on the local exchange, and the greatest part of that suspicion landed on the plump, dull woman in the booth. It was actually Marjorie he had come looking for, knowing that if anyone had let anything slip, before or after the boys got themselves killed, it would be Marjorie who would have picked up on it. He fixed her with his best lawman's glower, and strode in measured steps toward her. He slid into the booth across the table from her and removed his hat, checking the table for any spills before laying it down.

"So how about it, Miss Thompson?" he said, leaning back and running his fingers through his thick silver mane. "You heard anything interesting of late?"

Marjorie's hands began to pile up the bunch of trash movie magazines she'd been dining with. "I don't know nothing about any of those fellows. I gotta get to work." She grabbed her purse and pawed through it until she turned up a wadded dollar bill, which she tossed on her dirty plate. She grabbed her movie star rags and purse and began hefting herself along the bench, obviously intent on making a getaway.

"You hold on just one second there, missy." Bell set the flat of his hand down on the table, causing the utensils to clatter and Marjorie to startle. He reached the same hand up and pointed at her with his index finger. "Sit," he commanded. "We ain't done talking yet."

Marjorie obeyed, letting her bottom reconnect with the bench. "I don't know nothing about whatever it is." She pursed her lips into an unattractive pout. "I'll get in trouble if I'm late." Her forehead bunched up into accordion creases. Petulance did not become her.

"You might know more than you think," Bell said, changing gears. This woman, despite her age and size, was still a little girl on the inside. He'd get more out of her through flattery than with a whip. "As a matter of fact, I bet you know a lot more than anyone around here gives you credit for." He let his tone turn to honey. "Most folk in this town may not give you the credit you deserve, but I sure do."

She relaxed, reaching over to set her belongings next to her on the bench. Her forehead smoothed and she leaned in a bit toward him. "Credit for what?"

Bell smiled widely and shifted in his seat. "Credit for what?" he echoed her. "Goodness, young lady, if anyone knows how everyone in this area is connected to each other, it's you. I bet most times someone wants to be rung through, you know who they are calling before they even tell you."

Her dull eyes showed a tiny spark. "Well, yes, I reckon that's so. I mean, people tend to talk to the same people. You get to know, you know?"

"Well, maybe, but I bet you are better at remembering who talks to who than I'd be." He let his right hand wander across the table to the crown of his hat. "But with all these people phoning up the same people all the time, do you ever get curious when someone asks you to connect them to a different number than they usually ask for?"

Marjorie started to answer, then stopped herself. She leaned back and looked down her nose at him. "I ain't paid to be curious. Folks' business is their own. Not mine." Her words began to pick up pace. "I just put the caller through, and move on. What they talk about ain't none of my business. No, I just put them through and move on."

Bell had to force his eyes not to roll upward. Instead he leaned forward, speaking softly like he was about to offer up the most tantalizing secret. She, too, leaned in toward him, so he knew she was hooked. "No, no. Of course you don't listen in, but I bet you'd remember if someone put a call through. You'd just connect them . . . and move on, but you'd notice. You'd remember."

Her eyes shifted back and forth as she sought her answer. "Yeah," she began, her voice full of caution. "I'd probably notice."

"And remember," he said, and nodded to assure her.

She licked her lips. "Well, yeah."

"Good." He picked his hat up and put it on. He folded his arms and leaned into the table. "So, did the Sleiger boys call anyone or get a call from anyone they wouldn't normally have?"

She shook her head. "No. Their mama don't let them use the phone. She's told us not to let them."

From behind the counter Annie snorted. Bell turned back. "I thought you didn't listen in on customers," he said and turned away before seeing the effect his words would have on the waitress.

Marjorie seemed emboldened by the rebuke. "Why you coming in here and asking about the Sleigers for anyway?"

Bell considered whether now was the time to spread the word, to see if someone might come forward with something he could use. Telling Marjorie was probably the best way to do that. Better even than taking a full-page ad out in the newspaper. The newspaper had already come out and wouldn't publish again until tomorrow morning, but Marjorie would have the whole town buzzing before the sun finished its slide. He shifted. "I'm afraid the boys have gone missing."

"Missing in Conroy?"

Her question coaxed a genuine chuckle from him, but it quickly faded. Conroy was too small and its people too nosey for anyone to just up and disappear. No, Bell knew the boys were dead, too. He nodded. "And Dowd and Bob turned up dead out at the Vaughn farm yesterday morning."

"Killed? What, they shot?" she asked.

Seeing the twinkle in her eyes made Bell want to slap her. "No, not shot. Dowd was"—he struggled for the right word—"mauled."

"Like by an animal?" Marjorie made no attempt to hide her disappointment that Dowd's death might not be the result of murder.

"Well, yeah," he said, wondering if he should reward her with the rest of the story. Finally he plunged in. "But Bob. His head was ripped clean off, and his body was tied to the steeple over at Five Point."

She sat up straight and raised her eyebrows. "Really?"

"Yes," he said, again stifling the urge to strike her. Instead he leaned in close to her and whispered. "Really. So maybe you could help by keeping an ear out for things, if you know what I mean, if just for now." It wouldn't do for folk to hear him asking her to spy, so he lowered his voice even more. "And don't you tell anyone I asked you to, you hear me? You just let me know if anyone makes any calls that seem out of the ordinary. You call the office and ask for me if you hear anything." He doffed his hat, and slid out of the booth.

He stood and began heading toward the exit, when her voice caused him to turn. "But that don't make no sense, Sheriff," she called loudly after him. "You saying someone used an animal to kill Dowd?"

He slipped a thumb behind his belt and gave her question some serious thought. He shrugged. "Maybe. Know anyone capable of pulling such a stunt?"

"I do," Annie said from behind the counter, then looked around the room, seemingly for confirmation from the other diners who were looking on. "We all do, don't we?" There were a few silent bobs of the head around the room, but no one spoke up. "And you do, too, Sheriff." Annie stepped around the counter and scurried up toward him. "That weird old Charlie fella who comes in every Friday. The one with the cloudy eye. He takes those dogs of his with him everywhere." She began shaking her head, as if to underscore her point. "Those dogs are darn near wild. I bet they'd rip a man clean apart if old Charlie sicced them on him. You lookin' for someone crazy enough and mean enough to do it, Charlie's your man."

THIRTY-FOUR

Nola had no idea how long the knocking at her door had been going on. The incessant noise had worked its way into her dream, setting the pace of what she knew would bloom into a splintering headache if she let it rouse her. If whoever it was would just go the hell away, let her slip back into her dreams, it might never take full root. The banging continued, growing both quicker and sharper with each rap. She heard Frank at her side snort and mumble in his sleep.

It couldn't be Bayard. He'd passed out in the bar, and they had left him where he lay. If by some slim chance he had awakened, he would have started in on another bottle and carried on until the situation had been rectified. He wouldn't have come for a visit.

She wished for the instant and painful death of whoever was at her door, then for a blissful moment, the noise stopped. Her chest rose and fell in a sigh, but that exact moment was when the rapping started again, this time on her bedroom window. Her eyes worked open. She pushed herself into a sitting position and swung her legs off the bed. Through the crack in the curtains, she could see an eye watching her.

She put her hands to her head, trying to apply enough pressure to keep it from exploding. Then the bastard knocked against the glass again.

"Some of us work nights, you know," she snapped, pushing the words out with a dry and leaden tongue. She stood and, remembering her nakedness, pulled the sheet from the bed and draped it around her body, leaving Frank fully exposed. The sight of his masculine young frame usually stoked a fire in her. He took her with such desire that she felt young and beautiful. Under better circumstances, that fact alone would make her willing to live for him, to die for him. This morning she'd gladly kick his ass to the curb for five more minutes of shut-eye.

Whether it was her voice or the loss of the sheet, she didn't know, but Frank finally stirred. "What the hell?" was all he managed before another loud rap landed on the glass.

"You break that pane," she snarled as she stumbled toward the window, her feet getting tangled in her train, "and I will cut your pecker clean off with the smallest shard of it." She made it to the window and tore the curtain open, regretting it when the light flooded her eyes. For a moment she thought she'd vomit, but she closed her eyes tight and took a deep breath before pushing the window up.

She retreated into the cool shade of the room before slowly reopening her eyes. She recognized the man's hat before she placed his face. It was McAvoy, the old doctor. "What the hell do you want?" she asked as she took a few steps back and sat on the foot of the bed. Her wish for the doctor's death hadn't worked, but the thudding in her head made her consider praying for her own.

Beside her, her prince had drifted back into the land of nod. She reached over and shook his leg until he groaned and peeled open a single eye.

"What?" His one eye held enough anger for two. Nola pointed at McAvoy, who was now leaning in through the opening.

"I have been looking over half the county for you." McAvoy leaned in more.

"Ya found me. Now go the hell away."

"Frank, get up," the old man commanded. "You need to worry a little less about dipping your wick in that one"—he gestured to Nola dismissively—"and more about your duties. The Judge needs you."

"The Judge should learn how to goddamn wait until a reasonable hour," Nola said and pushed herself back on the mattress, collapsing against her pillow and throwing her arm over her face to block the light.

"Shut up," Frank told her. She'd have given him an evil look, but it would have required both moving her arm and opening her eyelids. Even one of those things would have entailed more effort than she wanted to consider. "What's he need?" Frank asked.

"He needs protection is what he needs," the old man called out with enough urgency to prompt Nola to move and open her eyes. "He's in a bad way. I think someone is trying to kill him."

Frank swung from dead-to-the-world to alert in a heartbeat. "Let me find my pants," he said, swinging himself into a standing position.

Even with the pain that threatened to pop her eyes clean from her head, Nola took in the sight of him as he stomped around the side of the bed looking for his trousers. It was a shame, she thought, when he lifted them from the floor and pushed in a leg. Frank lost most of his charm once his pants were on.

THIRTY-FIVE

McAvoy waited only long enough to make sure Frank was up, and headed out to pick up Bayard. He wanted to stop and check on Ovid before heading to Tupelo. He would need to take a sample of his blood for typing as well, although he worried his godson hardly had any left to spare. He'd tried to convince that Ford girl he knew what he was doing, but the truth was that he had no idea what was ailing Ovid. She was right; the Judge belonged in a hospital, but a public declaration of weakness would be akin to signing the man's death certificate anyway.

He followed the road from Nola's house until he reached the T it formed with Chamberlain Road, then turned north toward Conroy proper. The sun cut through the passenger-side window of his car, nearly blinding him. As he held up an arm to shield his eyes, he caught sight of an approaching red pickup truck in the rearview mirror. The red Ford was traveling much faster than what was safe for the road. McAvoy considered pulling over and letting it by, but the driver pulled into the oncoming lane with an obvious intent to pass. There were no vehicles heading toward them, so McAvoy decided to let off the gas and let the fool by him. Rather than pulling forward, the truck sidled up next to his car, slowing to match his exact speed. His peripheral vision pinpointed a younger man sitting in the passenger's side of the truck, and a flash of recognition caused him to look away from the road and glance at the other vehicle. It was Wayne Sleiger, and since you hardly ever saw the one boy without the other being nearby, he reckoned that meant Walter was the crazy driver.

The two vehicles traveled on parallel paths for a few moments, then Walter finally sped up and pulled ahead. McAvoy shook his head, wondering at the foolhardiness of the young. He let go of the breath he hadn't realized he'd been holding as the red truck returned to the lane and carried on until it was within forgetting distance. His mind had returned to attending to the Judge's needs when the pickup suddenly spun around and headed directly at him. In response, he hit the brake and turned the wheel, causing his car to slide off the road. His chest banged painfully into the steering wheel, and he winced. The pain told him he'd probably cracked a rib or two. He reached the gearshift and set the car to park, adrenaline forcing him to take heavy breaths in spite of the pain it caused.

Goddamn those fool boys, he thought as he tilted his neck back to look for their truck. The Sleiger boys had left their vehicle, he saw, and were walking toward him. In spite of the pain, he was struck by the strangeness of their dress. Though it was just about as thick and humid as it got in Conroy, both were wearing long sleeves, scarves, and gloves. Hats—battered, wide-rimmed ones like you'd see on a scarecrow—shaded their faces. They moved quickly toward him, and he was about to give them holy hell when Wayne opened his door without a word and pulled him out from behind the wheel. Walter popped open the trunk, then the brothers hoisted McAvoy up and dropped him inside. He got a brief look at their faces, pale and pitiless, before the lid slammed shut on him. He banged his fists against the metal above his head, only to hear a vehicle, which had to be their truck, peel out. For a moment he wondered if they were through with him, if they intended to leave him trapped in his own car on the side of the road. Then a sudden movement flung him back. The car lurched forward, the screech of rubber shredding against the blacktop announcing its departure.

THIRTY-SIX

Corinne trod into the kitchen, instantly slowing her steps as she took in the sight of the Judge's maid, Lucille, asleep with her head resting on her folded arms at the table. Corinne hated waking her; she knew the poor woman had weathered one hell of a night.

She could make her way back upstairs, let Lucille rest, and worry about McAvoy's more regimented schedule of shifts watching over the Judge going forward. She was about to spin on her heels and do just that when a lark smashed into the window, bloodying the pane and startling Lucille awake. The maid jumped, but she composed herself as soon as her eyes met Corinne's.

"I'm sorry," Corinne felt compelled to say, even though she knew she had nothing to do with the lark's fate. Lucille looked from her to the stain on the window. "It was a bird." The poor lark had undoubtedly flown its life to an early end. As a girl, it would have brought Corinne to tears, but she had spent too many days watching innocent humans suffer to mind the fall of every sparrow. That tally would have to be kept by God himself. She returned her focus to Lucille. "I'm sorry it woke you."

"How's the Judge?" Lucille asked, looking up at her with swollen, red eyes. So, she had not been sleeping after all. She had been crying. At first Corinne took the tears as a sign of Lucille's devotion to her employer, but then she realized something. The Judge's maid and the woman she'd seen in the colored waiting room at the train station were one and the same. It was possible that Lucille's distress could be related to the Judge's well-being, but something about the uncaring flatness of the woman's voice as she posed her question told Corinne it was unlikely. Something had been bothering her even before the Judge's condition had taken a turn for the worse.

Corinne's intuition warned her not to bring up their previous encounter. "He's still resting," she said, then reflected on the large dose of tranquilizers Dr. McAvoy had administered before taking off. "I suspect he may be sleeping for quite some time." Lucille gazed at her for several moments more without so much as a blink. "I'm sure Dr. McAvoy will be along soon," she said, trying to fill the silence. "He said to expect him first thing." Corinne stole a glance at her wristwatch. "I'm surprised he isn't already here."

At the sound of the doctor's name, Lucille stirred from her stupor. "Can I fix you something to eat?" Lucille's face showed her exhaustion; she seemed to be far too young of a woman for the purplish bags forming beneath her eyes.

Corinne felt guilty for asking the weary woman to wait on her. "Maybe a little coffee? But only if you'll join me."

Surprise animated Lucille's face. Her forehead bunched up and her eyes widened. "Oh, no, ma'am. I don't know about where you come from, but that isn't how things are done around here." She paused. "I'm sorry. I don't mean no disrespect, but I believe you will find things will go a lot easier for you in this town if you do as those around you do. Folk my color don't 'join' folk your color for anything."

"But that's ridiculous, Lucille, you must know that . . ."

"What I know, ma'am," Lucille said, standing, "is that when colored folk start thinking of themselves as a white person's friend, things tend not to end so well for the colored." Her head leaned a bit to the side. "Don't think I don't appreciate your kindness, but there are lines that are better left uncrossed. The longer you live around these parts, the easier it will be for you to see that." She pushed back her chair and stood. "You need to eat, too. You like eggs? I'll make you some eggs."

"What I'd really like is for you to explain to me what's going on here."

"Ma'am?"

"To start with, why am I here nursing a man who should be in the hospital? Why is Dr. McAvoy afraid to get the Judge the care he needs?"

"That isn't for me to say."

"Okay, then tell me about her . . . about Ruby."

"No, I'm sorry," Lucille responded, shaking her head, holding her chin high as she gazed at Corinne with something akin to panic in her eyes.

Corinne had no intention of taking "no" for an answer. "Please." She crossed over to Lucille, holding her hands raised as if in prayerful supplication. "I know she was special to my fiancé. I suspect very special. I found her photo at the Dunnes' home. And last night your employer called out her name. Please," Corinne repeated, forcing a smile to her lips. "People around here don't seem to like questions, and I fear you may be my only hope of getting a straight answer. Does the doctor's reticence about the Judge's proper care have anything to do with Ruby?"

Lucille held her hands up and shook her head. "I'm sorry, Miss, but this here is one of those lines best not crossed."

"Elijah and Ruby, they were lovers, weren't they?" Corinne pressed.

"That is a question best asked Elijah himself."

"Please, I need to know who she was to him. I need to know what happened to her." Corinne tried to take Lucille's hand, but the other woman stepped back. "I've even been dreaming of her . . ."

"You saw her?" Lucille's eyebrows raised, and she wrapped her arms around herself as if she'd caught a sudden draft.

"Well, yes. It had to be a dream, though. She's gone, isn't she?"

Lucille tilted her head forward, leaning in like she planned to share an intimacy. "There's gone, and then there's *gone*."

"I'm afraid I don't understand."

"I got no more to say. I could lose my job . . ."

"But it's more than that, isn't it?"

"You want to learn about Ruby? Well, it's like I said, you need to ask your Elijah. I don't mean no disrespect, but if you don't trust each other enough to talk about your pasts, you ain't got no business marrying each other anyway." She paused. "I don't understand you, Miss. Me, I don't got a lot of options, but a woman like you could go just about anywhere in this wide world. You willing to settle in Conroy, that must mean you love Elijah. And if you love him, you owe it to yourself to get the answers you needin'." She took her apron from the chair where she'd laid it and tied it around her waist. "I'll make those eggs now, then I'll go sit with the Judge while you rest up a bit." But before Lucille could follow through on her offer, the doorbell rang.

"It's probably the doctor," Corinne said. "Shall I get it?"

Lucille shook her head, a wary expression on her face. "No, ma'am. I'll see to it." The bell sounded again. A short, impatient ringing. "You wait here. If it's Dr. McAvoy, I'll bring him back through to you." Corinne's eyes followed Lucille as she made her way from the kitchen.

THIRTY-SEVEN

The lace curtain covering the door's window did little to prevent a ray of sunshine from piercing the dusky hall. Rather than the light pushing away the dark, the shadows seemed poised to attack the slim ray of brightness. Lucille had walked the length of the hall hundreds, maybe even thousands of times during her employment at the Lowell house. Still, despite the familiarity of the setting, and the light that bisected the center of the hall, Lucille was spooked by the thought of traversing it.

The bell rang a third time. This time it was only a quick buzz, but it was followed by the pounding of a fist against the door. Lucille was embarrassed by her own timidity, but she still scurried past the shadows on her way to the door. Through the lace-filtered glass Lucille recognized two of the Judge's men, Frank Mason and Bayard Bloom. As hard as Lucille tried to remain ignorant of the Judge's dealings, she knew these men acted as his muscle. Suddenly the shadows she had skirted seemed benevolent in comparison to what awaited her on the house's threshold. Still, she was glad it had been Frank knocking rather than Bayard. Frank could kill a man, slicing him open without a single pang of conscience, but Bayard Bloom was nearly legendary in the entire tristate area for his savagery. Sure, Frank would take your life, but he'd do it quickly. The experiences endured by Bayard's victims formed a canon of cautionary tales for any who'd consider double-crossing the Judge. Lucille braced herself, wondering what could have sent these two lowlifes to the Judge's door this early.

Frank leaned in toward the glass, seemingly intent on scanning the hall for signs of life. The brim of his fedora tapped against the pane, and he leaned back upon catching sight of her. A few steps behind him, and off to his side, lumpy, balding redheaded Bloom rocked with impatience like an angry child. Lucille opened the door, but offered no passage wider than her own body could block.

Frank was a tall, lean man. He might have been handsome, perhaps even devastatingly so, if not for the cutthroat look of his deep-set and narrow dark eyes. At the sight of Lucille, he removed his hat, revealing the straight black locks he kept slicked back. The rose scent of his hair oil wafted in on the warm air.

"Yessir?" Lucille slurred the words into one, letting herself slip into the role of the servile and respectful dark-skinned woman who readily acknowledged these white men's innate superiority. Let no one ever say she didn't know what was expected of her.

Frank leaned in and angled his face in toward the opening. "Doctor McAvoy sent us. Said the Judge might need a little looking after," he said, and then pulled his thin lips into a tight smile.

Lucille's shoulders collapsed under the weight of resignation. If McAvoy wanted these wild dogs here, she didn't have any choice but to welcome them. "Please come in," she said and stepped aside.

Frank crossed the threshold and held out his hat to her. She nodded and took it from him, placing it with exaggerated care over a hook on the coat stand. She turned back to see that Frank had stopped cold in his tracks, and was sniffing the air like a hound trying to track a scent.

"You baking?" he asked, his forehead bunching up, his eyes narrowing.

"No, sir," she replied, "but I'd be glad to fix something for you if you'd like. I was about to cook some breakfast for the Judge's nurse . . ."

"No," he said and pushed past her, drawing near the foot of the stairs. "You don't smell that? Kind of like cinnamon, but not?" He craned his neck and looked up the stairs. His hand moved beneath his jacket, allowing Lucille a glimpse of his holster.

She took a few paces toward him, drawing in a deep breath. She did catch a faint whiff of something, now that she was looking for it. She struggled to place it. No, not cinnamon. More like a flower. Dianthus? Maybe. No, not really. But what lay beneath the spice was the undeniable scent of decay. How had she not noticed it before? "No, sir," she lied. "I don't smell nothing unusual." Something about the odor frightened Frank, and realizing that scared Lucille out of her wits.

THIRTY-EIGHT

Elijah opened Corinne's empty suitcase and laid it on the bed. He turned to the chifferobe and yanked the doors wide, collecting her hanging clothes in a single scoop and tossing them on the bed next to the case. At first he made an effort to fold the dresses neatly, but he lost patience quickly and started dropping things in. He turned back and opened the top drawer, both a little excited and a little embarrassed as he reached in and took hold of her undergarments. He ran both hands to the back of the drawer so he could collect them in one go, but stopped cold when he felt the unmistakable shape of a pistol swathed within the softness of his fiancée's underwear. His hands released the clothes and took hold of the velvet bag containing the firearm.

The sound of the door opening from the kitchen caused him to release the weapon. "What's going on here?" his mother asked. She stepped out onto the sleeping porch and crossed over to the bed that held Corinne's case. She paused before it and, without looking at her son, removed the contents, laying Corinne's belongings next to it. Elijah watched without responding as his mother began to neatly fold the clothing before returning it to the case. "She'll be staying on with the

Judge for a while? Will we be postponing the wedding, then?" she asked, looking back at him without stopping her self-imposed chore.

"Ah, I see it's more than that," she said when he stayed silent. She must have read, or misread, the expression in his eyes. "You've had a change of heart? Or was it the young lady who did?" He held his tongue, knowing he was in for a scene the moment he told her that he would be packing a case for himself, too. That he was going to leave this place and never lay eyes on his mother again.

When he joined the army, he did it to run from what he believed Ruby had done to him. He knew he was running now, too, but this time he was separating himself from the lies he'd been raised to believe. He didn't want this farm. He didn't want these people. Since the TVA was hiring, he'd take Corinne to Tennessee. See if they could start a new life together there.

"Well, doesn't really matter," his mother said. "She wasn't right for you. Nor you for her. You need a wife who knows her place. A wife who knows how to be a woman. The pair of you will be saving yourselves a lifetime of regret. Besides, I think the girl is a bit off . . ."

"Corinne isn't off. There ain't nothing wrong with Corinne." The words broke free from Elijah's heart. "What's wrong is with you. And Daddy. And this place." His voice cracked. "How could you not tell me the truth about Ruby?"

His mother blanched at his words, her face frozen into a cautious mask, her lips a tight straight line, her brow smooth. Only her eyes betrayed the truth he suspected was buried in her soul. He waited, wondering if she would finally, and for the first time, be honest with him. "And just what truth is that, son?"

The screech of the screen door alerted them both to his father's arrival. Clay stepped onto the sleeping porch, his expression hard. The drink-fueled and gleeful aggression had been replaced by a smoldering hate that was all set to ignite. "You can stop your pretending, Ava. The boy knows he ain't mine. He knows you spread your legs for the Judge.

And he knows you'd've rather watched him marry his own blood than admit to your sins."

She turned and advanced on Clay. "Why? Ruby is dead. Why would you tell him now?"

"Maybe 'cause I'm tired of pretending the spineless bastard is mine. I mean, *look* at him. I tried to make a man out of him, but even the army couldn't do it." He smiled, causing the corners of his eyes to crinkle. He seemed almost happy to be finally spewing his venom.

Elijah pushed his way between them. "We're leaving. Corinne and me both. Today."

"Yeah, boy, that's right. Go on and run." Clay reached out and pushed him back and into his mother. "You've been nothing but a disappointment your whole life. Hell, I'd hoped you'd get yourself killed in Korea, so I could at least boast about 'my son the hero.' Maybe even get a few free drinks out of it. But Jesus Christ, you can't even get yourself shot right. They probably pegged you while you were running anyway."

His mother tore around him, and advanced on Clay. "You've been disappointed? You? Look at what happened to my life. I had no choice but to marry you, an unwashed, uneducated man who reeks of sour mash and dung." Her face turned red, but the blood drained from her pale hands as they bent into claws. She struck out and scratched long, angry red tracks along her husband's cheek. He took a step back, then slapped her hard enough to drive her to her knees. She pressed her hand over her reddening cheek and looked up at her husband. "I should have hanged myself," she said, rising. "I should've flung myself in front of a train. I should have pulled him out with a wire hanger before I ever married you."

Elijah had heard enough. He went to the chifferobe and opened the top drawer, feeling around inside until the texture of soft velvet met his fingers. He retrieved the bag from the drawer, then turned it upside down so that the pistol inside could slide out and into his open hand. A Walther PPK, a model he knew well. He checked the clip and took off the safety, aiming the barrel between his father's surprised eyes.

The older man laughed. "Go ahead, if you got the balls to do it," he said.

He faced his father, each moment causing his hand to quiver a bit more, every second weakening his resolve to end the man.

"You put that down now, Elijah," his mother said, her voice quivering. "We'll deal with this together. Just hand me the gun." Elijah caught his breath, then lowered his arm, and let the pistol slip into her waiting hand.

"Little pansy mama's boy," his dad said and laughed, not a happy sound, but one filled with anger and disdain. "Worthless bastard." Elijah felt like he'd been kicked in the chest. He focused on his dad's lined and weathered face, staring into this stranger's eyes. Elijah never noticed his mother lifting the gun. A bullet entered through the man's right eye, and his brains splattered against the window screen like oatmeal being flung against a sieve.

He jolted back and turned toward his mother. She stood there trembling, the knuckles of her hand white as she clutched the weapon. Her eyes were red, tears brimming. "I didn't mean any of what I said. I'd've never hurt you. You forgive your mama, okay?" Before he could move, she swung the pistol up and placed it against her temple. She squeezed the trigger, then she was no more.

THIRTY-NINE

"Yeah," Bell said to his deputy as they pulled up to Charlie Aaron's place. "Something sure as hell happened around here." They'd gone by the funeral parlor where Charlie worked before coming out here. Charlie was due to assist at a burial, but the owner of the funeral home hadn't seen hide nor hair of him. Charlie's boss figured Charlie was passed out—again—in a drunken stupor. Asked Bell to pass on the message to the old man that he was fired. For good, this time.

It looked like Charlie might have worse problems than being fired. Even from the car, they could see the broken windows and the dried blood that painted the concrete steps leading up to the porch of the old man's house.

"His truck ain't here," Deputy Rigby said as he put the car in park and killed the engine. Bell looked at him, barely able to hide his disgust. They hadn't even gotten out of the car yet, and the boy was already turning green around the gills.

"Just stay here," Bell snarled and flung open his door. Bell's joints felt stiff and his footfalls were heavy as he plodded toward the steps. The blood had dried, but flies still buzzed around, landing in the sticky residue. Bell squatted as best as his bad knee would let him to examine what he realized was a tooth. He stretched slowly up and placed his right hand over the back of his neck to block the sun's scorching rays.

He mounted the steps, doing his best to sidestep the blood. The front door was broken into splinters, providing a gaping entryway. He stepped inside, his senses affronted by the vinegary scent of Charlie's home. And riding over that unpleasant smell was something worse: the stench of coppery blood and decay. He watched his step, moving around the swipe of blood on the wooden floor that led from Charlie's living room and out to his porch. "Charlie?" he called, although he didn't know why. The old man was already dead. He felt that in his bones.

The heavy buzzing of horseflies caused him to look up and take a few more steps through the main room to the kitchen's doorway. Bell pulled a handkerchief from his pocket and held it over his nose.

"Shit," he said, catching sight of the mastiff's ruined body. What the hell was going on around these parts? Seemed as though the whole goddamned world was going mad. The sheriff backed away without taking his eyes off the dog's body. No way Charlie would've let someone get away with such a thing, which was another tip of the hat to his theory that the old man was dead. He turned and made a beeline for the door, this time not bothering to check whether he was tracking blood, be it Charlie's or the dog's. He broke free of the pungent scent that permeated the house and clambered off the porch, avoiding the stairs altogether.

"We got trouble," he called to Rigby, but no sooner had he said the words than the sound of a gunshot echoed across the fields.

Then a second.

Rigby bounded out of the car and looked over at him. "Hunters?"

He shook his head. "That was no rifle." He pointed toward what seemed to be the source of the sounds. "What's over there?"

"I'm pretty sure the Dunne place lies in that direction."

FORTY

Raylene tapped the hard-boiled egg on the railing of the steps of city hall, then rolled it between both hands until the shell shattered. "Here you go, boy," she said, holding it out to her son as he came walking up to her.

The boy looked ridiculous. He was swimming in his father's old coat, and wore his father's trilby with the brim angled down to shield his eyes. He'd taken a once-white, now gray, dish towel from the diner and wrapped it around his neck like a scarf. He'd forced his hands into much-too-small ladies' gardening gloves, powder blue with pink roses and daisies. Where he'd found those, she had no idea.

He seemed worried, or maybe just uncomfortable, shifting from foot to foot, not meeting her eyes. "Naw. Not hungry," Merle said, taking a drag off his cigarette.

Folk around here had criticized her for letting the boy smoke so young, but she figured it didn't matter very much one way or another. The angel done told them that the world they knew would soon be ending, and that a new Jerusalem would be built right here on this spot. "'So also is the resurrection of the dead. The body is sown in corruption, it is raised in incorruption. It is sown in dishonor, it is raised in glory.

It is sown in weakness, it is raised in power. It is sown a natural body, it is raised a spiritual body.' That's First Corinthians, boy," she said, realizing that Merle wasn't listening to her. His eyes were fixed on the city hall clock, and she knew he was willing the hours to speed by, until the sun would set, and he could shed the garments he wore to protect himself from its light.

That morning, the boy had been beet red when she cut him loose from the fence. As Ruby told her to, Raylene had covered him with a blanket, then walked him back into the shade of the house. As burned as the boy had been, within minutes of getting him inside, his skin had returned to the same freckled paleness it had always been.

Raylene had to struggle to keep up with him as they made their way into town. The boy pretty much ran, the hat pulled way down and his hands stuffed in the pockets of the coat, his pace not slowing until they stepped into the thick morning fog. For the first time Raylene found herself wondering why an angel of God should burn in the rays of His sun.

No. Her faith was unshakable. She buried the thought as quickly as it had arisen. "What you doin' here? I thought the angel had work at the diner for you today." She finished peeling the egg and popped it into her mouth whole.

Merle drew a puff on the cigarette and blew it out. His face pinched in on itself whenever he smoked. "I already did as she told me to." He paused, and she noticed his hand shook. It sickened her to see her boy's hand in the feminine glove. "It starts tonight. She told me to be ready. But she wanted me to come talk to you. Pass on a message." Merle watched her, alternating between biting his lower lip and taking drags. "She said ain't everybody gonna get changed. Just a few of us. The ones she says are worthy."

The yolk was dry, making it hard to swallow. *For many are called, but few are chosen.* The words came to her mind, but she didn't manage to speak them before Merle went on.

"I need to get back to the diner," he said, throwing his half-smoked cigarette onto the steps. Raylene leaned over and picked it up, sticking the stub behind her ear. When Raylene looked up, Merle's forehead had scrunched up, his eyes narrowed with hate. "She ain't changing you. You haven't been chosen. She says you're too old."

A tremor ran through Raylene, and she nearly teetered over. She grabbed the step she sat on with both hands, taking deep breaths while the world spun before her eyes. "Not chosen?" Like Moses on Mount Nebo, she was to die, looking into the promised land, but being denied entry herself. Raylene grabbed ahold of the railing and pulled herself up. She was a servant of the Lord. If this was His will, she would bow to it. She nodded. "'Neither do men put new wine into old bottles: else the bottles break, and the wine runneth out, and the bottles perish: but they put new wine into new bottles, and both are preserved.'"

She reached out for her son, but he pushed her hand away. Merle took a couple of steps back, reaching the foot of the stairs. "She says you worship false gods."

Raylene felt her knees buckle, and she caught the rail to keep from falling.

"From now on, folk around here are to worship her." He gave his mother a sour look. "Oh, and she said if you don't quit quoting that Bible crap, she's gonna rip your tongue out." A cruel, straight smile came to his lips; then he turned and ran off in the direction of the diner.

FORTY-ONE

Corinne jerked awake. In spite of her best efforts to remain vigilant, the warm band of sunshine that had stolen through the crack in the curtains, combined with the sleepless night, had caused her to nod off in her chair. She glanced at her wristwatch. It was well past noon, and Dr. McAvoy still hadn't come for a sample of the Judge's blood.

She rose and went to examine Judge Lowell. If he had regained consciousness at any point, she was unaware of it. She thought again about the high dose of sedatives the doctor had administered. It was almost as if McAvoy had subconsciously hoped to help his friend pass quietly into death rather than recover. Again, Corinne had to combat a sense of distaste in order to take the Judge's wrist. His pulse was still weak, although his breathing seemed less labored than it had before. He seemed to radiate an unexpected vitality that belied the gray clamminess of his skin.

The sound of men's voices drew her to the window, and she pulled the curtain back an inch or so, in order to see the yard below better. The two goons who worked for the Judge stood outside talking, very nearly arguing. The dark, slim one, Frank, leaned back against their auto as the clown called Bayard strutted, waving his arms and pointing angrily at his companion. Corinne couldn't make out their words, but the buffoon's anger came through clearly enough.

When Lucille had introduced them, she'd said that McAvoy had sent them to assist with caring for the Judge. Corinne found herself shaking her head as she watched Frank light up a cigarette, puffing away with no sign of concern over his buddy's tirade. What kind of care could these two possibly provide? What had she found herself mixed up in?

A sound, something between a moan and a whimper, caused her to turn back to the Judge. He seemed to be rousing, and was clutching tightly to the top of his sheets as if trying to drag himself back from a nightmare. He rose almost to a sitting position, his eyes open wide and flooded with terror. His lips moved, but no words came. Then he fell back and went still. Corinne rushed to his side and felt his wrist, following up with pressing two fingers against his carotid artery. After several moments passed, she closed his eyes and pulled the sheet over his face. Whatever the reason for his delay, the doctor would arrive too late.

FORTY-TWO

Bayard didn't like it. He didn't like it one little bit.

"Keep your head," Frank said and puffed on his cigarette. His annoying habit of squinting as he smoked, something Bayard could usually ignore, made Bayard ache with a desire to draw his partner's blood.

Frank opened the car door and climbed in. He sat sideways, hunched over, his legs hanging out.

"You *know* that scent," Bayard said, nodding in agreement with himself. "It's the same as how that Hollywood woman smelled."

Frank flicked ashes from the tip of his cigarette and glared at Bayard. "All right. I know. Damn it. I know. Shut up, so I can think."

But Bayard wasn't going to be hushed, not this time. "They ain't nothing to think about. Whatever was wrong with her was wrong with Ruby, too. And now it's got the Judge."

Frank didn't answer; he just kept sucking on the damned cigarette. It wasn't until it was mostly ash that Frank spoke. "We need to find out what's keeping the doc," he said and threw his cigarette to the ground. "You stay here and keep an eye on things. I'll start at his house, maybe head down to the hospital in Tupelo if he ain't home." He swung around on the seat and cranked the ignition.

Bayard lunged forward and grabbed the top of the door before Frank could close it. "If'n he was home, he would have answered the four times you called." Bayard blinked slowly, looking Frank up and down and asking himself how this pretty boy who thought with his cock had ever come to assume he was in charge. "And you ain't leaving me here." Bayard reached in over Frank and killed the engine. He took possession of the keys.

He had made the mistake of ignoring his gut in Hollywood. But unlike Frank, Bayard learned from his mistakes.

The memory of the day they'd spent in Los Angeles burned in him, and he suspected all the whiskey in the world wouldn't put the fire out. He'd left Frank in the room where the King woman, Myrna, had put them. Twenty minutes had passed in that fancy movie star cage without a sign of her. While Bayard had spent the whole time pacing, Frank had just sat there, nearly as still as a statue. Contact with the actress had left him acting like he was drunk. Useless. He barely even nodded when Bayard told him he thought they should investigate instead of just sitting around. Realizing he'd have to take care of things on his own, Bayard had slipped down the hall, moving real quiet like he did when he sneaked into houses to watch people sleep.

He made his way down the shadowy hall in the opposite direction from which they'd entered it. He moved from door to door, poking his head around the casements of those he found open, trying with a cautious twist the knobs of those that were closed. Then he realized his cautiousness would make him look more suspicious if someone were to catch him. Not that that seemed to be an issue—the whole damned place was deserted. He could make as much noise as he wanted, he decided, and if anyone stopped him, he could just say he was looking for a place to piss. He couldn't wait to find his boss's daughter and get them all the hell back to Conroy.

But then he found the white room. Even after all these months, every time Bayard closed his eyes he saw the room, with its glossy tiles that covered the ceiling and walls. The floor was concrete and sloped a bit inward toward a large drain at its center. He realized in an instant all the possibilities such a room could hold. Through his fantasies, he'd come to associate the bleach smell of the room with a feeling of happiness.

It was there in the white room where he'd found Ruby, bound to a gurney by thick leather straps, straps that looked way sturdier than what you'd need to hold down a slip of a thing like Ruby. He crossed over to get a better look at her, drawing his knife to cut the straps as he did so. Her eyes were open, but they were all glassy, the black spots at the center way bigger than they ought to be. He waved his hand over her face, but she gave no reaction. She was alive, he could tell, but they had her on something. That much was for sure.

He raised his knife to start cutting through the straps, but his eyes landed on another gurney that had been pushed into the corner. This one was empty. It was bent in the center, warped like it had been twisted in some kind of vise.

"Are you sure you want to do that?" Myrna said from behind him, her voice still sultry. He forced himself not to react, even though her silent approach had thrown him. "They can be so unpredictable when they reach this stage."

"What the hell have you been doing to her?"

Myrna didn't respond to his question. Instead she looked at him and smiled. She drew near and held out her hand, palm up. "May I?" she asked, looking at his knife.

Without a second thought, he held the handle out to her. She took it and held the knife's sharp blade to the light. She weighed it in her hand, seeming to admire its perfect balance. "Very nice," she said, then handed it back to him. He took it from her, a sense of amazement filling him. The thought hit him that he could love this woman.

"So you've come in search of this little chickadee?" she asked, crossing her arms and tilting her head as she did. Bayard felt his head nodding in reply. "Well, this is indeed a first." She turned to the gurney and traced a finger along Ruby's jawline. "Then this was a mistake on my hunter's part. I insist that only those who are alone in the world be brought to me. It helps us avoid so many complications." She looked back at Bayard. "Don't worry, the hunter will pay for his error." Her eyes sparkled, as if the thoughts of just how she'd make that happen excited her. "He's supposed to bring us the broken ones. The addicts. The penniless. The ones without family. Perhaps it's time for me to consider replacing him. He's artless in all this, you know." She raised her hands and motioned around the tiled room. "To him this facility is just a functional setup, a place to administer treatments and dispose of the . . ." She paused and seemed to search for a word. After a moment, she gave a girlish giggle and a slight shake of her head. "The empties, if you will."

She left Ruby's side and came closer. "But for an artist such as yourself, it could function as a veritable atelier." He didn't understand her ten-dollar words, and she seemed to read the confusion in his eyes. She traced her fingers down his forearm, across the back of his palm, along the flat side of his blade. "A place," she explained, "for you to work your *art*. To create your masterpiece." She raised her eyebrows, posing a question without saying the words. Somehow she had read him all the way down to the roots of his soul, and she liked the darkness she saw there. "It's even soundproofed, you know. As long as the door's kept closed, no one's gonna hear a peep. No disturbances, no need to creep around. You could conduct a symphony of your own creation."

"What kind of treatments?" Bayard asked. He never lied to himself, especially *about* himself. He was strong, but he didn't have much in the smarts department. He knew he would be willing to do anything she asked of him, but he worried that he wasn't mentally equipped to rise to the challenge. He felt now that he'd rather slit his own throat with the knife he held than disappoint her.

"Do you find me beautiful?" she asked, ignoring his question. Of course he did. He found her so beautiful he couldn't even form the words to tell her. Her smile told him that she understood. "Time is the thief of beauty. Every rose must fade." She turned and took a few steps away, and the separation physically pained him. She glanced back over her shoulder at him. "Or at least I used to think so. But I made friends who showed me it wasn't necessarily so." She spun around to face him. "Tell me. Do you believe in the supernatural?"

He shook his head, not in denial, but to show he didn't understand.

"Ghosts, witches," she said, the words very nearly reminding him of the dread he'd felt before stepping into this room, "vampires?" Her eyes widened as she said the last word in a breathless whisper.

"I don't know," he said, a part of his brain telling him he needed to shake it off, grab Ruby, and get the hell out of here. There wasn't much a man like Bayard feared, but his mama had scared him at night with stories of the witches who'd come and take him if he didn't stop pissing his bed. "Maybe," he said, realizing his grip had tightened on the handle of his knife.

"Your girl there." She motioned toward Ruby. "She came here oh so willingly. She was excited to taste a little opium. Ecstatic at the thought of participating in a scandalous little black-magic ceremony." She looked up, her excited eyes meeting his. "She has quite the taste for the outré, you know. Of course, in Hollywood, she and her beautiful boy are hardly unique. Finding young people looking to sell their souls to become stars is quite an easy thing to do. No, really. It's like shooting fish in a barrel. A never-ending stream of fresh, bright faces for your pleasure." Her eyes narrowed as her lips pulled into a thin smile. "She flung herself at us. Oh, but she thought she was so clever. She thought she'd worm her bumpkin way into our lives, turn our secrets to her profit. Thought she could control us through her petty homespun machinations. She didn't realize we could see right through her small-town schemes and tiny ambitions." She cast a glance at Ruby. "Now did you, dear?"

"It don't make no sense to shoot fish," Bayard heard himself protesting, but he wasn't sure if he'd said it out loud. If so, she didn't seem to hear, or perhaps she chose to disregard him. All the same, a small part of Bayard's brain had begun to protest. This woman was working on him, just as surely as she'd charmed Frank.

"I assure you, all of the purportedly imaginary creatures I've mentioned are quite real. Even vampires." She gave him a moment to consider what she'd said. "In fact, your young lady here is halfway on the path to becoming one. My associates, you see, have managed to reintroduce a being that had been hunted to extinction, wiped, as far as we can tell, from the face of the earth."

Bayard felt a cold shock jolt through him, then his armpits began to dampen. He cast a wary glance at Ruby. It was true; she didn't look quite right. Her skin shone a silvery blue and looked kind of waxy. The weirdest part was her eyes. Besides being too big, the black bits in the middle were dotted with tiny specks of blue, looking like they were about to break free and rise to the top, like bubbles in water that was nearing a boil.

"The movies don't get much right when it comes to vampires, but they are correct on one point. They can live forever, unchanged, immune to the ravages of time." Myrna returned to Ruby's side. "To ingest . . ." she began, but then chose a more familiar word, "to drink a vampire's blood can turn you into one of them, allowing you the gift of eternal, healthy youth." She winked at him. "Of course, there are drawbacks. First of all you fall utterly under the creature's thrall. Were I to taste the blood of a true, full vampire, I would be turning my will completely over to the beast." She reached her hands up to her temples and wiggled her fingers. "It allows them to get in here. To take control of your thoughts and actions."

She lowered her hand, and leaned in toward him as if she intended to share a secret. "And if that weren't bad enough, were you yourself to turn, to develop fully into a vampire in your own right, you'd combust at the touch of the sun and be forced to spend your 'life' as a leech, a captive to your own hungers." She reached over and ran her fingers through Ruby's dark hair. "Some might be willing to make such a trade-off, but I'm not one of them."

She tapped her index finger on the tip of Ruby's nose. "I'm just not one for extreme measures, now, am I?" she asked as if there were a chance Ruby might answer. "But my friends have stumbled upon a happy medium. Just as how they've learned to re-create the vampire, they've also rediscovered the method that allows one to reap several of the benefits of vampirism, without many of the worst drawbacks." She looked away from Ruby, returning her gaze to him. "The allure of eternal youth and the ability to influence those around us made any risk seem acceptable."

"Why's she so blue?" Bayard asked, wondering aloud at the unnatural tone of her skin. It seemed unlikely a body with an ounce of life in it could have that color.

"It's a rather lovely color, I think. I'm considering redoing the drawing room in a similar shade." A smile curved on her lips that made him wonder if she was only pulling his leg. When he didn't react, she shrugged. "A person exposed three times to the blood from a full vampire will most likely become a vampire themselves. But by employing certain measures, this transformation can be slowed down.

"We take advantage of the vampire's innate allergies, certain metals, like silver in its colloidal form—the cause of the bluing of her complexion—and natural phenomena, such as sunlight." Bayard didn't understood a word she was saying, but his eyes followed when she pointed to some kind of opening in the ceiling above Ruby. She flipped a switch on the wall. "These things help to keep it in a weakened, manageable state. A few moments a day beneath this skylight, in heavily filtered sunlight, helps keep the beast at bay," she said as a panel lowered, exposing a window covered by a red shade that was thin enough to let a dim light pass through.

The dull light bathed Ruby's body, and she began bucking up and down against the gurney. "The poor dears do detest this part so." Ruby never seemed to wake from her stupor, but still she squealed and strained against her restraints. The King woman flipped the switch, and as the sunlight faded, Ruby fell still.

Bayard had never seen such a beautiful thing in his life.

The King woman stood there, taking in his reaction. Their eyes met, and she smiled. "In rare cases," she said, her brow rising and her eyes taking on the look of a tent revival preacher's, "the process can be held in stasis." She balled up her hands in frustration, seeming to realize that she'd lost him once again. "It can be put off. Stopped, leaving the infected in a type of bardo, a state between living and undead. The blood we take from the beings in this in-between state is the trick to enjoying the benefits of vampirism without the extreme drawbacks. This in-between blood, it doesn't change us. It merely fortifies us. We aren't anywhere near as fast or strong as full bloods, but then again, we don't have to die or lose control of our own will, so it seems to me more than a fair tradeoff.

"Under some extremely rare circumstances, the infected person doesn't turn, but instead becomes a living, breathing fountain of youth, if you will." She glanced back at Ruby. "I believe our girl here may very well be one of those exceptional cases. Of course, if she does prove to be *special*, she will be sent off to someone much higher in the pecking order than I am." Her lips pursed, and she shrugged. "There is a hierarchy to all this, after all, an organization much larger and more well connected than you'd perhaps believe. In spite of my movie star status, I guess I'm what you might consider middle management. So, even if she is one of the special cases, I would still have room for you in our little enterprise."

"And if she ain't?"

"Then she will have to be destroyed long before she completes the change. We're being extra careful with her." She pointed at the warped gurney. "We were a tad too slow with her pretty boyfriend. He, too, had shown promise, but . . . Well, suffice it to say that if he hadn't been so beautiful to look at, we might have moved sooner. We just had such high hopes for him."

"You killed the boy?" A sense of disappointment flooded Bayard. He would've liked to see what the kid looked like on the inside.

"No. I'm afraid his change came too quickly. He overpowered his keeper. Drained him as dry as a nun's knickers, and escaped." She turned on him, one eyebrow raised and her eyes narrow and angry. "The boy surprised us all. It usually takes them much longer to regain full control of their bodies. It isn't like there's a prescribed timetable for any of this."

It sounded to Bayard like she was trying to defend herself, like she thought he'd been finding fault with her, but then her gaze softened and fell away.

"Still, it's odd that his case was the first time our precautions failed so completely. I've been left to wonder if the boy's keeper himself didn't play a role in the escape. Love does lead one to do the craziest things." She held up her hand as if trying to silence a protest. "Not to worry. He will be caught and captured. And when we do, he will be disposed of quickly. It's a bit of a shame, though. He's probably the first unattended vampire in two, perhaps three hundred years. Part of me would like to see what he'd get up to. But no, he's fully turned. It would be too dangerous to *play* with him.

"However"—she licked her lips and looked at him through sparkling eyes—"when they are in this halfway state," she said, motioning toward Ruby, "they're so helpless. So compliant. You can take your time with them, you know. Before they turn, they're a bit disoriented, graceless. Their muscles simply won't do what their brains tell them to do, because, well, because they are dying, leaving the poor dears incredibly strong, but incapable of harnessing that strength. Still, they can survive trauma most ordinary people cannot."

She drew a step or two closer. "Imagine it. As long as you leave her heart and head intact, you could take your pretty miss apart piece by piece, and she could be there *with you* as you did it. Of course, she needs her head to feel your passion. And leaving the heart untouched will let her body react to stimulus. You wouldn't want her to just lie there." She winked. "Or then again, maybe you would." She paused just beyond his reach. "Of course, as I've said, she may be bound for greater glory, but we could build you a new toy for your games. I'm afraid your friend the deliveryman has already been extinguished, but we could have great fun with your other pal."

Bayard felt his pulse begin to pound as a portion of his blood supply headed south beneath his belt buckle. He'd often wondered just which part of Frank he'd cut off first, if he ever found a reason to start cutting. Her eyes fixed on him, making so many promises. She had seen into the darkest recesses of his soul, and was tugging the twisted roots of his desires out into the light of day. "Shall we go fetch your friend?' she asked as his mouth went dry.

He wished now that he hadn't hesitated when the door to the white room eased silently open behind her back. He wished his mouth had opened to warn her. He should have gone with his gut, but he'd stalled like an overheated car. "No need. I'm already here," Frank said from behind her. She spun toward the door, and Frank put a bullet deftly into each of her eyes. The second took the back of her skull clean off, and her exquisite body fell dead to the beautiful concrete floor, where it continued to twitch for much longer than it should have.

FORTY-THREE

Bayard stood with his head cocked back and tilted a little to one side. His cheeks were flushed as he watched Frank through barely open slits. His tongue hung limp over his bottom lip. Frank had only seen his partner look at him like this once before—that day in Hollywood, when he knew Bayard had nursed some serious thoughts about killing him. Frank sat stock-still, trying to figure out just what his next move should be. He tried to focus on the situation at hand, but the memory of that day in California kept pushing its way into his mind, like it had some kind of answer to give him.

Frank had come to, snapped out of whatever spell Myrna King had put on him. When he did, Bayard was gone, and Frank didn't have a clue what had happened to him. Deep in his gut he knew that Crane was dead, and he suspected his partner might be too.

Frank had no idea what was going on in this house, what Ruby had gotten herself caught up in, but there was no way in hell he'd just roll over and die without taking that Myrna bitch, and anyone else she might have helping her, with him. He pulled a knife from his pocket and started to cut strips from the heavy golden drapes that had so fascinated him earlier. When Frank had a good pile lying on the floor, he crossed the room and pulled the door on a liquor cabinet that stood in the corner. Finding it locked, he slid his pistol from its holster and used its handle to smash the glass. He grabbed a decanter and took a good swig before emptying half its contents on the sofa. He knelt on the floor next to the shredded fabric and stuffed the strips into the decanter until the remaining booze had been absorbed and the bottle itself was full.

He stood and fished his cigarette lighter out of his pocket, flicking the wheel until it lit. He held the flame beneath the portion of the drapes that still hung in the window, and they caught fire as if turning to ash had been their lifelong dream. As they fell away, he noticed something that he hadn't from the outside: the windows were barred by decorative but functional wrought iron. If that were true of all of them, there was one less option for escape. He probably should've formed a more coherent plan before acting, but it was too late to worry about that now. He had no choice other than to carry on with the course to which he'd committed, and he couldn't deny that a part of him liked it when there was no turning back.

He made his way to the door, stopping only to light the couch's alcohol-drenched fabric. He watched a race of blue flames spring into life, but then the smoke began to burn his eyes. He stepped out of the burning room and closed the door behind him.

The hall was empty, but by the way the hairs on the back of his neck raised up against his collar, Frank knew he wasn't alone. After the brightness in the other room—both from the flames and the light streaming in through the window—it took some moments for his vision to adjust to the relative darkness of the hall. He moved to the side of the hall, pressing his back against the wall.

Although smoke had not yet seeped into the hall, its aroma was unmistakable. Instinct drove him in the opposite direction from which he'd come. If Bayard was still alive, he wouldn't have just turned tail and run. Bayard was nothing if not single-minded. He would have gone looking for Ruby. Then, at the end of the corridor, Frank perceived three figures blocking the exit he would have needed to use if he'd intended on making a simple escape. Maybe it was just a trick of the shadow, but Frank could've sworn their eyes glowed with a faint silver-blue light. The three moved in unison toward him, then stopped as if they'd hit an invisible wall.

They turned toward the door Frank had closed on the burning room. The one closest to it reached for the knob, but hissed as the hot metal burned his hand. The second, evidently braver than the first, twisted the knob and flung the door wide, shrieking as the heat of the flames flooded out around him. Smoke billowed into the hall, blocking the three from Frank's sight, but he could still hear them. In addition to cursing like any angry man would, they hissed . . . a sound you'd never expect to hear from a person. They shouted for the King woman, and Frank glanced around him to see if she were near, but she was nowhere to be seen.

Through the smoke, three pairs of faint lights were approaching. One set moved low to the ground, as if they were slithering across the floor. The second approached along the side of the hall, and the third shone down from the ceiling. The smoke parted, revealing the three men with glowing eyes—one of whom was indeed crawling along the floor, while the second clawed its way along the wall, and the third hung upside down from the ceiling.

Frank began sliding down the hall, trying to maintain the space separating him from these otherworldly apparitions, one hand clamped onto the rag-stuffed bottle, the other cradling his lighter. He began to spin the wheel of the lighter, sending a shower of sparks into the haze, but the lighter refused to produce a flame. "Shit," Frank said under his breath, realizing it was out of fuel. He let the cool metal slip from his sweaty hand. He flung the decanter, managing to bean one of the trio, but it didn't have the explosive effect he'd been counting on. He reached for his pistol and fired three quick shots, one right between each pair of glowing silver-blue eyes. Each shot met its mark, and the lights faded in quick succession.

He sped down the hall, stepping into each room on the way, gun first. Each was empty. No Crane. No Ruby and no Bayard either. Chances were indeed good that all three were dead by now. He was about to give up and settle on finding his own way to safety when he saw it. One room, near the end of the hall, looked different from the rest. Its door stood out, looking more like something from a factory than a house. He gripped his pistol in his right hand and carefully slid the door open. He found himself standing face-to-face with Bayard in some kind of white-tiled kitchen or something. Myrna was standing with her back to Frank, like she'd been gift wrapped. She turned. Frank pulled the trigger, thinking he was saving Bayard, but the look that came over Bayard's face was one of total loss, loss that hardened into hatred and a desire to do harm. A desire to draw blood. In that moment, Frank had thought he might have to use his last bullet on Bayard himself, but then his longtime partner had stood down.

◆　◆　◆

That day, Bayard had seemed unsure of himself. Now, it struck Frank, Bayard had come to some kind of decision. Yes, there was no denying it. The look Bayard was giving Frank now was the same one he'd given him after he'd plugged the King bitch. Though Frank was unsure of the reasons behind Bayard's renewed deliberation, Frank felt certain of the outcome. *Who knows?* Frank wondered silently. *Maybe it was always going to come down to this, even if we'd never gone to California.*

"Gentlemen." A voice from the porch snapped Frank out of his thoughts. He craned his neck to see around Bayard. It was that nurse. Frank crawled out of the car and circled his partner. He hadn't really gotten a good gander at her before. In spite of everything, Frank found himself appraising her. She was a sturdy-looking thing. Frank figured she could take a good hard ride. His eyes drifted up from her hips to consider her ample bosom. Her hair, brown, was pulled back, leaving her ears to stick out a little too much for his liking. Her face was plain, but not unattractive. She tilted her head forward a tad, so those serious gray eyes met his. Something in them warned him the news would be bad. Frank's attention turned to Bayard as Bayard took a few halting steps toward the porch. "If you wouldn't mind coming in?" she said.

Hell yes, he would mind going back in there. Frank remembered the shrieks Ruby had made as he dragged her out of the King house and into the sunlight. She hadn't shut up until long after they'd closed her up in the cool of the van, the same van they'd ended up driving clear across the country back to Conroy. He could face whatever was about to go down between himself and Bayard, but there was no way in hell he'd face anything like that ever again. If the Judge had taken a turn in that direction, well . . .

"Everything all right?" he asked, trying to maintain his cool.

"He's dead," Bayard called out, "ain't he?"

Corinne's head nodded once in response.

"Then there ain't much more that we can do around here," Frank said and looked at Bayard. "How about it?"

Bayard nodded. "Could we go down to the river? The bend where we used to swim when we were kids?"

A slight smile curled on Frank's lips. So the old swimming hole was where Bayard intended to end it. "Sure thing, buddy. Anywhere you like." He held out his hand. "But give me the keys. I want to drive."

FORTY-FOUR

"I've called the funeral home, to have them come for the body," Corinne said, placing her hand gingerly on Lucille's shoulder. "If Dr. McAvoy wants to examine the body before signing the certificate of death, he can do so at the mortician's." It was hot, and the body soon would begin to give off an unpleasant odor. There was no need for anyone to suffer through an unnecessary indignity. "They're sending a car over." She had sensed no attachment to the Judge on Lucille's part, but the maid had insisted on sitting with the body. Corrine reminded herself that not everyone had grown as inured to death as she had. For some, it still held a kind of mystical or sacred import. For her, after witnessing the death of so many, it was just another passing. She'd watched younger and—judging by the company he kept—better men die.

"I'll stay with him till they get here." Lucille looked over her shoulder and placed her hand on Corinne's.

Corinne nodded. "I'm sorry for your loss."

Lucille turned in her chair until the two women were facing each other. "Oh, it is no loss to me. That man. He thought he owned me. He swore he'd never let me leave him." She turned back to face the sheet-covered corpse. "No, this here is my emancipation. This here is my Independence Day. And I ain't taking my eyes off of him until they cart him out of here feet first." Lucille paused, her complexion going gray. "I'm sorry, Miss. It was wicked of me to say such a thing." Her dark eyes moistened. "Please don't tell anyone."

"Of course not. I understand." Corinne didn't understand, but having never been in a position similar to Lucille's, she couldn't. "I'll be downstairs. I'll let the funeral people in when they arrive."

The women locked eyes for a moment. Corinne sensed there were a great many things Lucille wanted to share with her, but the other woman's lips pulled tight and she looked away. In spite of the heat, Corinne felt a sudden chill. She pulled her arms tight around herself. That was when she noticed the scent. Not the normal smell of decomposition, but some sort of spice. No. An incense. Myrrh. *The odor of sanctity.* Catechisms, long thought excised from her soul, rose up before conscious thoughts.

She forced herself to shake off the sense of dread that had begun to descend on her. "I'll be downstairs." She was repeating herself, but Lucille didn't seem to notice. She stepped out of the room, closing the door quietly behind her, and made her way down the hall, the sound of insistent knocking causing her to hurry down the stairs. It was still full light outside, but the sun had passed over to the far side of the house, leaving its entryway gloomy. She switched on a lamp to bring light to the shadowy hall.

She had expected to see a proper mortician in a black suit. The two young men looking back at her through the door's upper window certainly didn't match her expectations. Of course, who knew what passed for proper in these parts? They both wore wide-brimmed hats and dirty, long-sleeved shirts that looked more like you'd expect to see on factory workers. The oddest thing was that both had wool scarves tied around their necks.

"We're here for the Judge," the one closest to the window said.

She opened the door.

"Where is he?"

Corinne was even more surprised to see that both men were wearing gardening gloves. "Come in. The body," she said, feeling uneasy, "is upstairs. Shall I show you?"

"Not necessary," the second man said. "We'll find him." As they trudged up the stairs and vanished into the Judge's room, Corrine turned to shut the door, gasping out loud when she saw that, rather than a hearse, the mortician had sent the men in a red pickup truck that was a dead ringer for the one that horrible Charlie Aarons man drove.

She barely had time to shake off her surprise when the two reappeared at the top of the stairs. They'd rolled the Judge's body up in a sheet from his own bed, and the studier of the two had hefted the corpse over his shoulders. Corinne struggled to hide her distaste, but a part of her felt she should voice an objection. Lucille followed behind them, a confused look on her face.

One of the men brushed past Corinne and opened the door; then the one bearing the Judge strode out without a single word. "Ladies," the first said and doffed his hat before closing the door behind them.

Lucille turned to Corinne, her mouth agape, a crease running down the center of her forehead. "Miss, I thought you called the funeral parlor."

"Well, I did . . ." Corinne said, flustered.

"Then why did they send those Sleiger boys?"

FORTY-FIVE

McAvoy came to, cold and hurting. He didn't know where he was, but he felt earth beneath him. He struggled up to his side, then onto his knees. Something held him by the leg.

He was surrounded by absolute darkness. No, there to his left, a pair of tiny blue flames burned, but they illuminated nothing. He tried to make out their source, but gave up as a wave of nausea hit him. He then registered the fact that his head felt as if it had been crushed in a vise. When he reached around to the back of his head to search for the source of the throbbing, he felt the stickiness of congealed blood. He listened to the sound of his own breathing, trying to piece together what had happened. The last thing he could remember was being pummeled by the Sleiger boys. *What in the hell possessed them?*

A loud whistle sounded, and white sparks floated up before his eyes. He winced in pain. He knew that sound. It was a train wailing out its approach. The length of the whistle's shriek told him it was probably drawing near the unprotected crossing just south of Conroy, as conductors familiar with the line liked to give a good long warning before reaching that point.

He managed to stand, pushing himself up from what his hands told him was a dirt floor, but felt a cold bite on his ankle when he tried to take a step. He bent over and felt around. A chain. He'd been chained by the leg to an iron loop set in a large concrete block. He tugged on the chain, but it was a hopeless endeavor. He licked his lips, preparing to call out and see if anyone might come to his rescue, but before he could make a sound, a familiar voice reached his ears.

"You wouldn't believe how they tortured him. I listened to his screaming again and again. It must have gone on for hours. It may have gone on for days. I don't know. It all blurred together after a while."

McAvoy clutched his chest, very nearly teetering over. It was Ruby's voice, although it sounded different than when he'd last heard it, drier and with a slight rasp. Still, it was unmistakable.

"Tortured?" His voice croaked, but his question would go unanswered.

"He was so smart," Ruby said. "So beautiful. So bored. You purchased the pleasure of his body, and when your money stopped being enticement enough for him, you introduced the drugs to keep him dependent on you."

"I couldn't bear the thought of losing him," McAvoy confessed, guilt bringing hot tears to his night-blinded eyes. "He would've never left on his own. Not if he hadn't had you to prop him up."

"He didn't belong in a town like Conroy. Neither of us did. It was his idea to get away from here. To get away from you. He said we could be stars. God, what a cliché." Ruby let loose a mirthless laugh. "We left here hoping to make something of ourselves, but there were others out there who were even worse than you. Hollywood chewed us up and spat us out. And what can I say? The studios didn't come calling." Her words slowed, her voice grew more faint. "The money went so quick. And the drugs were everywhere. We both ended up selling ourselves—sometimes for the cash, sometimes for release. Sometimes separate, sometimes together." For several moments there was silence. "When the great

Myrna King took an interest in us, I thought maybe, just maybe, things would work out after all." A bitter laughter filled the unfathomable darkness around him. "I figured maybe my face wasn't meant for the silver screen after all, but there would be other ways a girl like me could get ahead. I couldn't wait to meet her fancy friends. To learn *all . . .*"—the word danced in the darkness—". . . their secrets." Her cold, glowing eyes pierced his soul. "Oh, and I learned their secrets all right. All of them."

McAvoy began weaving under the weight of his guilt. He rocked back and forth in the darkness, moaning until the words finally came to him. "What did they do to you out there?" He had intended to ask what they had done to Dylan, but his courage failed him.

"They turned me into this." Her voice boomed as the light of her eyes swooped in on him. He flung his arms up before his face to hide himself from those lights. "Or at least they started the process. You finished it."

"When you came back, you were so ill. You would be fine one moment, and then you'd start speaking absolute nonsense and the darkest of slander the next."

"But that isn't why you killed me, is it, Doctor? It wasn't because you were afraid that I might speak the truth about you. It was because I took Dylan from you."

"I gave you a gentle death." His voice trembled. He felt a cold hand brush his swollen cheek.

"I'm sure you'll understand why I can't find it in my heart to return the favor." The intense beam of a flashlight burst to life, the brightness stunning his eyes. The light traced along the floor to find a bundle wrapped in a white sheet. "It may take hours or it may take days, but when he wakes up, he'll be awfully hungry." Something metallic skidded along the floor and bumped up against his foot. The flashlight's beam shifted to the spot. It was a straight razor, its blade glinting in the light. "If I were you, I'd use this on myself before he comes to." And then the light died.

FORTY-SIX

Bell was left to do the driving. Rigby, his damned fool of a deputy, had been nearly in a trance since they'd left the Dunne farm. Bell tried to cut Rigby some slack. He'd grown up with Elijah Dunne, even spent time out on the family's farm. But the deputy had been misfiring on all his cylinders for days. Maybe he just wasn't cut out for police work, and maybe it was getting near time to tell him so. Bell needed to find Elijah first, see to it that justice was served, and then he'd deal with Rigby.

The Dunnes were both dead. And it wasn't either of them who'd done the shooting, since they found the gun a good fifteen yards from the bodies, lying out in the yard in a pile of women's clothing. That left Bell to think he must have been wrong about the boy. He would've bet his bottom dollar Elijah was as innocent as a lamb, but he should've known better. Should've seen the signs. Something had caused Elijah to snap. The sheriff had seen it happen to soldiers before, after World War II. Young men would come back changed by battle, unable to flip the switch and return to the niceties of peacetime. Yes, the more Bell pondered the recent turn of events, there could be no doubt about it: Elijah had killed his best friends, and now his parents.

Old Charlie Aarons had been dragged from his home and ripped apart in the woods that separated the house from the Dunne farm. That brought the murder count up to at least five. The Sleiger brothers were still missing, so they'd likely been casualties of Elijah's madness, too. Bell didn't need any more headaches, but as he turned the wide curve down by River Road, he realized he had another problem.

"Up ahead," Bell said, tapping the dashboard to get Rigby's attention. About a hundred yards in front of them, at the bend, the car he recognized as belonging to Frank Mason had taken on an ancient oak and lost. "Damn it," Bell said, easing the patrol car up behind the wrecked vehicle. He put the car in park, and scratched his head as he leaned out the window. "Stay here," he ordered Rigby, although there was nothing to indicate the deputy had planned on moving.

He swung open his door and climbed out, pausing for a moment to take in a breath as his feet contacted the earth. He ambled toward the car, not really wanting to get close enough to see what had become of the Judge's boys. The car's passenger side had clipped the oak, so he made his way to the driver's side. The seat was empty, but what was left of Bayard was slumped over in the seat next to it. His head had connected with the dashboard and busted open like an overripe melon.

"Not quite sure what happened, Sheriff." A voice caused Bell to turn, nearly jump. Frank Mason was reclining in the tall grass only a few feet from the wreck, smoking a cigarette. "I think maybe someone messed with the steering." Frank inserted the cigarette between his lips and scrambled to his feet. "Don't suppose you could give me a ride into town?"

Bell bit his lip. Frank and Bayard had been partners for years and, Bell believed, friends since boyhood. Still, Frank showed no distress over Bayard's demise. "Can't do that, son," Bell replied. "I'll radio in for an ambulance to fetch your buddy, but since you can still walk, I ain't got time to taxi you around. I've got a man out there killing just about everyone close to him."

"Really?" Frank's eyes lit up with interest. Bell forced himself not to react. He turned and took determined strides back to the patrol car, the sound of Frank's footfalls alerting Bell to the fact that he was being followed. He looked back over his shoulder and reached in to grab the radio's microphone.

"Who you looking for?" Frank asked, craning his neck to get a gander at Rigby.

To hell with it. "Elijah Dunne, know him?"

Frank straightened. "Course. He and Ruby used to date."

Yes, of course, that makes sense, Bell thought to himself.

"His new woman, the nurse, she's out at the Judge's house right now."

Bell flung the radio's microphone back to the seat, striking Rigby. The deputy didn't react. Bell jumped in and slammed the door behind him. He cranked the engine and shifted into reverse to clear the wrecked vehicle, then peeled out forward, leaving Frank in a cloud of dust.

FORTY-SEVEN

The patrol car sent a piece of gravel shooting straight into Frank's shin. "Son of a bitch!" Frank yelped in pain and bent over to grab his leg. The stone's sharp edge had connected hard enough to put a hole in his pants and take a bite out of his skin. "Son of a bitch," Frank repeated, this time thinking of the officer who'd caused his problem.

Frank started limping down the dusty road toward Conroy. He cursed the sheriff, cursed the heat, then cursed the damned horsefly that had begun buzzing him, dogging his every step. His hand managed to connect with the fly, swatting it hard to the ground, where it rested on its back for a couple of seconds, only to begin kicking its legs and rocking itself back into an upright position. Its wings began to flutter, and Frank raised his foot to crush it when a singular thought stopped him. "That you, buddy?" he asked. He knew it was madness, but for the tiniest slice of a second he wondered if it might be possible that Bayard had slipped into this pest. But no, that was just regret speaking.

There hadn't been a choice, not really. He'd known from Bayard's expression that it was finally time. All those wrestling matches and drunken fistfights between them that had ended in draws, neither of them managing to piss any higher on the tree than the other. They'd both always wondered, and they'd both always known, they'd have to scratch that itch someday to find out. Frank had long suspected it would come down to smarts, in which case he'd win. But not knowing, well, that was what kept life interesting. Now a part of him was missing. Killing Bayard had felt a lot like cutting off his own right arm. *If thine eye offend thee*—words from a nearly forgotten Sunday school lesson flitted back from nowhere, buzzing around him like the horsefly that was once again circling, a tad more distant than before.

He carried on down the road, still swatting at the bug but with less vehemence, until he registered the sound of an approaching car. A blue station wagon piloted by a prim middle-aged woman with puckered lips and disapproving eyes moved just fast enough to kick up a low thin cloud of dust around it. He clambered out into the road and waved his hands to signal her to stop. She hit the gas and swerved clean but close around him. He jumped back. "Son of a bitch," he repeated for the third time, like he intended to seal a charm.

He was about to set off again when another vehicle came around the bend. This one slowed as it approached him, though he hadn't even tried to catch the driver's eye. Two young guys in a rusting red pickup.

"That your car back there?" the one on the passenger side leaned out the window and asked him. It was one of the Sleiger brothers. Frank thought it was Wayne, but he didn't know the boys all that well.

"Yes. Yes it is." Frank noted that they seemed dressed for deep winter, even though it was probably ninety-five degrees in the shade. At the same moment, the fly that had been circling him zipped away like it suddenly remembered it had a previous appointment.

The two men turned to face each other and exchanged a few words that Frank couldn't make out, then the passenger stuck a gloved hand out the side and motioned with his thumb to the bed of the pickup. "Hop in back. We'll drive you into town."

Frank hesitated, but only for a moment. "Much obliged," he called out, and hefted himself over the side of the truck and onto the bed.

FORTY-EIGHT

Elijah moved like a man in dream, seeming to watch himself from the outside, from a distance. When his mother's body slumped down, the pistol fell and skidded along the floor, sliding right up to the toe of his boot. Without thinking, he picked it up and placed it in Corinne's suitcase, piling in the rest of her belongings along with it. He closed the case and sealed the latches. He grabbed the handle, and without looking down, he turned and stepped over the man he had once believed to be his father.

He exited the house, dragging his feet so that he tripped and tumbled down the back stairs. He landed on his hands and knees, the suitcase hitting its side and tumbling some feet away. He stood, surprised to see his jeans had torn and his knee was bleeding. He felt no pain. He felt cold. Very cold. He bent over and reached for the case, missing its handle once, twice, before clutching it, but as he lifted the handle, the case fell open, Corinne's clothes—and the gun—tumbling back down to the ground. He dropped the case and walked away, his only goal to reach the truck.

He knew he should go find Corinne. Take her away from this place. Never set foot in Mississippi again. Yes. He would do that. But first, there was one place he had to see once more, almost like he was being called there. Almost like he had to go there to break a spell that had been put on him.

He wove across the gray grass to the drive where his father's—Clay's—truck was sitting. This time he didn't meander. He drove straight to the Cooper house, but he very nearly didn't stop. Still he killed the truck's ignition.

It all looked wrong. That smell he'd noticed before inside the house had filtered out so that the air seemed dirty with it. The world felt strange. Time moved too quickly, the sun sliding across the sky in what seemed to Elijah to be mere minutes.

The pull to come here had been strong, irresistible even, but now that he sat before the house, his stomach churned. It wasn't the smell that nauseated him. It was all those times he'd tried to get Ruby out here alone, hoping his friend the hoot owl might offer an encore performance. Thank God she'd been too prissy to drink stolen shine and wrestle in the back of a truck bed at an abandoned house. His hand trembled as he ran it over his beard. He'd almost bedded his own sister. Sowed his seed in her.

They'd come close—many, many times. His manhood pressed tight against her, only a few layers of spun cotton between them and incest. She had always stopped him. She wanted to wait, she would remind him, until they were man and wife. Man and wife. Right now he couldn't decide whom he hated more. The Judge? Clay? Or maybe his own mother. She'd knowingly let him carry on with his own sister. He hated Clay for lying to him to cause him to break things off with Ruby, but hell, at least the man had done something. In his own horrible way.

He watched purple shadows fall and claim the world around him. Did the Judge know he was his father? He must have some suspicions. Elijah's eyes darted to the rearview mirror, using the last few moments of twilight to scan his reflection in search of any traces of the Judge. Ruby had inherited the Judge's dark coloring and fine features. Elijah looked exactly the opposite. Blond hair. Blue eyes. Strong, nearly hooked nose. High forehead. None of these features marked him as Ovid Lowell's boy. Maybe the Judge figured if Ava had spread her legs so willingly for him, she'd spread them for a lot of other guys, too. No. It was entirely possible the Judge didn't have an inkling.

His eyes were still affixed to their own reflection when he thought he heard a man call out, with more than just a touch of fear in his cry. Probably just an owl, but still Elijah dropped his gaze and spun around to search for the sound's source, surprised to see the dusk around him lit up by a whirling, fiery red light.

A patrol car, its siren silent, but its beacon burning, was pulling up to the house. It came to a stop, and its driver killed its engine. "I told you he was probably out here," said the voice of his one-time buddy, muffled only by the drone of crickets he hadn't even taken note of moments before.

"Yep, boy," the sheriff's gravelly voice rumbled. "You might not be a total waste of county funds after all."

FORTY-NINE

"Looks like the boys are putting in overtime," Barbara Jean said as she swept into the diner. She removed her head scarf to reveal a freshly peroxided mound of hair, parted in the center with massive curls on each side of the part. "This darned fog is gonna ruin my hair." She patted the side of her head. Annie couldn't see through the thick haze that had swallowed the diner, but she could see through Barbara Jean; she was fishing for a compliment.

Annie focused on the milky white pressing up against the window and made a show of refilling a customer's coffee. Barbara Jean was late. "The mill has 'em working double shifts," Annie said. "At least that's what I heard earlier."

Barbara Jean dashed behind the counter and slid her purse, a flashy turquoise bucket bag with a poodle appliqué, onto the shelf beneath the cash register. "Just let me grab an apron," she called to Annie before she slipped into the kitchen. She took her precious time making her way back. She came out, still working on tying her apron.

"Merle tell you the sheriff came by today?" Annie asked. Barbara Jean looked at her with widening eyes. Annie knew Barbara Jean's surprise didn't stem from the sheriff's visit. Without a doubt, word about Dowd's and Bob's grisly deaths had spread over half the county within minutes of the sheriff's visit. Annie knew that what surprised Barbara was that Annie would volunteer to talk about it. To be honest, Annie was a bit surprised at herself. It wasn't like her to gossip, but something about the way the fog blotted out the sun left her less than less than happy to be on her own. She couldn't understand it. Usually Annie liked the fog. She liked how it hid her from everyone, and how it hid the sight of Conroy from her, obliterating the familiar landmarks and erasing the foolish faces.

"Oh, darlin', that is old news," Barbara Jean said with a shake of her newly minted curls. "The latest is that someone messed around with Frank Mason's car. Got wrapped around a tree. Bayard's dead. And ain't nobody seen Frank." She tapped the side of her nose with her index finger. "Looks like justice was served."

"I don't understand," Annie said, untying her own apron.

"I'm just saying that someone must've finally decided those two boys went too far. Dowd and Bobby. They had friends around here."

"But," Annie said, disappointment setting in, "I thought the sheriff figured Charlie Aarons was behind Dowd and Bob." All afternoon, she'd been playing out a scene in her head, a scene where the sheriff came by her house, alone, just to thank her for the tip she'd given him. She'd invite him in. Offer him a cup of coffee. He'd accept and tell her it was the finest cup of coffee he'd had in forever. He'd say Mrs. Bell could learn a thing or two from her, and he'd place his hand on her hip . . .

"Darlin', I don't know what you're going on about. What would that half-blind old coot have to do with any of this?" She approached Annie, coming closer than she ever had. Annie didn't like her nearness. She began to take a step back when Barbara Jean leaned in and whispered. "No. You mark my words. The Judge and his boys are on their way out around here. When it all comes out in the wash, we're gonna find out things are changing. Out with the old, in with the new. There's a new boss in town. We'll know who soon."

Barbara Jean spun around, leaving Annie to fold her apron. Annie went behind the counter to retrieve her purse from her customary pigeonhole. She emptied the cup, where she kept her tips, into the purse and, without another word, made her way out of the diner and into the mist.

Eight blocks, only eight blocks east and three blocks south, between the diner and her home. Even when she took her time, when she let herself lapse into a daydream about how life could be, it took her at most ten minutes or so. Tonight she set out with a quick and determined pace, the Elks Lodge next to the diner soon swallowed by the mists behind her, the Woolworth coming into view. She cast a glance in through the window. The store was closed, but she could see a young fellow sweeping and another stocking goods on a shelf. Walt Kimble, the man she recognized as the manager, stood by the open cash register. Walt was a regular at the diner. He'd brought the boys by, too, for lunch just this afternoon. As she passed, the three stopped their actions and walked in unison to the window. They stood side by side, staring at her. Annie looked away and picked up her pace.

There weren't many people on the street. That was good. She nodded at the women she knew by name. When a man passed, she turned her gaze downward. She didn't fear they'd leer or make an advance under the cover of the fog. She feared their eyes would fall on her, and they'd hurry away.

Four blocks. Only four more blocks. She'd turn onto her street. Soon she'd be home. She'd make a cup of tea. Just like every night. Maybe tonight she'd do something special. Put a splash of her father's leftover bourbon in it. She'd put on her mother's robe, pull the cat onto her lap . . . no, of course, she'd poisoned the cat. She patted the pocket in her uniform, to feel the bottle of thallium still there. She decided then and there that tonight would be the last night she'd face alone. Tomorrow she'd wait till the lunch shift when the place was full of those dirty mill workers. Then she'd slip it in. A bit in the coffee. A bit in the stew. A bit in the gravy. Maybe she wouldn't get many of them, but she'd take more than a few with her. They'd know then. All of them. They'd know how badly they'd hurt her. And by God, they'd be sorry.

But the best part was that it would finally be over. All over. She'd never hear another snicker. Never hear a whispered word of sympathy. *Bless her heart.* Never catch the sight of her own ugly reflection.

A man's hand caught hold of her arm, and she jumped back. Over the years, the few hands that had reached out for her were always rough in their handling, intending to taunt or terrify her, never to caress or soothe. She didn't scream. She'd learned not to. Something about screaming egged them on. Still her heart pounded.

"Hold up," he said as she tugged, trying to free herself from his grasp.

"Let go of me," she snapped, realizing that the man who held her was no man at all. It was Merle, the teenager who washed dishes at the diner. Something was off about him, though. Merle had dark eyes. But here in this foggy twilight they now appeared to be filled with tiny blue sparks.

Merle held tight.

"Let go of me. What do you want?" She gave another hard tug, and she slipped from his grasp.

"She wants to know why you won't help her."

"What are you going on about? Help who?" She pulled her arms around herself and stepped back.

"Miss Ruby," the boy said, his spotted face leaning in close.

Annie had had enough of the boy. She only knew one Ruby in Conroy. "You talking about the Judge's Ruby?"

Merle nodded.

"You're crazy, you know. Ruby Lowell is dead. Has been for months now." She turned, but again she felt his hand on her. It slid into and from her pocket before she could react.

"I knew you had it." He held the bottle up before her eyes. "I guessed what you were intending when I saw your cat losing its fur." He shook the bottle. "You have enough for one or two people maybe, but you don't have anyone close to you. That meant you planned on taking a bunch of folk with you, but you don't have enough to kill everybody. Not here. You'd end up cutting it too much to take a bunch of folk out quickly." He held the bottle out to her. "Besides, in small doses this stuff takes time. I went to the library in Tupelo. Read up about it. That's why I never told the sheriff about it. But when Miss Ruby came to me, I told her about it. I told her about you."

She reached out to snatch away the bottle, but Merle was too fast, sweeping it back beyond her grasp. He smiled, then again held the bottle out, this time letting it drop without guile into her palm. She shoved it into her pocket. "Ruby is dead. And you're crazy."

"No," Merle replied, his sparkling eyes taking on an intensity she'd only seen before in Pentecostal tent revivals. "They put her in a casket, but she wasn't dead. Not really. Not in the way you and me think of as dead. I know, you see, 'cause we live right next to the cemetery. One night, I just felt her. Standing out there in the moonlight. She's my friend now, so I told her about you. She got the idea from you."

Annie felt the pulse in her neck, even as her extremities turned cold. "What idea?"

"To use the diner. See, if she's right there with you, looking at you, there ain't no way you can refuse her. She's too beautiful to say no to. You love her too much." His expression softened, his eyes took on a distant, smitten look. "You'd do anything for her. Give her anything." He tilted his head and leaned in as if he were about to make a confession. "But if she ain't with a person, she can't make 'em do as she wants 'em to. Until you taste her. Once you taste her"—his tongue slid out and ran slowly across his lower lip—"she owns you." He reached out, squeezing her hand. "You gave her the idea to spike the food with her blood, so everyone who eats at the diner will do as she wants 'em to, without her having to be right there watching over 'em." His voice grew quiet. "You handed her the goddamned key to the city"—he paused, squinting at her—"but you never eat what the diner serves. You never, even once, eat at the diner."

"Of course not," she said, growing angry. "I've been in the kitchen."

Merle laughed, although she meant it as a sincere explanation. "It doesn't matter now anyway," he said, as a pickup truck turned on to the street and came to a halt next to them. It took her a second, but she recognized it as belonging to old man Aarons. There were two men inside, though. Her stomach lurched as she recognized the Sleiger boys. The doors to the truck opened, even though they left the engine running.

Annie broke out into a cold sweat. "You two best get out of here and leave me be," she called out as they drew near. "The sheriff, he's looking for you." She felt her body tensing, preparing to run if they took a single step closer.

"Don't be afraid," Merle said, his voice calm, soothing. "Miss Ruby, she's got a special reward for you. You're gonna serve her. She's chosen you as her handmaiden. She's gonna take you herself, and when you wake up, you'll never have to worry about growing old or dying. Ever again. You'll live forever. As long as you please her. As long as you serve her."

"But I don't want to live forever," Annie said, bursting into tears.

"Don't be silly," Merle said, "nobody wants to grow old and die. Everybody wants to live forever."

"Not in this body. Not with this face." Before she could take a step, the Sleiger boys had her and were stuffing her into the cab of the truck. In that moment, she believed what Merle had told her. The realization of what was about to happen to her slapped her across the face, and as it did, she let herself scream, not even caring if the Sleigers enjoyed the sound of her cry.

FIFTY

Francis examined her reflection. She wore her favorite robe, a faded rose one Dylan had chosen as a Christmas present for her some years ago, back before he had picked up any of his bad habits. Back when he was still her little sweet-faced angel boy. She tugged the side of her curler cap down, and twisted off the lid of her cold cream. She applied a dab on the forehead, then smoothed the cream into an even coat. A dab on each cheek, on the chin. She gently worked the cream up, then ran her hands under warm water.

It had taken her an hour in a hot tub to help her relax after nearly hitting the fool who'd been standing in the road. She'd barely managed to swerve in time. She forced the thought from her head. No use getting herself all worked up again over it.

She tightened her robe and turned off the light, padding down the stairs in her new slippers. The old ones, the ones her husband had bought her as an anniversary present before he grew ill, had worn clean through, so she found a new pair that somewhat resembled them. She wouldn't allow the unfamiliar to creep into her house. When Dylan finally returned, she wanted him to feel at home, to know this was where he belonged.

Oh, how she rued the day she allowed that Ruby girl beneath her roof. Originally, she had approved of a liaison between them. It seemed like the two might be a good match, both socially—Ruby was, after all, the daughter of a judge—and physically, too. Her dark eyes and raven hair were diametrically opposed to Dylan's Apollo-like radiance, though her features were indeed exquisite. But her beauty didn't go any deeper than what a body could see. Ruby had been a carnal girl, lacking entirely in spiritual and intellectual qualities, a taste for which she had done her best to cultivate in Dylan. Francis watched helplessly as the horrid girl dragged her beautiful son down, forcing her attentions on Dylan. Seducing him. Soiling him. Stealing him away.

Francis did what she could to intervene. She even had Reverend Miller come and speak to the youth and try to appeal to his higher nature, but the change in Dylan happened all too quickly. Francis could never have imagined that Ruby's despicable influence would act with such alacrity, undoing a loving mother's years of guidance seemingly overnight.

Francis flicked on the kitchen light and pulled a small saucepan from a drawer. She filled it with water and placed it on the stove. The igniter had stopped working reliably, sparking only around half the time, so she took a match and touched it to the burner; the gas flamed to life. She slid the pot to the burner, and glanced at the clock on the wall. Half past seven. She'd fix her nightly cup of Postum and warm up the radio. Dylan's favorite program, *Suspense*, aired tonight. His father had never approved of the program, but neither had he expressly disapproved of it, so she and Dylan had enjoyed listening to it together ever since Dylan was a boy. Francis would listen to it tonight, just as she did every week at this time. It made her feel closer to Dylan, knowing that he, too, wherever he was, would undoubtedly be tuned in.

She opened the cabinet where she kept the Postum, and a sense of sorrow, greater than even what she felt at her husband's passing, descended on her. She had done this how many weeks now? How many years? Keeping the home fire burning. Holding everything still and in place. Early on, it had been easy to hold on to the faith that Dylan would begin to see through Ruby and her lascivious ways. That he would grow to miss the wholesomeness of his own hometown. That he would come to miss his mama as much as she missed him.

But then Ruby had returned. And Ruby passed on. Between those points, the Judge had refused to let Francis pose her own questions to Ruby, claiming that the two had drifted apart early on, and that Ruby had no knowledge of Dylan's whereabouts. Despite the assurances of Dylan's well-being that Clarence had passed on to her from beyond the veil, despite Chief Little Feather's promises of Dylan's safe return, Francis felt unsure. Tonight, for the first time, she allowed herself to question whether her boy could be gone for good, lost to her forever. She watched the steam as it began to rise from the pot of water.

She found a spoon and ladled the mix into her cup. A knock sounded at her door. For one delirious moment, her heart leapt. Could it be? She stopped. Of course not. She was being ridiculous. Another, more insistent knock set her in motion. She followed the sound of the rapping to her front door. Using one hand to secure the upper portion of her robe, and the other to grasp the doorknob, she opened the door a crack, just enough to get a glimpse at the caller on its other side without having to reveal too much of herself.

"Hello again, Mrs. Sawyer."

"Marjorie," Francis said, rather surprised to see the hapless woman for the second time in one day. Marjorie had struck her as a complete creature of habit, showing up every day or so, always with a cake carrier in her plump, sweaty hands. Never before had she come calling twice in one day. "It's rather late for a visit, I think. I was just preparing to turn in." This time the girl came without pastry, her gaze cast downward. She seemed rather upset. Francis realized it was her Christian duty to inquire. "Is everything all right?"

"May I come in?" Marjorie replied. She stood there on the stoop, looking for all the world like a lost child. Downcast. With one hand, Marjorie fingered the bow around the waist of her dress. She had something small clutched in the other, and because of the way she kept slipping it backward, nearly hiding it behind her, Francis surmised that this object was more than likely the cause of the simple girl's consternation. "Please?"

Francis came close to refusing, but relented. "I suppose it would be all right, but only for a few minutes." She stepped back and allowed the girl to enter. She remembered the pot she'd left on the burner, and turned. "Come through, and please close the door behind you." Francis made her way to the kitchen, not bothering to wait on her dowdy guest to trudge along behind her.

She turned off the stove. The water had boiled, so she left it in place to cool a bit before adding it to her cup. She glanced at the clock. Still plenty of time before the program. With any luck she could wrap up Marjorie's bundle of misery and parcel her back out the door before the announcer began speaking.

Marjorie appeared suddenly behind her, startling her. Even though Francis was well aware of Marjorie's presence, the stealth with which she approached demonstrated none of the lumbering, ungainly qualities Francis had come to expect of her. She suppressed a gasp. "Do sit." She motioned toward the kitchen table, circling around to its far side and pulling out her own chair. Marjorie did as requested, dragging the chair so that the legs scraped loudly against the linoleum Dylan had chosen for the room. Francis nearly protested, but something about the girl's expression stopped her. Marjorie's hand shot out and grasped the edge of the table as she fell, collapsing into the chair. "Dear, are you quite all right?" Francis said, noticing how pale the girl seemed. "Are you ill?"

Marjorie's head shot straight back, and her eyes opened wide. They struck Francis as odd, but she couldn't figure out exactly how. Marjorie's breathing grew labored, as if she had just finished sprinting a mile. Then, through gritted teeth, she began screaming, the veins in her temples jutting out. Her hand reached up and came slamming down on the table, shards of glass escaping as the small brown bottle she had been secreting shattered. Blood dripped from Marjorie's hand as she raised it, and Francis jumped up to get a towel to wrap it in. "What is wrong with you, child?" She grabbed a dry cloth from beside the sink and turned to use it as a bandage, but stopped at the sight of a portion of the bottle that remained on her table. She dropped the towel.

The red diamond poison warning stared accusingly up at her. But how? She'd disposed of the bottle behind the diner. Years ago now. The night that Dylan left. The night he'd threatened to turn her in to the police.

Her brother had been a chemist working for the pulp plant before he died in the war. He'd had a few bottles of it in his possession. She'd used the others. This one had been the last. She had held on to it, just in case. She never really thought she'd use it.

"You drove him away," Marjorie said. Her face had bunched up in on itself, shriveled into a mask of rage. "I know it now. I know everything."

Francis backed away until she bumped up against the sink.

Marjorie stood and walked to the drawer where Francis kept her cutlery. She slid the drawer open. "You poisoned Mr. Sawyer. That's why he got sick. That's why he died."

"You don't know what you're talking about. You don't know what you're saying." Francis slid along with her back to the counter. Once she got a clear shot for the door, she'd . . . she'd what? Go to the sheriff? What if they listened to this girl?

Marjorie reached into the drawer and pulled out Francis's best carving knife. "You poisoned your husband. You found out he was planning on leaving you. Leaving Conroy. So you poisoned him to keep him around." Marjorie took a step closer. The overhead light glinted off the blade.

"I don't know how you got these crazy ideas in your head . . ." Francis said, sliding to the end of the counter. The entrance to the kitchen was now a straight shot.

"Ruby. Ruby told me." Marjorie stood before her, her chest heaving. "And Dylan told her. Dylan, he told her that you poisoned Mr. Sawyer so he couldn't leave you. Then Dylan caught you trying to do the same thing to him, so you could keep him around."

"When did Ruby tell you this?"

"Tonight. Just now. I hear her in my head. She's laughing. She wants me to ask you if you'd like to talk with Chief Little Feather."

"That harlot is dead, and you are crazy."

"I am not crazy," Marjorie cried and lunged at her. Before Francis fully realized what she was doing, she grasped the handle of the pot she'd left on the stove and flung the still-scalding water into Marjorie's eyes.

Marjorie howled and dropped the knife. She fell to her knees, then over on her side, pulling her legs up into her chest. "I'm not crazy," she said between sobs.

Francis stood frozen in place. "I never meant to kill his father." She hadn't expected to admit it, but the confession spilled from her, surprising her with how good it felt to say the words. "I was so very careful to keep the dosage low. I just couldn't let him leave me. I couldn't let him leave us. A boy needs his father." Her own legs began to feel weak, and she slid down to the floor next to Marjorie.

"I only wanted to protect Dylan. He was putting himself at such a risk with those drugs she started him taking. He was putting himself at such risk . . . *being* . . . with that undoubtedly syphilitic whore. Is there a man she didn't spread her legs for?" A flash of anger filled her. "One day I heard them talking. Talking about leaving Conroy. I knew if she took him away, she'd destroy him. I'd never see my baby boy again." Her own sobs rose to match and then drown out Marjorie's. She realized her companion had fallen silent, the realization causing her to regain her own composure. "I only wanted to make him a bore to her long enough that she'd lose interest in him and move on. I would never have harmed him. Not really. He was my son. He was the love of my life."

Francis pushed herself up, then crawled the few feet to the stove. She opened the oven door, peering in. She drew a breath and puffed out the oven's pilot light, then turned the gas up high. She looked back over her shoulder and took one last look at the girl, still writhing on the floor. Still on her hands and knees, Francis made her way around Marjorie, and finding the knife had damaged the linoleum, picked up the blade and plunged it into the girl.

Francis pushed through the blood that had begun to puddle around Marjorie. Francis put her head inside the oven and then, closing her eyes and thinking of her son, began taking deep breaths.

FIFTY-ONE

Corinne spotted the patrol car's arrival through the two large picture windows that had been set one on each side of the station's double-door entrance and emblazoned with the city's seal. She couldn't help but reflect on the fact that while the building's higher and smaller windows were barred, these two large windows were not. Had the architects reasoned Conroy's criminal element would respect the integrity of the large festooned panes?

She and Lucille had been waiting there for hours, ever since the sheriff had shown up at the Judge's house, telling her that the Dunnes had been murdered, and that it'd been Elijah who'd done the killing.

Now the three men entered the building one by one. The deputy, who was first in the procession, opened and held one of the double doors, allowing Elijah to be pushed through by the sheriff. "Elijah," Corinne called. She tried to grab hold of his sleeve as the sheriff maneuvered him past her and toward the large cell that lined the back of the office.

"Step back, please, Miss Ford," Bell said, this time having no trouble remembering the family name Corinne had planned on leaving behind.

Corinne searched Elijah's eyes for even the slightest sign that any of this could be true. That the kind and gentle young man she had intended to marry—had this really shifted into the past tense?—could be responsible for the bloodshed Bell wanted to lay at his feet. She saw no guilt. Only confusion. Pain. Corinne shuddered as she wondered if Elijah had learned of his parents' murders from men who thought him responsible for the act.

"Sheriff," Corinne said, inserting herself between Elijah and the cell into which the sheriff had intended to place him. "Look at him. Can't you see he had nothing to do with any of this?"

"Your loyalty to your fiancé is heartening, ma'am, but I do need you to step out of the way."

The deputy—what was his name?—took her by the arm and pulled her to the side. Keys jangled and metal scraped metal as Bell unlocked and opened the cage. He gave Elijah a rough shove, causing him to lurch past the bars, and pulled the door closed with a loud clang.

Corinne rushed forward and reached through the bars. "This is madness," she said, turning her gaze from Elijah, whose eyes refused to meet her own, to Bell, his deputy, and finally to Lucille, who had wedged herself into a corner, looking like her one hope in this entire mess was to be forgotten. Corinne spun back to the man she'd come to this hell to marry. "Elijah, tell them. You didn't hurt anyone."

Elijah shook his head and mumbled, "I didn't. I didn't hurt nobody." Finally he raised his eyes off the floor and looked at her. "I didn't."

"Take a seat," the deputy said and tried to strong-arm her into a chair.

Corinne flung him off. "Do not touch me." The deputy's face blanched, and he took a quick pair of steps back. *That's right, tough guy,* Corinne thought. To her surprise Lucille had joined her at her side.

"Please, ma'am. This won't help anyone." Lucille said.

Corinne felt her heart tumble into the pit of her stomach. Something in Lucille's expression, the way her brow rested low over her downward shifting eyes, the calm acceptance in her voice, spoke of a hopeless resolution. "Once they made up their mind . . ." Lucille began to whisper, but then her words faded away under Bell's withering glance. Corinne scowled back at Sheriff Bell, who seemed nearly varnished by satisfaction. He had already tried and convicted Elijah. Lucille gave her arm a gentle tug. "Please, you'll just make it worse for him and yourself."

A stunned-looking Elijah drifted back in the cell until he bumped up against the metal frame of a cot on its back wall. His knees buckled, and he collapsed, taking a seat on the thin mattress as the frame that held it squeaked.

"Where are they?" Bell said, advancing on the cell. Elijah sat still, staring blankly at the floor beneath his feet. Bell pulled his baton from his belt and banged it against the bars.

Elijah jolted to attention. "Who?" He licked his lips and squeezed the bed frame until his knuckles went white, like he was trying to grab ahold of the real world and pull himself back from this nightmare that his life had become.

"The Sleiger boys," Bell said, and punctuated his words with another strike against the bars. "What have you done with them?" he said before the metal stopped ringing.

"I don't know . . ." Elijah began.

"The Sleiger boys?" Lucille asked, releasing her hold on Corinne and stepping a foot or so closer to the sheriff. "They were just at the Judge's house."

"That's right," Corinne said, feeling a shimmer of hope rise within her. "The mortuary sent them to pick up the Judge's body."

"Them Sleigers ain't got nothing to do with the funeral home," the deputy said, his eyes widening, and his hand clutching his holster as if for reassurance.

Bell tossed a look of disdain at his deputy, then turned back to Elijah. "Okay, boy," Bell said as he returned the baton to a loop in his belt. "How about you tell me what's been going on around here, all nice and slow and honest like?"

"I don't know," Elijah stammered. "It don't make no kind of sense." His gaze lost focus as he seemed to consider all the possible explanations. A few moments passed, then his eyes darted up and locked on Bell's.

Bell leaned back a bit and crossed his arms over his chest. "Okay, let's start with you telling me why you killed your folks."

Elijah jumped up from the cot and lunged toward the bars, grasping them so tightly his knuckles began to whiten. "I done told you, I ain't killed nobody. My ma . . ." His words died out. He looked to Corinne. "That gun you brought with you." His face flushed red as his tears begin to fall. "My pa. He said things. Bad things. She shot him. She shot herself."

The sheriff spat on the floor and drew closer to the cell. "You expect me to believe a fine woman like your mama would do something like that? Hell, boy." He turned and walked back toward his desk, stopping before it and hooking the keys to his belt. He turned back to face Elijah. "If your mama did the killing, you tell me why you tried to hide that gun."

"I didn't hide anything. Honest, I don't even know where it is."

"Oh, don't you worry. We got it," Bell said. "We found it in the yard with the miss's clothes and case."

Elijah's forehead creased, then his eyes drifted down as if he were trying to remember. He focused on Corinne. "Yeah. I was going to bring you your things. I was going to take you away from here."

"So your intent was to flee."

Corinne rolled her eyes. "Sheriff, I would hardly say that leaving the gun lying in the middle of the yard for all to see constitutes 'hiding.' And as for being a fugitive, he doesn't seem to have put much effort into escaping. Where did you find him, parked in the Dunnes' driveway?"

Bell flashed her an angry look and pointed his index finger at her. "Maybe you need to simmer down, little lady. If I felt like listening to a hysterical woman, I'd call my wife."

Little lady, indeed. She was not going to be silenced by this musta-chioed ape, especially with Elijah's life on the line. "Listen. I have no idea what happened at the Dunnes', but you want to work your way to the bottom of things, I suggest you figure out what the Sleigers"—she cast a glance at Lucille to confirm the name, Lucille nodding her assent—". . . what the Sleigers are up to. Why they've been hiding out. And why they'd take the Judge's body, because I bet if you'd take the time to ring the mortuary, his remains are not there." The sheriff ran his hand over his mustache. He was finally listening, so Corinne contin-ued. "They are up to something strange, and it looks like they're trying to implicate Elijah." She stopped in midthought as a new realization struck her. "McAvoy. He never arrived to look after the Judge. Could these Sleigers have done something to him as well?"

"But by Elijah's own account, they didn't have anything to do with his parents' deaths. As for Dowd and the others, what motive would they have?"

"Besides, I've known the Sleigers for forever," the deputy said. "They ain't killers."

"You've known me forever, too, Fred," Elijah snapped, the despera-tion of a cornered man biting through his words. "Am I a killer?"

"Under the right—or wrong—circumstances, I think we're all killers," Bell said. He didn't seem ready to entertain even the slightest inkling that the man he had arrested could be innocent, even if the real killers were delivered gagged and bound at his feet. Corinne wondered if it was his pride keeping him entrenched in such certainty, or if he was just too intellectually lazy to care about uncovering the truth.

"I'm just saying the Sleigers sure ain't criminal masterminds," the deputy said. Bell shot him a sharp glance, and the deputy lowered his head and slinked away, taking a seat at one of the office's two desks.

They all turned in unison as both of the double doors eased open to reveal the black emptiness of night. There was no movement beyond the doors, no wind to have opened them or kept them in that splayed position. Corinne took a step forward, intending to investigate.

"You just wait right there, Miss," Bell commanded. The authority in his voice caused her military response to kick in; she obeyed the direct order.

The sheriff's right hand slid down to his holster. "Rigby," he said in a calm voice, and motioned with his left hand, his pointer and middle finger extended toward the door. The deputy shook his head as if he didn't understand, but Corinne intuited it was sheer cowardice that kept him from rising. Bell's face flushed and his eyes rounded beneath raised brows. He motioned once more toward the open doors, this time removing the gun from his holster as he did so. Corinne couldn't tell if he did it to indicate he would cover the deputy, or if he was threatening to shoot Rigby if he didn't obey. The look in the deputy's pleading eyes told Corinne that she wasn't the only one having trouble making the distinction.

Rigby's chair squeaked as he stood, the sole sound in the peculiar silence that had descended upon the room. The deputy nearly tripped over his own dragging feet, recovering just before toppling over, and made a few slow and furtive steps toward the doors. Then he stopped and pulled his pistol from his holster, craning his neck in an attempt to peer through the darkness, even though he was only a yard or so from the position where he'd started.

"Rigby." Bell's voice spurred the deputy into taking a few more steps. But he punctuated each step by casting a glance over his shoulder at the sheriff, each pause a question as to whether he had gone far enough. Corinne didn't know whether to feel sympathy or disgust when she saw the way the man's hand trembled around his gun.

"Enough," Corinne said, although she wasn't sure if she'd actually voiced the word. She stepped forward, relieving the deputy of his weapon as she pushed past him. She strode toward the opening and looked out. Nothing. She took a step out onto the landing. "Corinne," she heard Elijah's voice call out to her. "Come back." He was frightened for her. She was not. The only fearful thing in this moment was the thought of leaving the group's safety in the hands of men like Bell and Rigby.

The doors were open so wide there was no room for anyone to hide behind them, and even if there had been, the panes on their upper halves would have revealed anyone over three feet tall. Still, she tugged on the handle of the one on her left. The door resisted at first, but a moment later it shut with a loud clack.

"There's nothing," she called, her nose turning up at the cloying scent of the pulp factory. She was about to reach out and close the second door when she noticed a bank of fog, the thickest and most pungent she'd ever witnessed, begin to coalesce and draw near. She stepped back over the threshold, the heavy night air pressing up against her. Underneath the skunky scent of pulpwood rode another smell. Sweet. Woody, but with a chemical undertone. She had smelled the odor earlier in the Judge's room.

At the bank's edge, she discerned an animal movement. Her eyes had adjusted enough to the dark to make out a canine form lurking at the edge of the miasma, almost like it was herding the fog to the station's steps.

Sensing movement behind her, she looked back over her shoulder. Rigby and Bell had joined her at the entrance, Rigby having regained enough confidence to step out from behind her skirt. The sheriff holstered his gun, and then reached out and relieved her of the deputy's pistol.

At the edge of the fog, the hulking beast drew close enough for those gathered just outside the station's doorway to make out its brindle markings. "Isn't that . . ." she began.

"Tac, is that you?" Rigby called out, taking a few steps out toward the dog. "Sheriff, ain't that Charlie's dog, Tac?" Rigby squatted on his haunches. "Come 'ere, girl." The dog padded forward. "Where's Toe, girl? Where's your brother?"

"I ate him." The words came from the dog's mouth seconds before it lunged at the deputy, dragging him off behind the veil of fog. From his screams, Corinne could tell he was being dragged across the road and beyond the field; then the sound ceased abruptly. The sheriff shot wildly and indiscriminately into the fog, emptying his gun's chambers. There was no sign that any of his bullets met their mark.

Faces began to appear through the mist. "Who are these people?" she asked Bell without taking her eyes off the arrivals. "These people," she had said, because their forms appeared human, even though her instincts cried out that they were something else entirely. Many of them appeared to be limp puppets, incapable of ambulation under their own steam, and dragged along all the same by some kind of invisible strings. A few seemed to be more their own masters, standing taller and moving with more grace, but there was still something wrong with them. It was their eyes. They glowed blue like gas flames. All carried an assortment of pipes and pans, garbage can lids, sticks, which they began to sound and clack and clang in unison. Small fires began to sprout up among them, bobbing up and down in the distance. "Are those torches? Actual torches?" No sooner had the words escaped her than an odd cacophony began—car horns and clanging pipes, breaking glass. "Sheriff, what is this?" she asked, daring to look away from the spectacle before her to see the cross of confusion and concern that had spread over his face.

"Tell me. Were you and Elijah supposed to marry today?"

It seemed impossible, but it was true. "Yes."

"Then this here, this commotion," he said without taking his eyes off the growing crowd, "is shivaree. And I think they're coming for your Elijah."

"What?"

"You need to get back inside," he said, unhooking the keys to the cell from his belt loop and passing them to her. "Do your best to get Lucille and Elijah away from here. When you find a phone, you call the state patrol. You hear me?" He reached down and pulled his pistol from its holster. "I take it you know how to use one of these?" He held the gun out to her.

"Yes, but . . ."

"Good God, woman. For once in your life will you just do as you are told?"

Corinne shifted the heavy ring of keys to her left hand and tightened her grasp, taking the gun in her right hand. She tossed one last quick look at those who had gathered in the fog. They formed an advancing arc. Although she couldn't see them, the way the noises carried and echoed told her that there were others behind the building as well. The ones she could see walked in a type of lockstep, stopping and advancing as if controlled by a single mind. Corinne gathered from their actions that she stood inside a constricting circle of which the jail served as the center point. She began to turn away and follow the sheriff's orders when she heard him call out.

"Frank, boy," the sheriff called, his voice coming out strained, high. "Mason? That you? What the hell happened to you, boy?" Frank Mason pushed forward to the front of the crowd. He moved awkwardly, lurching forward like he was being yanked along against his will. "I don't know what you think y'all are up to, but you need to get out of here. Get all these folk out of here."

As Corinne stood focused on Frank, a blur—a rush of wind—gyrated before her, then Bell, too, disappeared into the night. This time Corinne heard no cry, no wail, only a woman's familiar laughter riding on a wave of the shivaree.

FIFTY-TWO

Corinne stumbled backward through the door, slamming it shut behind her. Lucille met her there and shoved the bolt in, locking the door into place. Their eyes met. Bolting the door was a hollow gesture, and both of them knew it. Corinne found herself cursing the station's builders once again.

"What is wrong with this place? What is wrong with these people?" Corrine said, not really expecting an answer.

"It's Mississippi," Lucille responded all the same.

Corinne slid to the side of the window to see if she could spot the sheriff among the shuffling crowd. "It looks like the entire town has gone mad." She turned back to Lucille and Elijah. "We have to get out of here."

She sped to Elijah's cell, fumbling through what seemed to be an infinite collection of nonfitting keys. The noise continued growing louder. Corinne knew the circle was tightening. A heavy stone shattered one of the windows, then all fell silent except for the sound of a woman's laughter.

"Ruby." Elijah's voice reached out to her from behind the bars. He stood there, whiter than the fog itself, his hands clutched around the bars that held him. "I'd know her laugh anywhere."

"That is not possible," Corinne protested aloud. "It isn't," she repeated, but this time silently. She continued to work through the keys; finally one she must have tried a hundred times already slid into place.

"They closed her in a casket," Elijah mumbled to himself. "Buried her with her mama."

"And yet she's still out there," Lucille said, fixing them both in her terrified gaze. "She's taken the rest of them. Everybody who done her wrong. And now she's gonna come for us."

Corrine focused on the task at hand, turning the key until the lock clanked. She grasped the bars and swung the door open, but Elijah didn't move.

"Why, Lucille, you know I wouldn't harm a hair on your head."

Corinne turned back to the entrance. The door, in spite of having been locked, had slid silently open.

"Sweet Jesus!" Lucille exclaimed and fell back as Ruby floated in on a cloud of roiling fog. Until now, Corinne had never believed in magic or monsters, but all that had changed in an instant.

"You were like a mother to me," Ruby continued as her feet lowered to the floor, making light contact. "You, on the other hand," she said, approaching Corinne and tracing a cold finger along her cheek, then her jawline. "I'm afraid the Dunnes' little tiff done ruined my special surprise for you. You two were supposed to be married by now. We were coming to serenade you outside your bridal chambers. Interrupt in the moments before you surrendered your precious maidenhead." She laughed and feigned a wide-eyed surprise. "Or could it be you aren't intact?" Her nose wrinkled up as she shook her head. "Naughty, naughty girl.

"I was gonna kill you," she said smiling, her lip curling back to show an unnaturally sharp pair of canines. "Oh, yes, I was." The words poured forth with a touch of glee. "But you done made me like you, what with the way you came stomping out there all on your own while the menfolk were in here pissing themselves. I think I might find a better use for you, darlin'." She threw back her head and let loose a laugh that caused Corinne's blood to run cold. Corinne shuddered as she noticed the blueness of the skin that stretched across Ruby's otherwise lovely throat.

The weight of the gun in Corinne's hand reminded her of its presence. Her hand ached to raise the pistol; her finger twitched at the thought of squeezing its trigger. Ruby's blue flame eyes shot at her, all mirth gone from them. "I wouldn't even think it," she said, and then the gun fell from Corinne's grasp. Ruby pinned her with her gaze. "And there went your last chance to for us to be friends."

"Ruby," Elijah called, causing this beautiful yet unholy creature to turn away. "How can it be?"

"Don't ask how, my love, just be happy that it is." Ruby glided toward him, her arms outstretched in a welcoming lover's embrace, but Elijah stood frozen in place, looking at the cage's door as if he were considering pulling it closed in an attempt to keep her out. "You are happy to see me, aren't you, sweetheart?

"When I awoke," she said, "all I wanted was to come to you, the one person who loved me. The one person who would be missing me. I wanted to tell you that I was fine. That we could still . . ." Ruby paused, the words seeming to fail her. "But I was so weak at first. I had to build my strength. I wanted to be whole, to be strong. Then I learned you were to be married. To this." She shot a contemptuous glance back at Corinne, turning as if she planned to advance on her. But then she stopped and turned her face upward.

"I can feel it. I can feel Daddy waking." She paused, seeming to listen to something that Corinne couldn't hear. "Now he's mine forever. And I will come to him every night, and I will hurt him. Just like he hurt me."

She turned back to Elijah. "Your mama cheated me out of finishing her husband, but I've punished everyone else who came between us." She lifted a few inches up off the ground as she spoke, gliding into the cell. "I've punished everyone who's betrayed me. I've made them all pay. All except one. You."

Her hand shot out and took hold of Elijah's forearm. "I wanted to see if you would wed that woman. Or if you would walk away. But since the nuptials got interrupted, I'm going to give you one last chance, right here, right now," she said. "One last chance to make the right choice. Tell me you love me"—she paused—"and you better tell me the truth, 'cause I know the difference between the real feeling and the infatuation this thing inside me uses to make people stand still when it's hunting."

Elijah's lips moved without making a sound, as if he were waiting for the words to catch up with them. "Ruby." Her name finally formed. "I don't understand none of this. I don't know how this could be happening. But of course I love you. I've only ever really loved you." Corinne's heart broke when she saw the look in his eyes. What he was saying was true. "There is no one else I could ever love like you. But I thought you were dead. I thought I'd lost you forever." He placed his hand over her hand that held him. "I want to be with you. I do." Corinne watched as a tear fell from his eye. "But there's something you have to know." His voice lowered. "I'm your brother. The Judge. He was my father."

"Oh, darlin'." Ruby's voice curled through the air. "I know that. I've known it for years. I knew before I ever set my sights on you." Ruby reached up with her free hand and placed it lovingly on Elijah's cheek. "You know how much your daddy liked getting all liquored up. Once Dylan found him stumbling around outside Nola's." Her voice turned into a low purr. "Dylan liked hanging around there. Plenty of drunk, lonely men to take their pleasure in his pretty mouth." She lowered her hand, a cruel twist to her lips. She was playing with him. Tormenting him even as she demanded his love. "Dylan said your daddy cried like a little girl when he told Dylan about you." She released his arm, and took a step back, as if she wanted to get a better view of his reaction.

Elijah's face fell at the sound of her words. His gaze turned toward Corinne, his face burning red with shame. "You have to let them go," he said, nodding toward Lucille and Corinne. "We can be together. I'll do anything you want, but you have to leave them be. Lucille—she ain't ever done a thing your daddy didn't make her do." He reached out and pulled Ruby into his arms. "And Corinne. You know she ain't you. Hell, just look at her. But she's a good person, and she helped saved my leg back in Korea. She never came between us. Not really." He leaned down and placed a gentle kiss on Ruby's lips. "She helped get me back to you."

Ruby's eyes flashed on Corinne. "Well, there you have it, sugar. You are one hell of a lucky girl. Elijah just bought you one final chance. Get out of here. Get out of Conroy," she said and then turned her gaze toward Lucille. "Both of you. If either of you are here tomorrow at sunset, you won't live to see another dawn."

The world around them began to tremble as the sound of an enormous blast tore apart the night. For a moment Corinne struggled to pull the pieces of what was happening together into a rationally acceptable situation, but a sudden realization caused her to let all the nonaligning pieces tumble to the floor.

Ruby and Elijah were gone.

FIFTY-THREE

"'Babylon the great is fallen, is fallen, and is become the habitation of devils, and the hold of every foul spirit . . .'" Raylene's voice carried in the unnatural silence of the morning, all the way from the city hall steps throughout the streets of Conroy.

Corinne jumped at the sound of the words. Lucille patted her hand. "Looks like for once that crazy bitch is right," Lucille said, and Corinne broke out laughing. Lucille only smiled at first, then she laughed, too.

Dawn found the two women huddled together outside the train station. It was the only place where they could wait together. By formal law, Lucille could not join Corinne in the white waiting room; unspoken law among the whites dictated that Corinne not join Lucille in the colored. They had one goal, and that was to get out of Conroy. They didn't need any misstep preventing them from achieving that goal. But neither could they bear to separate, not after what they had witnessed together. Left alone, they would begin to question their sanity.

They were leaving Conroy with nothing other than the cash Corinne had concealed in her brassiere. Lucille had chosen to walk away from the meager belongings that remained at her own house, unwilling to risk that something might happen to prevent her from joining her babies up north. The words "As he came forth of his mother's womb, naked shall he return . . ." played in Lucille's mind.

The ticket seller had refused to give Lucille a ticket without a hefty bribe, so Corinne had been forced to part with more than the regular cost of two tickets. If word of the Judge's death hadn't made it around the town, thanks to Corinne's call to the undertaker, Lucille knew she would never have been allowed to board the train. But now she had her ticket in hand, and she would be, praise the Lord, leaving this place. Once they were safely away, Lucille would write the pastor. Warn him to warn the others.

Even though the sun had risen, the air remained chill and pungent now with the clinging scent left by the explosion at the pulp plant. News of the plant's destruction was on the lips of all who passed.

The blast had been bigger than any faulty boiler could have caused, managing to take down a good part of the building. Fifteen men on the night shift were confirmed dead. Many others had been wounded or remained unaccounted for, including the Sleiger boys, who worked maintenance on the boiler and hadn't been seen for a couple of days. Suspicion was falling on them, as many were of the opinion that the place looked like it had been purposely bombed. No one had been able to locate either Sheriff Bell or his deputy, so many of the townspeople worried that they had somehow been caught up in the event. All worried that the closure of the mill might sound Conroy's death knell.

But none of this held any meaning for Lucille and Corinne anymore. They sat silently, letting the conjectures and consternations of those who passed them float by like the song of so many morning birds.

"He didn't mean it, you know. Elijah, what he said. He just didn't want her to hurt you."

Corinne laughed, but this time there was no humor in the sound. "Oh, he meant it all right. Every word. I knew it, and that creature knew it. That's why she let us go." Corinne took Lucille's hand. "It doesn't matter. I don't care what any of these people think about me. Including him."

The shrill cry of a train whistle carried through the crisp morning air. "Won't be long," Lucille said to her new friend. "Train's just a bit south of here."

FIFTY-FOUR

What with Frank up and disappearing, the Judge's death, and the disaster at the mill, Nola felt like she had somehow survived the end of the world. News about the deaths at the mill intertwined with rumors about the Judge's passing, spreading through the town before the milk could be delivered. As far as she knew, the whereabouts of the Judge's body remained a mystery. Some unknown Yankee woman had called and reported the Judge's death to the funeral home, but by the time they got their best hearse washed and over to his house, there wasn't a soul there. Even his maid had flown the coop. A few folk were questioning whether the Judge was really gone, but Nola knew if he were still alive, sick or no, he'd never be able to resist presiding over the investigation into the explosion at the mill.

Conroy was a small town, which meant everyone was touched by the deaths at the plant. If an unforgiving God had chosen to punish Conroy for its sins, He couldn't have picked a better place to strike. An impromptu wake hatched at Nola's the moment she opened the door, and what with nearly everyone in Conroy out of work and wanting to raise a glass in someone's memory, Nola had been on her feet from three in the afternoon until one-thirty in the morning. It'd been a hell of a night, and it was damned good to be home.

The Judge's passing had been overshadowed in a way Nola knew he'd find most displeasing. *Full pomp and circumstance*, she thought as she reached behind herself to undo the zipper of her dress. The Judge would have wanted full pomp and circumstance to mark his passing. Now his death was just one of many, not so special anymore, and from the talk at the bar, not many would miss him. "Here's to you," she said with only a slight tone of sarcasm as she took a sip of her whiskey.

She usually hung around the bar long enough to count out the till and supervise cleanup. Not tonight, though. She'd headed right out at closing time. For all she knew, with the Judge gone and Sheriff Bell missing, the state police would be closing her down come daybreak anyway. No use wasting her time and energy until she knew how the chips were going to fall.

She undid her bra and let it fall to the floor. She turned to view herself in the mirror of her vanity. Tits were hanging a bit, not as high as they once were, but they looked as good as any woman her age could hope for. God, she envied those Hollywood starlets who filled the magazines at her hairdresser. Some of those damned bitches never seemed to age. She turned sideways to examine herself from that angle. Her stomach showed just a bit of padding, a softness Frank claimed to enjoy. She ran her hand down the length of her stomach, the thought of Frank causing her fingers to reach a bit lower. She'd miss that man all right.

She'd never see Frank again, of that she was certain. He'd plowed his car into a tree, killing Bayard, then skipped town to avoid the consequences. Bayard. No one had come to toast Bayard's memory. Nola had hated the bastard, who'd scared her to death on a regular basis, but now that he was gone, she found it in her heart to toss back the last of her whiskey in his honor. She sat the glass on the vanity table, then went to the closet, pulling a clean nightgown from a hanger and slipping it over her head.

She crossed to her bed and reached down to extinguish the lamp on her nightstand, when a knock, unmistakably *his* knock, sounded on the front door. Her heart fluttered as she raced to answer it, but she remembered herself and slowed, taking her time to cross the darkened living room and find the door. She flipped the switch to illuminate the porch light, planning to give Frank holy hell for up and disappearing, before she let him take her into her room and lay her down.

She flung the door open, but the sight of him caused her words to catch in her throat. He stood there before her as moths flitted into his halo. She didn't know why. Maybe it was only because she'd thought he was lost to her. She had always wanted him, for pleasure, for company, but she had never before realized how much she loved him. Her heart nearly broke at the sight of his oddly pale skin.

"Are you all right?" she asked. "Were you hurt?" She paused, a little taken aback by a flicker of tiny blue specks dancing in his dark eyes. Something was different about him; something was strange. "Why are you dressed like that?" she asked, finally taking note of the police uniform he was wearing. Never in a million years would she have expected to see him dressed as an officer of the law.

He cocked his head and smiled at her, a delicious mischief in that smile spiking her desire. "Ain't you heard? There's a new sheriff in town." He leaned toward her, placing a hand against the outside of the door frame. He was so close, and she wanted him so badly. "Come on, sugar, it's getting late," Frank said, his lids narrowing seductively. "You gonna invite me in or not?"

ACKNOWLEDGMENTS

I would like to thank the amazing team at 47North, especially Jason Kirk for having faith that a rough stone might shine, and Nicci Jordan Hubert, for her patience and elbow grease. Thanks also to my friend and fellow author, Roberta Trahan, for the encouragement that helped *Shivaree* grow from a short story to the novel you now hold. Of course, the biggest thank-you goes to my spouse, Rich Weissman, without whom none of this would have ever happened. Finally, much love to my furry co-authors: Duke and Sugar.

ABOUT THE AUTHOR

Photo © 2015 Boone Rodriguez

J.D. Horn was raised in rural Tennessee and has carried a bit of its red clay with him while traveling the world, from Hollywood to Paris to Tokyo. He studied comparative literature as an undergrad, focusing on French and Russian in particular. He also holds an MBA in international business and worked as a financial analyst before becoming a novelist. Along with his spouse, Rich, and his furry co-authors, Duke and Sugar, he divides his time between Black Butte Ranch, Oregon, and San Francisco, California.

24296089R00182

Made in the USA
Middletown, DE
19 September 2015